Praise for

Delia Parr's

novels

"Parr's cozy writing style will help all readers, no matter what their situation in life, to identify with the characters in this novel. Grandparents raising grandchildren is a timely and relevant topic, and Parr explores the subject in a sympathetic manner."
—*Romantic Times BOOKreviews* on *Day by Day*

"Parr draws readers in from the first page, making them care about these midlife ladies and their life-altering situations."
—*Library Journal* on *Day by Day*

"Parr is to be commended for her character development."
—*Publishers Weekly* on *Abide with Me*

"Realistic issues with concrete solutions will keep readers engaged."
—*Romantic Times BOOKreviews* on *Abide with Me*

"Well crafted. Readers will immerse themselves in the lives of these three women in midlife whose Christian roots help them overcome life's challenges and rejoice in its joys...a homey feel reminiscent of Jan Karon's Mitford series."
—*Library Journal* on *Abide with Me*

Delia Parr

Carry the Light

Steeple
Hill®

Published by Steeple Hill Books™

STEEPLE HILL BOOKS

Steeple
Hill®

ISBN-13: 978-0-373-78635-0
ISBN-10:   0-373-78635-2

CARRY THE LIGHT

Printed in U.S.A.

Dedicated to
the memory of
Gizmo Jane:
The Panda Pup,
The Cheese Dog
and
Friend to All

Chapter One

Escape was only a few steps away.

With that thought, Ellie Waters maneuvered through the maze of high school students reluctantly edging to their next period class, slipped inside her office and shut the door behind her. The room was not much more than a supersized closet, but it was her own space and she loved every crowded inch of it.

She made her way past two cartons of new textbooks sent by publishers to be considered for adoption, eased into the wooden chair at her desk, leaned back, closed her eyes and took a deep breath. Ten quiet minutes; that was all she needed to regroup and replenish her sagging energy.

It was only noon, but she had already taught four classes, met with her supervisor for her annual performance review and had a parent conference. By hiding here and managing the paperwork that was only a part of her duties as the language-arts department head at Welleswood High School, she might be able to finish the school day in peace. In quiet. And without interruption. She sighed, fully hopeful her plan would work.

Until the telephone rang.

She opened one eye, stared at the offending instrument

and wondered if there was an alarm attached under her chair that alerted the outside world that she finally had some downtime. When the telephone continued to ring, she opened her other eye, resisted the urge to answer and let out another sigh.

Just once, she would love to have ten minutes to unwind after changing hats from classroom teacher to department head. She had been the language-arts department head here for seven years now, but she had been teaching here for over thirty-five years. From experience, however, she knew that the pace of the school year was rapidly heating up now that March had arrived, and peace and quiet would be very precious commodities.

At the moment, she didn't want to think about the school-board election next month or whether the community would vote to accept or reject next year's budget. Nor did she want to think about the pressure she would soon be under from parents eager to make sure their children were recommended for advanced classes next year. But she did have to think about parent conferences scheduled for that evening, which made for an extra-long day today and an extra-tired day tomorrow, a Friday. Fortunately, she had the weekend to recover, and she looked forward to spending two very quiet, very peaceful days at home, grading the mini research papers she had collected this week.

The telephone continued to ring. Apparently, the caller was not giving up, but Ellie, just as determined to finish her paperwork before the parent conferences tonight, was letting the call go to voice mail. This year's senior awards for the department had to be reviewed and organized for her supervisor, and if she didn't make a plan to ration the department's supplies, they would run out long before June.

When the telephone finally stopped ringing, then started up again less than a minute later, she let out one final sigh, gave in and reached for the receiver. "No peace today," she muttered, and glanced down at the bottom desk drawer, where she kept a stash of candy. Not every telephone call was a problem or an emergency, but she was ready for either.

When she finally answered the telephone and heard her mother's voice, she opened the drawer. She made a mental note to replenish her stock, and took out three dark-chocolate kisses. "Yes, Mother, I have time to talk now," she said, unwrapping a kiss.

"I left three messages for you earlier, and one just now. You never called me back," Rose Hutchinson grumbled to her daughter.

"I'm sorry. I've been teaching classes and I had meetings all morning. I haven't had time to check my messages. Why are you whispering?" she asked, trying to divert her mother's attention away from her criticisms. She slipped the chocolate kiss into her mouth and let it begin to melt slowly against the inside of her cheek.

"I'm talking as loud as I can manage," her mother replied. "I'm sick, which you would have known if you'd bothered to call me today."

Ellie straightened her back and swallowed the last of the chocolate kiss. "But I just talked to you last night. You were fine then. What—"

"I know I was fine. Until this morning. I feel awful. My neck hurts and my jaw hurts and my chest hurts. I called Dr. Stafford's office and told the receptionist that I think I have the flu. He can see me this afternoon at four o'clock, but I just don't think I can make it there by myself. I'm feeling too weak. I need you to take me," she whined.

She went on before Ellie could respond. "Unless you're too busy. Then I'll have to take a cab. I'm sure the driver won't mind helping me into the cab or waiting for me while I'm at the doctor's office. Phyllis's daughter always takes her to the doctor's for her appointments, but then, her daughter has the sense to not be working anymore. She's retired now, you know, so she can spend a lot of time with her mother, not that you would consider retiring—"

"I'll take you. Of course, I'll take you," Ellie insisted, interrupting before she was compared unfavorably, again, to her mother's friend's near-perfect daughter.

Resigned, Ellie gave up any idea of taking a catnap this afternoon between the end of the school day at three and the start of parent conferences at six-thirty. Despite her contentious relationship with her mother, she did not resent her responsibilities as an only child. Taking her eighty-five-year-old mother to the doctor had become a frequent task in the past year.

Assuming Dr. Stafford saw her mother on time, which he usually did, and assuming her mother prolonged her appointment for a good fifteen minutes by arguing with the doctor, which she usually did, Ellie would be able to take her mother home, pick up whatever prescription she might need at the pharmacy, bring it back to her mother's home, and still be on time for parent conferences tonight.

Unfortunately, dinner did not fit into this scheme, which meant Ellie would have to rely on the teachers' traditional cookie tray for sustenance tonight—if someone in the administration had remembered to order it.

"I'll probably need you to stop at the store for ginger ale, too. I'll have to drink lots of clear fluids if I have the flu," her mother said.

"I took you for your flu shot, Mother, remember?" Ellie asked, rather than point out that flu season was nearly over.

"Certainly I remember. I'm old, Ellie, but I'm not senile. And just because I had a flu shot doesn't mean I don't have the flu. Last year, Alice Williams got the flu shot and she came down with the flu, if you'll recall."

"I can pick you up at quarter to four," Ellie replied choosing not to continue the argument. "Is that all right or do you need me to come over now?" she asked, with one eye on the mound of paperwork and the other on those two chocolate kisses sitting on top of her desk.

"Quarter to four is fine, but only if you're on time."

Ellie pursed her lips, cradled the telephone against her shoulder and slowly unwrapped another kiss. "I'll be on time."

"Well, I certainly can't do anything about it if you're not. With all the responsibilities you've had at school for the past umpteen years, I can't imagine how you've survived without learning to be more punctual. Unless it's just because I'm not important enough—"

"I'll be there. Quarter to four," Ellie interrupted again. She waited until she heard her mother hang up, then popped the kiss into her mouth.

Enduring her mother's criticism was nothing new for Ellie. She honestly could not remember a single moment in all of her sixty years when she had truly pleased her mother. Rose Hutchinson had already lived a long and full life, and Ellie reminded herself that each day her mother was here was a gift. Each day, however, was also one more day for Ellie to be reminded again of how she had disappointed the one person who mattered most: her mother.

She bowed her head and knitted her hands together. She prayed for patience, for strength and guidance, so that she might find the path that would lead her to discovering the love and acceptance she still desperately wanted from her mother.

At four o'clock, Ellie and her mother were sitting in Dr. Stafford's office. Dressed conservatively in black slacks, a black top and a plaid blazer, Ellie was also still wearing the sensible, lace-up oxfords she wore to school every day. In contrast, her mother had chosen to wear a bright aqua dress, calf-length and ultra-feminine, which did little to comple- ment her full figure, along with pumps, a matching handbag and costume jewelry that included a large turquoise brooch, bracelet and dangling earrings.

Half an hour later, after Dr. Stafford had examined Rose Hutchinson and rendered a tentative diagnosis, Ellie fervently wished that her mother indeed had the flu. "Are you sure?" she asked the doctor. "Mother has absolutely no history of heart trouble, and her cholesterol level has been dropping since she started her new medication. When I talked to her earlier today, she wasn't complaining about pain in her chest or arm. Aren't those the signs that would have told us—"

"Don't argue with the man," her mother interrupted, as if she reserved that right exclusively for herself. "He's the doctor. If he thinks I had a heart attack and I need to go to the hospital, then it's best if I go—even though I'm not convinced he's right, mind you. If you're worried about getting back to school in time for those conferences, you can drop me off at the emergency room. Or I can always go by ambulance, can't I, Dr. Stafford?"

"I do think getting you to the hospital as soon as possible would be best," he said firmly, repeating his earlier recommendation, "although I don't think it's necessary to call for an ambulance."

"I'll drive her to the hospital right away and stay with her," Ellie replied, clarifying her intentions.

"Good. I'll call ahead so they're waiting for you," the doctor said. "Now remember, I'm sending you to the hospital as a precaution, Mrs. Hutchinson. I don't want you or your daughter to jump to conclusions or to panic. The only way we'll know for certain if you suffered a mild heart attack earlier today is to get you checked out thoroughly." He looked at Ellie. "Not everyone has the classic symptoms you described, especially women, but based on what you've told me and what I've observed during my examination, I think we should be cautious and let the hospital run a few tests."

Ellie watched as he and her mother bantered back and forth for a few minutes. After treating her for nearly thirty years, Dr. Stafford knew exactly how to handle Rose Hutchinson, a skill Ellie sorely needed.

He smiled at one of her mother's heated rejoinders. "I suppose it's possible you've got the flu. Let's find out, shall we? If you're right and I'm wrong, I'll make it up to you," he promised.

Her mother's eyes lit up. "How?"

"I'll make another donation to the Shawl Ministry at church."

"We do need the wool," her mother replied, and looked at Ellie for confirmation.

Ellie nodded. Working together with her mother and other volunteers, knitting shawls and afghans for members of the congregation who were celebrating special occasions or needed consolation during difficult times was one way Ellie tried to fit volunteer work into her hectic schedule—and spend time with her mother, too. Unfortunately, with a full-time job and tons of paperwork at night, she had not been as active as she would have liked, yet another bone of contention between her and her mother.

Her mother let out a long sigh. "All right. I'll go to the hospital, but you need to write out your check first, Doctor Stafford. I'll take it with me."

Chuckling, the doctor left the room to make arrangements for them to be met at Tilton General Hospital. While he was gone, Ellie used her cell phone to call the school. Once the automated system picked up, she tapped in her supervisor's extension, left a voice mail message and then left another message for her principal, telling both her colleagues that she would not be at parent conferences tonight after all.

As she finished, the doctor returned and handed her an envelope. "Give this to the emergency-room physician and be sure to have Dr. Marks paged. He's expecting your mother.

He's an excellent cardiologist, and I'm certain he'll be able to help her."

Ellie tucked the envelope into her purse and helped her mother to her feet. When she looked into her mother's eyes, she was surprised to see the same fear that was making her own heart beat a little faster. Apparently, despite her show of bravado, her mother was not quite as confident she had the flu as she had let on. "Everything is going to be fine," Ellie whispered, and prayed she was right.

Life was good. Life was grand. Especially when life was filled with one of God's finest blessings: chocolate!

Humming softly, Charlene Butler tied a bright pink bow on the gift package she planned to deliver tonight after closing her shop and heading out to the highway for her forty-mile ride home to Grand Mills, a small rural community in the Jersey Pinelands.

Inside the gingham-lined wicker basket, she had tucked all sorts of the chocolate specialties that had made Sweet Stuff one of the most popular stores on Welles Avenue, as well as the very center of Charlene's lifelong dream to own a candy store.

Double-dipped, dark-chocolate-covered pretzels sprinkled heavily with pink jimmies, chocolate-raspberry fudge, chocolate-dipped strawberries and milk-chocolate-covered cherries were favorites she included in all the gift-basket orders she received for new mothers of baby girls, and this basket was no exception.

Although this basket had not been ordered at all. It was going to be a surprise gift from Charlene to Melanie Arbor, a member of her congregation whose adoption of two-year-old Kelsey had been finalized this morning.

When Charlene heard the shop door open, she stepped away from the worktable in the rear of the shop, walked into the main room and grinned as she navigated around one of the glass display cases filled with chocolates. "Aunt Dorothy! This is a surprise. I thought you were going on a bus trip today."

"I did. Just got back. I thought you were supposed to close at five o'clock. It's nearly six. You probably haven't had dinner yet, either, and you have a long ride home," she admonished gently as she stopped in front of the hutch that displayed a wide variety of vintage-era candy. "Makes a girl worry, you know."

Charlene looked at her aunt, a girlish eighty-one-year-old spinster, and pouted. "I thought we had an agreement. You weren't going to worry about me commuting to Welleswood, and I wasn't going to worry about you living all alone," she teased. Although her aunt's dark gray hair was neatly permed and she wore her trademark scent, Tabu, Charlene did notice that the elephant pin on the collar of her aunt's coat had lost several rhinestones. There was also a dark stain on one of her sleeves, which was unusual, since her aunt was usually very fastidious about her appearance.

Aunt Dorothy's hazel eyes twinkled behind her glasses, but since the lenses were a bit smudged, it was questionable how much good the glasses did to improve her vision. "You'll get no argument from me there. As a matter of fact, I was hoping you were still here. Annie Parker was on the trip. You remember Annie, don't you? We worked together at the factory. Started the same day and retired the same day, as a matter of fact."

"Sure I do. She lives at the Towers, doesn't she?" Charlene asked, referring to the senior-citizen's high-rise just down the avenue at the other end of town.

Aunt Dorothy nodded and started to help Charlene straighten the display of old-fashioned candy and gum, all in total disorder thanks to the numerous children who had stopped in after school today. "She had to give up the family home after Philip died a few years back. But to get to my point, she's feeling a bit low. Today's her daughter's birthday.

Jill would have been fifty-five, if she hadn't been killed in that awful car accident two years ago. I would have forgotten all about it if I hadn't been on the trip with Annie today. I feel terrible about forgetting. I should have done something extra nice for Annie to make today easier for her."

Charlene cocked her head. "Something *extra* nice?"

"Maybe a gift basket. Just a little one. I know it's late and you need to be getting home and you don't really have any baskets made up because you like to personalize each one, but—"

"I've got one. I mean, I just finished making up a gift basket. You can take that one."

Aunt Dorothy's eyes lit with surprise. "I can? You wouldn't mind?"

"Wait right here," Charlene instructed. Within moments, she returned with the gift basket she'd made for Melanie, along with a white shopping bag. "How's this?" she asked, and held the basket up for her aunt's approval.

"It's perfect, of course, but didn't you make that up for someone else?"

"I was going to surprise Melanie Arbor on my way home, but I have time to make another. It's Daniel's bowling night. He won't be home until late," Charlene explained. She was more relieved than disappointed to have time for herself on her husband's night out. Whether she spent that time at home or here in the shop mattered little. She set the gift basket into the shopping bag, handed it over and wrapped her hands around her aunt's. "Here. My treat. Take this to Annie and tell her my thoughts and prayers are with her today, too."

When Aunt Dorothy looked up, her eyes were moist with tears. "Thank you, Charlene. You might not be much of a businesswoman, since you wind up giving away almost as much candy as you sell, but you are a very precious woman. You know that, don't you?"

Charlene swallowed hard and smiled. "It's a family tradition. Makes a girl worry, you know, about being as good as her role model."

Chuckling, Aunt Dorothy tiptoed up a bit to kiss Charlene's cheek. "You're twice as good as I am, which you'd know for sure if you ever found out some of my secrets. Which I'm hoping you won't," she teased. "I'm heading across the street to pick up some supper for me and Annie. Do you want me to get something for you to eat on the ride home?"

"Thanks, but I have half a sandwich left over from lunch. I can drive you to Annie's if you like," she offered.

"You need to get yourself home. Somebody's bound to be at The Diner who can drive me. If not, I'll call a cab," her aunt insisted. "I'll stop by and see you tomorrow. I'll get up early and make some of those caramel brownies you like so much," she added before heading to the door.

Charlene followed her aunt, locked up behind her and watched the elderly woman cross the street. Aunt Dorothy did not seem to have her usual bounce to her step, but after such a long day, neither did Charlene. She waited until her aunt had gone into The Diner—a family-friendly restaurant that had anchored the Welleswood business district for years—before heading back to the workroom again.

An hour later, with her heart still glowing from her visit with the Arbors, Charlene headed toward home. When she hit the highway, she polished off the half sandwich left from lunch and chased it down with a diet soft drink. Dinner on the run was a frequent occurrence in her life now, but that, too, was a blessing of sorts. She did not manage to get home for dinner with Daniel very often these days. Her hour-long commute each way solved the problem of sitting at the dinner table each night in silence with the man she had married forty-one years ago.

Once their two children had grown up and left home, the awkward quiet between them was like an uninvited guest, at first. Now the silence was an invisible, integral part of their relationship, a testament to the struggle of maintaining a marriage that neither of them seemed to know how to revive.

Dwelling on the sorry state of her marriage, however, was not how Charlene wanted to spend the rest of her drive home. Using her hands-free cell phone, she called her son, Greg, a physical therapist living in Bucks County, Pennsylvania, with his wife, Margot. When he did not answer, Charlene left a message and tried reaching her daughter, Bonnie, now a high-school guidance counselor who had moved to New York City straight from college to share an apartment with several friends who also had a love for the faster-paced city life. No answer at Bonnie's, either, so Charlene left a message.

She often played telephone tag with the children, and it seemed that this, too, was another sign that the pattern of her life had changed. After being a full-time homemaker and stay-at-home mother, she found owning and operating her business just as demanding, but in different ways. Her mothering days might be well behind her now, but she was blessed to have the kind of store where she could channel her instinct to nurture to her customers.

Nothing, however, seemed to ease the yearning in her heart for the happy marriage she had once shared with Daniel.

For the better part of an hour, she concentrated on the heavy traffic and set her worries aside. When she finally pulled off the highway onto Magnolia Road, she hesitated for a moment, then called Daniel to let him know she was just fifteen minutes from home. To her surprise, he didn't answer, so she left him a message, too, and then remembered that he was bowling with friends this evening.

A few moments after she hung up, her cell phone rang. She answered without reading the display screen, keeping her eyes on the road.

"Is this Mrs. Butler? Mrs. Charlene Butler?"

Charlene stiffened at the sound of the unfamiliar voice. Aside from her family, no one called her on her cell phone for one very simple reason: she never gave out the number. She rolled her eyes, resigned to the idea that telemarketing had invaded the world of cell phones, too, and made a mental note to see if she could add her cell phone number to the national Do Not Call list. "What can I do for you?"

"Is this Mrs. Charlene Butler?"

A deep sigh. "Yes, I'm Charlene Butler, but I can assure you that I am definitely not interested in buying anything you might be selling. As a matter of fact—"

"Mrs. Butler, this is the emergency room at Tilton General Hospital. Your aunt, Dorothy Gibbs, asked that we call you. She arrived here about twenty minutes ago and—"

Charlene's heart pounded hard against the wall of her chest, and her mind raced with questions that she hurled at the caller. "Aunt Dorothy? Are you sure? I was just with her. She was fine. What's wrong?"

"The doctor is with her now. She appears stable at the moment, but she's asking for you. We couldn't reach you until she found the paper she had written your cell number on. Can I tell her that you'll be coming to be with her?"

"Yes. Absolutely. Of course I will," Charlene cried, blinking back tears as she looked for a place to turn around. "Tell her I'm on my way. It'll take me an hour. Just tell her I'm coming," she directed, praying that the good Lord would continue to keep watch over Aunt Dorothy.

Chapter Two

Charlene pulled into a parking space in the visitors' lot across the street from Tilton General Hospital just after nine o'clock—well ahead of her husband, who was on his way from the bowling alley to meet her. She slammed the car into Park, grabbed her purse and locked up with a quick click of the remote.

She practically jogged toward the emergency room on the east side of the hospital, where she could see the steady pulse of the flashing red lights on the ambulance parked at the entrance. Her purse, which hung from her shoulder, swung in a short arc with each pounding step, mirroring the emotional pendulum that dragged her from fear that Aunt Dorothy might be seriously ill to the hope she had just had another one of her little "spells."

When Charlene finally reached the entrance, she paused to whisper a prayer before passing through the automatic double doors. Inside, a security guard seated behind a desk cocked a brow, and she shifted the strap of her purse. "My aunt… Dorothy Gibbs… They brought her here… I need to see her," she stammered.

His gaze softened when he handed her a visitor's pass.

"Information desk is straight ahead. Then take a number. Take a seat."

She swallowed hard and glanced around the emergency room to get her bearings. Like most people, she supposed, she was not fond of hospitals. She had been fortunate to have raised two active children without ever needing to visit an emergency room.

As she might have expected, the air was heavy with anxiety and suffering, but also held a peculiar sense of boredom or, perhaps, a sense of resignation that she found disturbing.

Straight ahead, a bank of signs hung from the ceiling over a long, low counter in front of a series of five small, semi-partitioned areas. One sign read Information. Three were labeled Patient Registration. One read Intake. Non-medical personnel in business attire toiled with computers and paperwork at their stations, serving visitors and patients at the counter.

Charlene got in the information line behind two women and looked around. Through an opaque wall behind the security guard, she could see a good two dozen people seated in a stark, gray-painted waiting room, but Aunt Dorothy was not among them. Several children were lying on the floor, coloring or reading, while other youngsters raced back and forth between the restrooms and the water fountain.

The gray plastic chairs along the walls were nearly all filled with patients and their loved ones. An elderly woman sat alone in a wheelchair in the corner. Another woman lay on a gurney, her face to the wall. Everyone was waiting for medical attention. Charlene didn't know if Aunt Dorothy had had to wait, too, or if she had arrived by ambulance. Either way, Charlene's heart trembled with regret that she had not been by her aunt's side.

At that moment, a pair of metal doors swung open on Charlene's right, revealing the very heart of the busy emergency room, where she caught a glimpse of medical personnel hustling to care for patients behind curtained treatment rooms.

"Next."

With her visitor's pass in hand, she stepped up to the counter, where a middle-aged woman with frizzy orange hair sat filing a broken fingernail. Her name tag read Joy Wohl, but her bored expression was certainly joyless. "My name is Charlene Butler. I got a call from the emergency room saying my aunt had been brought here and that I needed to come right away. Dorothy Gibbs. Her name is Dorothy Gibbs," she explained, anxious to see her aunt as quickly as possible.

Without making eye contact, the woman slowly turned and pressed a few keys on the computer with the tip of her emery board. She sighed, put down the emery board and handed Charlene another visitor's pass, this one blue.

"Press the button to open the double doors. Once you're inside, there's a small waiting area to your left. Wait there until someone comes for you. You'll need to keep this pass visible at all times," the woman explained as she picked up the emery board again and resumed filing her nail.

Charlene nodded, peeled the backing from the blue pass and pressed it on her coat. She proceeded exactly as she had been told.

Too anxious to sit down in the waiting area, Charlene remained standing at the entrance, watching medical personnel hurry from a central station in and out of the treatment rooms. After waiting for five long minutes without any offer of help, she approached the central station. Not one of the three women behind the counter stopped working to acknowledge her; instead, an older woman dressed casually in khaki pants and a matching sweater approached, wearing a gentle smile. "You look like you need some help. I'm Kathryn Campbell. I'm a volunteer with the hospital's spiritual-care team."

"I'm trying to find my aunt, Dorothy Gibbs."

The woman's smile broadened. "Then you must be Charlene. Your aunt's been asking for you."

Charlene sighed with relief. "Then she's fine. Will I be able to take her home?"

Kathryn Campbell's smile deepened. "She's in the emergency room, so I'm not sure I'd say she was fine, but she is resting comfortably. You'll have to speak to the doctors about her medical condition. I've been checking in on her while she was waiting for you. She's alert and oriented, and she's feeling much better. She had a bit of an ordeal, but I'll let her tell you all about that. To be honest, I think she's still pretty frightened. If you'll follow me, I can take you to her. She's right down the hall."

Charlene followed the volunteer down the hall to the third room, where the woman peeked in and then motioned for Charlene to enter. "She's in the first cubicle. The curtains have been pulled to give her privacy, although she's the only patient in the room at the moment. While you visit, I'll see if I can find Dr. McDougal. She's been treating your aunt. One of the nurses will probably be in to check on her shortly, and I'll stop back later, too."

"Thank you. Thank you so much," Charlene murmured. Unsure of what to expect when she saw Aunt Dorothy, she caught her breath and entered the room. An off-white curtain framed the far side of the hospital bed where her aunt lay, eyes closed, clutching her battered purse to her breast. The cubicle, like all of the emergency room, reeked of alcohol and medicines.

Aunt Dorothy appeared paler and smaller than usual, and uncharacteristically frail. Charlene approached the bedside slowly, and smiled when she caught the scent of her aunt's perfume mingled with the pungent smells of antiseptics and medications. Relieved to see the gentle rise and fall of her aunt's chest, Charlene ignored the monitors at the head of the bed, since she couldn't make sense of them, anyway.

She slipped off her coat and placed it and her purse on top of the plastic chair beside the bed, trying not to make a sound.

When she turned back to the bed, a pair of hazel eyes, dulled by fatigue, greeted her. Charlene stroked her aunt's head, damp with perspiration. "I was trying not to wake you up."

"I wasn't asleep. Just resting," her aunt said, and smiled weakly. "I'm sorry. It looks like you might have to wait awhile for those caramel brownies I promised you. I don't think I'll be up to making them by tomorrow."

Charlene returned the smile. "Don't worry about the brownies or anything else right now."

Aunt Dorothy closed her eyes and sighed. "I'm sorry to be such a bother. After your long day, the last thing you needed was to drive all the way back here." Her hands trembled as she shoved her purse toward Charlene. "Take this for me, will you, dear?"

"You're not a bother," Charlene insisted as she laid the purse near her own. "What happened? Why didn't you call me earlier if you felt ill? I would have brought you to the hospital. Makes a girl worry, like maybe you had somebody else you liked better," she teased.

Aunt Dorothy kept her eyes closed, but smiled again. "I really didn't think I needed to come to the hospital. Not at first. I was visiting Annie, just like I told you earlier. We'd just been sitting around after dinner, talking, when I started feeling woozy. Then I had one of my little spells."

Aunt Dorothy opened her eyes and blinked away a few tears. "Poor Annie. She didn't quite know what to do. I started coughing and coughing, and I just couldn't stop. Then I started sweating and I couldn't catch my breath and my heart just started racing faster and faster. That's when I got scared, too, so Annie called nine-one-one. The next thing I knew, I was in the ambulance. Let me tell you, riding in one of those things is not much fun. I never realized they were so bumpy," she grumbled, but managed a lopsided smile. "The emergency medical technicians were a nice bunch of young fellas, though."

Charlene chuckled. "You didn't flirt with them, did you?"

Aunt Dorothy attempted another grin, but didn't quite succeed. She looked out of energy. "Only a little. They were a tad on the young side, but they were awfully strong. They got me to that ambulance easily enough, and they took good care of me all the way here—all except for going over all those bumps." She pointed to a basin of water and some cloths on the table by her bed. "I'm still feeling a little pasty. Could you wipe my face for me, dear?"

"What does the doctor have to say about your spell?" Charlene asked as she moistened a cloth.

"Not much yet. They did some tests, but I haven't heard back on them yet."

Charlene gently wiped her aunt's face, looking tenderly at the aged features that were so dear to her. "Did you take your insulin today?"

Aunt Dorothy's eyes flashed. "I never forget my insulin. You know that. Between the trip and going to Annie's for dinner, I probably just overdid it today. I'm sure I'll be fine."

"Yes, you will," Charlene murmured, and set down the washcloth.

A nurse entered the room with a cup of ice, looked from Aunt Dorothy to Charlene, and smiled. "You must be Dorothy's niece. I'm Sandy. I'm helping to take care of your aunt," she explained before turning her attention to her patient. She scanned the monitors and checked Aunt Dorothy's IV. "Feeling better?"

"Better, but I'm not feeling like myself at all. I don't think I'm up to going home tonight," Aunt Dorothy replied, surprisingly admitting to a frailty when she was usually so unwilling to be anything less than independent.

"Whether or not you go home tonight is up to Dr. McDougal. She'll be here to see you again in a bit. In the meantime, I've brought you those ice chips you wanted."

Aunt Dorothy took the cup of ice chips. When she tried to sip at some, her hand shook so hard she spilled a few onto her chest. "Look at the mess I'm making."

The nurse scooped up the spilled chips and tossed them into a trash can. "No problem. The mess is gone. Do you want some help?"

"Charlene can help me," Aunt Dorothy informed her.

Under the nurse's watchful gaze, Charlene held the cup steady while her aunt took some ice chips, sucked them away and then took some more.

"Is there a preliminary diagnosis to explain my aunt's spell?" Charlene asked.

The nurse looked at Aunt Dorothy. "Is it all right to discuss the diagnosis or test results with your niece?"

Aunt Dorothy swallowed the ice in her mouth. "Of course."

"We're still waiting for test results, so we can't be sure," the nurse began. "We're concerned about her lungs, of course. They're congested, which is why we're limiting fluids for the moment, at least until we get the results of her chest X-ray. And we're concerned about her heart. The symptoms she's exhibiting are all consistent with CHF, but they may or may not indicate she's had a heart attack. The electrocardiogram was inconclusive, but we'll know from the blood test whether or not she actually suffered one."

Charlene furrowed her brow. "CHF?"

"Congestive heart failure. According to what we've learned so far from her primary physician, your aunt was diagnosed with CHF over two years ago. We have some brochures about it that you can read, if you like, and Dr. McDougal will be glad to answer all of your questions once there's a final diagnosis."

Charlene looked at her aunt. "Why didn't you tell me?"

Aunt Dot shrugged. "They've got fancy names for everything these days. All that CHF means is that my heart is slowing down and doesn't pump as good as it did when I was younger. I'm eighty-one years old. Everything is supposed to slow down. For all the money they charge, the doctors should tell me something I don't know."

Charlene shook her head, but directed her attention to the nurse. "I'll take one of those brochures, and I'd like to speak to Dr. McDougal as well. Do you think they'll be admitting my aunt, or will I be taking her home tonight?"

The nurse patted her arm. "I wouldn't plan on taking her home tonight. We're hoping to transfer her to a regular room, as soon as one becomes available. We'll know more when we have all the test results, which won't be until morning. If you'll excuse me, I need to check on another patient. Just buzz if you need me to come back," she instructed before leaving the room.

"Honestly, I don't mind staying. They're taking good care of me," Aunt Dorothy admitted. "I'm sorry you had to drive all the way back here, but I wanted to talk to you about my papers and such. Just in case."

Charlene cocked her head. "Just in case?"

Aunt Dorothy sighed and patted the side of her bed. "Sit with me. I need to tell you where I keep my important papers, just in case I don't get to go back home at all. And I need you to stop at the bank first thing in the morning, if you wouldn't mind."

"I have money, but I shouldn't think that you'd be needing any," Charlene said.

"No, but I do need my living will," her aunt whispered, and closed her eyes.

Chapter Three

In less than a week, every aspect of Ellie's existence had been flipped upside down and twisted inside out. Organizing the chaos in her life was her most urgent priority, and she had only today to do it.

She closed and locked the door to her office late Wednesday afternoon at the end of her first day back at work. She was carrying a briefcase full of student papers that the substitute teacher had collected for her to grade, along with a list of parents who needed to be called because she had missed parent conferences for the first time in her career.

She tried to be content, knowing that the substitute teacher was fully certified in language arts and was hoping to be hired for the upcoming year if there was an opening, so Ellie's students had been left in very capable hands. She also tried to resist the sense that she'd let down her colleagues—she'd done her best to handle the overflowing papers in her mailbox and on her desk by relegating them into stacks labeled: To Do, To Distribute and To File.

The only thing not overflowing when she had returned had been her voice mail. The entire system had been shut down now for three days, much to the amusement of the faculty and staff, who watched the failed attempts to repair the system by the novice technicians the district had employed instead of calling in seasoned professionals.

Ellie hurried down the empty school corridor to the parking lot and carefully avoided the mini piles of dirt and dust left by the custodians as they swept their way from classroom to classroom. At her car, she stuck her briefcase in the trunk next to a small suitcase packed with comfortable clothes for her mother to wear home from the hospital tomorrow, and then plopped into the driver's seat. The afternoon was so warm she was tempted to put down the top on her convertible, but since she would only have to put it right back up again at the hospital, she decided against it…for all of two seconds.

Grinning to herself, she put the top down anyway. After all, what good was having a convertible if you didn't use it when you could?

She headed out of the parking lot and turned toward the avenue. At a red light, she kept time with the sound of her blinker by tapping her left foot as her mind raced back over the past few days and ahead to the next few weeks. Starting tomorrow, her routine would change. Drastically.

With the diagnosis of a mild heart attack confirmed, Ellie's mother would be released from the hospital in the morning. Tests had also confirmed that she had coronary artery disease, CAD, and given her advanced age, the doctors had agreed against an aggressive course of action, deciding to treat her condition with only medication, a change in diet and a mild exercise program. If all went well, after recuperating for a few weeks, her mother would be living back in her own home again, although none of the doctors would speculate on how much time she might have left.

In the meantime, Rose Hutchinson was moving in with Ellie, which was a bit like inviting the wolf to move into the chicken coop and expecting the chickens to celebrate.

Ellie accelerated the instant the light turned green, hung a left and headed south toward the hospital. Before tomorrow morning, she had to turn the small den on the first floor of her stately old Victorian into a bedroom for her mother, put fresh linens in the downstairs bathroom and clean the house. She also had to stock the pantry with appropriate foods for a woman with heart disease, which meant a trip to the grocery store.

Somehow, she had to find time as well to stop at her mother's house for more clothing and toiletries. Grading papers and preparing next week's lesson plans would simply have to wait until the weekend.

Feeling overwhelmed and definitely in need of a friend who might help her face the challenges ahead, she eased into the visitors' parking lot at Tilton General, took a ticket from the automated machine and found the last open parking spot at the far end of the lot. Then she turned off the ignition, pulled out the key and bent forward to rest her forehead on the steering wheel.

Reorganizing her life at home and at work would only mean her days would be temporarily more hectic. Coming face-to-face with the fact that her mother's illness was progressive and ultimately terminal only increased her anxiety. She had called both of her sons twice to inform them about their grandmother's condition. Alex and Richard had each promised to keep in closer touch by telephone and to come home soon. In the meantime, Ellie knew that if she hoped to establish a loving relationship with her mother, the time was now.

After praying for the gift of the time she and her mother needed together, Ellie put the convertible top up again, locked her car, grabbed the suitcase out of the trunk and headed across the asphalt parking lot.

Inside the hospital, she followed the now-familiar route to the visitors' desk for a pass, took the elevator to the fifth floor cardiac unit and went directly to her mother's private room.

She tapped on the half-open door. "Mother, it's me, Ellie," she said as she nudged the door open.

Straight ahead, wearing the aqua dress she had worn to the doctor's office, her mother sat in a wheelchair with her hands clutching her handbag and her lips set in a forlorn frown. A large plastic bag sat on the floor at the foot of the freshly made bed. The heavy smell of disinfectant filled the air.

Her mother's bottom lip quivered. "You took your sweet time getting here. I was afraid you'd changed your mind and decided to send me to a nursing home."

Ellie put the suitcase on the floor, laid her purse and the visitor's pass on the overbed table, and moved a chair to sit down next to her mother. "I told you that I had to go into work today, but that I'd be here by five o'clock. Why are you dressed to go home? The doctor said you wouldn't be discharged until tomorrow, and I took the day off to bring you home with me," she said gently, concerned that her mother seemed to be getting more forgetful.

"I got discharged right after breakfast this morning," her mother countered. She opened her purse and pulled out a wad of papers. "See for yourself. I've been cleared to go home for hours and hours, but I guess you were too busy at work to leave. I would have called Phyllis's daughter, but she took her mother to New York City today to see a Broadway show. The nurses were awfully nice to me, though. They gave me lunch and dinner, even though I wasn't supposed to be here."

Ellie skimmed the paperwork and sighed with frustration. "No one called me. Why didn't anyone call to tell me you'd been discharged early?" she asked, more upset with the hospital than with her mother.

"They probably left a message for you at school. You just never called them back, which doesn't surprise me. You never seem to call me back before I leave five or six messages."

Ellie gritted her teeth. "I gave the hospital my cell phone

number so I could be reached immediately," she argued. "Can I take you home with me now, or am I supposed to let someone know you're leaving?" she asked as she skimmed through the discharge orders, the diet plan her mother had to follow, more prescriptions than Ellie had ever seen at one time and a stapled set of papers that included information about the nurse who would be coming to the house.

"I think you're supposed to tell someone. I don't think you're allowed to take me downstairs by yourself," her mother said. "But do hurry. I'm getting sore from sitting in one spot all day."

Ellie handed the papers back to her mother. "Keep these for now. I'll check about what to do, and be right back." She retraced her steps to the nurses' station. Not recognizing either of the two nurses on duty, she kept her anger in check. "My name is Ellie Waters. My mother is Rose Hutchinson, in room four seventeen. I understand she's been discharged, and I can take her home now. Is that correct?"

The younger nurse, who looked like she might have skipped high school and graduated from nursing school yesterday, at age sixteen, wore a badge that read, Cindy Morgan, R.N. Without speaking, she pulled out a chart and bounced over to the counter where Ellie was standing. "Your mother was discharged hours ago," she said, frowning, "It's too bad she had to wait all this time for you to pick her up, but at least you're here now. Unless you'd like to go over her discharge instructions or her new prescriptions, all I need to do is call an aide to take your mother downstairs and wait with her while you get your car."

Ellie drew in a long, deep breath. "I can look the papers over when I get home, but I would have come to the hospital immediately if I'd known she'd been released. Is there any reason I wasn't called?"

The nurse flipped open the chart again and skimmed the paperwork. "I see they tried to reach you three times this morning. I tried once when I came on shift a few hours ago, but no one answered."

Ellie let out a sigh. "Our phone system is down, but I specifically asked to be called on my cell phone. Do you see that listed anywhere?" she asked, using her assertive teacher voice, which kept all but the most defiant students in line.

Cindy the child nurse skimmed the paperwork again and had the decency to blush. "Oops. Sorry."

"Oops," Ellie repeated, shook her head and decided that incompetence was quickly overtaking obesity as a major health concern in America.

Any doubts she might have had about bringing her mother home with her rather than sending her to a care facility of some kind quickly vanished. "I'll be waiting with my mother in her room. How long do you think it will be before an aide can come?"

"Ten minutes," the nurse promised, her cheeks still pink with embarrassment.

Ellie checked her watch, smiled and marched back to her mother.

Precisely six minutes later, the aide arrived, stood right in front of the wheelchair and put his hands on his hips. "You see now, Miss Rosie, I told you that you'd be going home today before I did!"

"If someone had bothered to tell *me,* we'd all have had a better day," Ellie grumbled to herself as she left for the elevator carrying her purse, her mother's suitcase and the plastic bag with all the disposable whatnots her mother had collected during her stay.

Forty-five minutes later, Ellie had her mother resting on the sofa in the living room with the TV remote in one hand and the cordless telephone in the other. "I won't be long," she promised. "I have to go to the pharmacy, make a quick stop at the store to get a few groceries, and get some of your things from your house for you."

"Don't forget to turn out the lights before you leave my house," her mother cautioned before a yawn interrupted her. "You never did have any consideration for the electric bill."

"I won't forget. If you need me while I'm gone, just hit the seven on the telephone. I have it programmed to call my cell phone."

Her mother yawned again, turned on the TV with the remote and adjusted the sound. "I'll be fine. I'll watch the news," she said, but Ellie could barely hear her over the high volume of the TV.

Thirty-five minutes later, Ellie emerged from the pharmacy with nine prescriptions, four over-the-counter drugs and pill organizers in different colors. She also had acquired the sincere belief that only someone with a master's degree in science would be able to read the paperwork for each medication and organize the pills her mother would be taking three times every day.

She fared better at the grocery store. She was not a health-food purist, but she did prefer fresh fruits and vegetables when she cooked, and had no trouble finding a nice selection of produce. She picked up some lean, skinless chicken breasts and fresh tuna to add to the lean beef and pork already in her freezer, and a few low-fat dairy products, all in accordance with the dietary guidelines she had been given at the hospital.

Last stop: her mother's house.

Ellie pulled into the driveway next to the darkened house, and turned off the ignition and headlights. She sat in the car for a moment, recalling childhood memories that were still painful. The tiny bungalow where she had grown up as an only child had always been her father's house. After his death nearly a dozen years ago, it had become her mother's house, but Ellie had never, ever thought of it as home, then or now.

She twisted the slim gold wedding band she still wore on her left hand. Home was where she had lived with her husband, Joe, and experienced the wonder of unconditional love for the first time in her life, until his unexpected death six years ago this past November. Home was where she and Joe had raised their two sons while they both pursued careers they loved. And home was where she lived now, surrounded by joyful memories, her faith and the fulfillment she still found in her career as an educator.

With loving thoughts of her late husband and her children and her little grandchildren tucked in her heart, she got out of her car and made her way into the house. She flipped the switch next to the front door for light. Little in the modestly furnished living room was familiar, since her mother redecorated as frequently as most women changed their wardrobes.

At the moment, the room was awash with tones of beige and white—on the walls, carpet and furniture. Instinctively, she slipped off her shoes and wiped her hands on her overcoat, surprised at how easily she could reclaim habits she had acquired as a child.

Turning on lights as she walked, Ellie heard echoes of her mother's critical words, and recalled her father's ever-present silence. In the front bedroom, more pale earth tones greeted her. She made quick work of choosing the clothes her mother would need for the next two weeks, grabbed some toiletries from the only bathroom in the house and placed everything in a large suitcase.

Lugging the suitcase, she turned off lights on her way back to the living room. With her shoes back on, she flipped the switch to turn off the last of the lights and locked up the house. Heading to her car, she prepared herself to go home and try one more time to win her mother's love and approval.

She had the faith she needed to guide and sustain her, and after she made one stop tomorrow, she would have the only other thing she absolutely needed during the next two weeks: her own little replenished supply of her favorite candy.

Chapter Four

After seven seemingly endless days, Charlene felt as if she had spent an entire week in a playground, stuck on one end of a seesaw. The neighborhood bully sat on the other end and constantly taunted her by pushing her up into the air and holding her there before jumping off again and again, slamming her hard and fast to the ground.

In reality, she had spent every waking hour for the past week at Tilton General Hospital, a bizarre playground filled with mysterious flashing and beeping equipment, where Aunt Dorothy was recovering from her little spell—a mild heart attack.

Days, when Charlene was encouraged by the promise of her aunt's progress, were invariably eclipsed by days when the bully, aka CHF and diabetes, yanked her down from hope to fear and doubt. Other than taking time to retrieve her aunt's living will from the bank, she had taken only one other break, the morning that two women from the Shawl Ministry had stopped by to visit her aunt and deliver a lap shawl they had made for her. Charlene was also able to grab an hour alone when Annie Parker and Madeline O'Rourke, her aunt's closest friends, came by each afternoon, which deepened Charlene's desire for a supportive friend of her own.

Charlene was pleased, however, that once she had called her children, both Greg and Bonnie had come to the hospital to see Aunt Dorothy, although they each had had to get right back to their homes and had been unable to stay overnight to visit longer with Charlene.

Yesterday, her aunt had stabilized enough that the doctors discussed discharging her. Now, on Friday morning, Charlene and Daniel were in Aunt Dorothy's room for a meeting with the hospital social worker, Denise Abrams. Fortunately, her aunt's roommate had left earlier for a test of some sort, so the group that gathered about Dorothy Gibbs's bed had plenty of privacy.

Charlene glanced at the faces and smiled to herself. No one was under fifty. Over the past week, she had seen a multitude of doctors, nurses, technicians and aides. Most of them were young enough to be her children, and she shuddered to think that at fifty-nine, she could be a grandmother to some of them. Although they all appeared to be competent and qualified, Charlene felt more comfortable with hospital workers who had been alive long enough to know that the best way to eat a Mary Jane was to suck on it and to remember a time when a chocolate bar, with or without almonds, cost only a nickel.

Aunt Dorothy sat in her bed, obviously enjoying being the center of attention. For the first time since she had entered the hospital, her hazel eyes held a bit of sparkle again, but she still looked forlorn and bedraggled.

Her pale blue hospital gown hung loosely around her narrow shoulders. Mottled bruises surrounded the small white bandages on the back of both her hands and at the crease in her elbows. Her complexion was pasty. Her dark gray curls were flattened in some spots on her head, while unruly clumps stood up in other places, making her look as if she was wearing a broken tiara.

She was a queen held captive on her throne. An IV line snaked from the back of her hand to several bags hanging on a stainless-steel pole, and wires linked her to monitors that measured her heart rate and blood pressure. A urine bag and catheter tubing were discreetly concealed beneath sheets near the floor, and bars on both sides of the mattress gave her something to hold on to, helping her to shift more easily in bed.

Charlene stood next to the pillow, resting a hand on her aunt's shoulder. Daniel held on to the top rail with one hand on the other side of the bed. Charlene studied him as he told her aunt about the young boys' basketball team that was coming to camp in the state park this weekend.

The crisp white sheets on Aunt Dorothy's bed offered a stark contrast to Daniel's perpetual tan, acquired from a lifetime working as a park ranger. He was a stocky, well-muscled man with dark, wavy hair. He had passed on his cleft chin and love of the outdoors to their son, Greg, while their daughter, Bonnie, had inherited his fabulous blue eyes and the tendency to be reserved and not to reveal thoughts and emotions.

Standing with him, as she had done for more than forty years, Charlene realized again how physically unlike one another they were. She had often said that her figure resembled a salt-water taffy: plump from top to bottom. She had pale skin and hair she'd kept light, long after time had darkened it and later turned it white.

Her life, since she'd married Daniel, had been built around her home, her children and her church. Unfortunately, by the time the nest she and her husband shared was empty, they had become strangers who had two children in common, but little else—except that they both loved Aunt Dorothy.

Grateful for his support during the past week, Charlene glanced at the end of the bed, where Denise Adams stood next to the papers she'd brought to the meeting and stacked in neat piles on the table Aunt Dorothy used to take her meals. For a woman who spent a good part of her professional life helping patients and their families make the transition from hospital to home, the social worker had an unusually stern and rigid turn to her mouth, and the expression in her light brown eyes was pure business.

Charlene was not impressed—until Daniel and Aunt Dorothy finished their conversation and Denise started the meeting. "As you know, Dorothy, Dr. Marks feels you're just about ready to leave the hospital," she said in a sweet, soothing voice that immediately set Charlene at ease.

For the life of her, however, she would never get used to hearing the hospital staff refer to her eighty-one-year-old aunt by her given name. Unless requested by the patient, titles and last names, Charlene had learned, were taboo under new guidelines that were supposed to guarantee patient privacy. But no one had asked Aunt Dorothy what she preferred.

"I wouldn't mind staying a few days longer," Aunt Dorothy murmured, clearly reluctant to return home and resume the independent life she had always led.

"We've got a number of options for you and your family to consider, which is why I thought it best that we all be here together," Denise replied. "I thought I might briefly explain what those options include. First and most importantly, we all realize you're not quite up to living alone again."

When Aunt Dorothy nodded, Charlene lightly pressed her fingertips against her aunt's shoulder to offer support. She was relieved that the social worker had not come right out and said Aunt Dorothy would never live alone again.

Denise smiled. "We have several alternatives you can consider."

Aunt Dorothy stiffened and blinked back tears. "Not a nursing home. Please. I—I never, ever want to give up my home and spend my last days in a nursing home," she whispered.

"You really don't need to move permanently into a long-term-care facility," the social worker assured her, clearly avoiding the words "nursing home." "You could benefit from a short-term stay in any one of the rehab facilities in the area, if you have the resources. While you're there, you could consider selling your home and moving into an assisted-living facility. I could help you and your family in that regard, as well."

Charlene, seeing the devastation and panic in her aunt's eyes, didn't hesitate—not even to consult Daniel. "Aunt Dorothy, you can come live with us until you're strong enough to go home again," she offered.

Relief flooded her aunt's features. "I wouldn't be in the way. Not for an instant. And I'd be good and quiet, too," she promised, looking from Charlene to Daniel and back again.

Charlene smiled and glanced at her husband, albeit belatedly, for his approval.

He looked at her aunt, instead, and smiled. "You can live with us for as long as you like."

The social worker frowned. "As I recall, the two of you don't actually live in Welleswood," she said to Charlene.

"I have my business here, but we live in Grand Mills," Charlene replied, wondering why that should make any difference.

"Near the edge of the Jersey Pinelands," Daniel added.

The woman's frown deepened. "That's a good hour away. Being that far from Dorothy's physicians could present problems. When she experiences another episode, which seems likely given the progressive nature of her illness, there might not be time for you to bring her back here."

"You could change doctors for the time being. People do that all the time," Daniel suggested. "I'm sure the hospital could transfer your records to a closer facility."

Aunt Dorothy blinked back a fresh wave of tears. "But then we'd have to change back again when I move home.

That's an awful lot of trouble for everybody." She sighed and worried the tissue in her hands. "It seems to me the good Lord should just call me Home, but He doesn't appear to want me yet."

Before Charlene could comment, the social worker responded, "Perhaps a better alternative would be to hire someone to live with you at your own home, assuming you have both the room and the resources. Whether you choose a home health aide or a companion, you'd receive the help you need and be able to keep the same doctors."

Aunt Dorothy's face lit with interest before she dropped her gaze.

Charlene swallowed hard. Hiring anyone to live with Aunt Dorothy full-time was well beyond the elderly woman's means, but even if it wasn't, Charlene could not imagine letting a stranger care for her beloved aunt. "We're family. We take care of one another," she murmured, patting her aunt's shoulder. "I have to come to work in Welleswood five days a week anyway, so why don't I just move in with you, temporarily, until you're up to living alone again," she suggested, unable to bring herself to suggest that Aunt Dorothy would never actually be well enough to live by herself again.

Based on the literature she had read, and what the doctors had told her, the progressive nature of CHF—combined with the complications of aging and diabetes—meant that Dorothy Gibbs would probably never be self-reliant again. But pointing that out now, when her aunt was so vulnerable, just didn't feel right to Charlene.

She looked over at Daniel again. "You could come and stay with us for weekends, couldn't you?"

He winked at Aunt Dorothy. "Why not? You're still my best girl, aren't you?"

"I can't ask you two to uproot yourselves like that," Aunt Dorothy argued, but her voice was soft and unconvincing.

"You didn't ask. We offered," Charlene countered, grateful for her husband's support.

"I've been promising you all winter that I'd come take a look at that backyard of yours once spring came and clear it out for you," Daniel added. "It would probably be a whole lot easier for me if I had a few weekends where I could work in the yard without driving back and forth."

Aunt Dorothy batted her lashes at him and smiled demurely. "I haven't had anyone over for Easter brunch for years. Not with the yard so overgrown. It's lovely to think we could have brunch by the creek again this year. Do you think Greg and Bonnie could come, too?"

"The kids aren't coming home for Easter this year, remember?" Charlene prompted, to remind her aunt that they had talked about this when Greg and Bonnie had visited her.

"Greg and Margot are spending the holiday with her parents and Bonnie is going to Spain as a chaperone with the Spanish club at her school," Daniel added. "Charlene and I will be there, though. I can't promise to have the yard cleared out by then, but I'll try."

"You're such a strong man. I just know you'll have my yard looking better than it ever did by Easter," Aunt Dorothy said confidently.

Watching her husband and aunt chatting, Charlene blinked hard. Aunt Dorothy was actually flirting with Daniel, and he was absolutely beaming!

"I think you've found a wonderful solution." The social worker smiled proudly, as if the idea had been hers. "I'll speak to Dr. Marks this afternoon. From what he told me earlier today, our patient might even be able to go home tomorrow," she offered. Then she packed up her papers and left.

"My house keys are in my purse. You took that home with

you, didn't you?" Aunt Dorothy asked as she took a fresh tissue from the box beside her bed.

"As a matter of fact, I still have it in the trunk of my car. I wasn't sure if you'd need anything in your purse or not."

Her aunt smiled. "Good girl. Instead of staying here all day, why don't you go to my house and air it out a bit? You could move a few things around to make up the spare bedroom for you and Daniel to use while you're staying with me. Just stick anything in your way up in the attic or anywhere else you find room. I'm afraid there isn't much in the refrigerator, either, except for a few old leftovers that probably need to be tossed out."

She paused to mop her brow with the tissue. "Unless you need to get to Sweet Stuff. You haven't been at your store all week."

"The store is fine. Ginger King offered to work full-time for me this week so I could be here with you. I'll get your house ready, instead," Charlene reassured her.

"What about you, Daniel?" her aunt asked.

"I'm afraid I have to get back to work. I'm on duty this weekend, but I can start on that yard of yours next weekend," he promised.

"Well, go on, then," Aunt Dorothy said, waving them both away. "You two have important things to do."

After a round of hugs and kisses, Charlene walked to the elevator with her husband. "Thank you," she murmured as they waited side by side for the elevator.

He nodded, but kept his gaze on the arrows over the elevator. "Sure. Nothing else made much sense."

The down arrow lit up, a bell sounded and the elevator doors opened. "It won't be for long," Charlene offered as they stepped into the empty elevator, saddened to think Aunt Dorothy's days on this earth were nearing an end.

He shrugged and pressed the button for the lobby.

"Maybe it might do us both some good to spend a little time

apart during the week," she said, giving voice for the first time to the fear that the indifference that had marked their marriage these past few years might be too great to overcome.

He let out a long, deep sigh. "If that's what you want," he said hoarsely.

And her heart trembled.

Maybe that's what he wanted, too.

Chapter Five

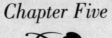

Still shaken by the notion that living with Aunt Dorothy might also be an odd, unexpected trial separation of sorts, Charlene walked up the slate walk to her aunt's house on Lady's Creek Drive. Dwarfed on either side by a copse of majestic oak and maple trees older than Welleswood itself, the one-story cottage looked sadly neglected.

Using the set of keys retrieved from Aunt Dorothy's purse, Charlene unlocked the front door and stepped into the living room. Memories of happier times assailed her, and she swallowed hard, praying there might be more time to share with her aunt and more memories to create.

Once her eyes adjusted from the bright sunlight to the dim interior, she pulled up the shades on the windows to let in more light. The living room was dated, yet neat, and was obviously in need of a good cleaning, just as she had suspected. Before she could continue walking through the house, however, there was a sharp rap at the front door.

She recognized the visitor standing on the porch and wished she had not bothered to answer the door at all. "Hello, Mrs. Withers," she murmured, and managed a smile for her aunt's elderly next-door neighbor.

A pair of curious brown eyes tried to see past Charlene into the house. "When I saw your car in the driveway I came right over," she said, holding her buttonless coat together with both hands. "I heard poor Dorothy has passed. Is it true?" she asked, her eyes filling with tears.

"No, it's not true. Not at all. Aunt Dorothy is recovering from a slight heart attack. She's coming home tomorrow, we hope," Charlene said, anxious to correct the woman, who had a well-earned reputation for gossip and exaggeration.

Agnes Withers furrowed her brow. "Really? I heard she had a real bad heart attack. Then I heard—"

"I'm sure my aunt will tell you all about it when she's home and up to having visitors," Charlene interrupted. "I just came by to straighten up a bit for her." She decided not to share more, for fear of adding to the gossip.

The neighbor leaned forward a bit. "You need to move in. That's what you need to do," she whispered, as if someone might be lurking behind the overgrown bushes to overhear her. "Dorothy won't admit it to anyone, not even her doctor, but the poor dear can't see well enough these days to take her insulin right. Half the time I'm here, she either fills that needle with too much or too little, and I have to fix it for her. Sooner or later, if that heart of hers doesn't give out first, she's going to take an overdose or go into one of those diabetic comas, all because she can't see to get her dose right."

"I hadn't realized it was a problem," Charlene admitted.

"Well, it is a problem, but you can't tell her I tattled. She'll get mad at me, and I couldn't bear losing my very best neighbor."

"I won't say a word."

"And don't mention I heard she was dead, either. She'd really get mad at that," the woman added.

"No, I won't," Charlene promised, eager to send the woman on her way.

Mrs. Withers apparently had other plans in mind, and took

a step closer. "I'd be glad to help you straighten things up for Dorothy," she offered.

Charlene tightened her hold on the door frame. "That's so kind of you, but I don't want to impose. I'm sure I can take care of things here, but maybe you could do something else for me…and for Aunt Dorothy."

"Of course," the woman replied, although disappointment laced her words.

"Considering the rumor that she had passed on, maybe you could call your friends to reassure them that she's doing much better and that she'll be coming home very soon."

"Absolutely. I will. I'll make the calls right away." Good as her word, she turned and walked away.

Relieved and convinced Agnes Withers would put the rumors to rest, Charlene went into the dining room, where more memories greeted her. Then she headed into the sun-drenched kitchen, where light poured onto the cracked red-and-green linoleum floor through a pair of windows facing the overgrown backyard. On the red Formica countertops that had faded to pink, Aunt Dorothy had new hypodermic needles and used ones. The room itself was orderly, but like all the other rooms, it needed a good cleaning.

Charlene opened the refrigerator and found a few Styrofoam boxes of leftovers on the shelves, beside all sorts of single-serving condiments. The freezer was packed with more Styrofoam containers covered in ice crystals and frozen meats dating back as far as two years.

She inspected the bedrooms on the other side of the house. She poked her head into Aunt Dorothy's bedroom, where she detected the stale smell of Tabu, but instead of going inside to pull up the shades, she flipped on the light with the switch near the door. As she expected, the room was as tidy and as sadly worn as the others and just as needy of a cleaning.

Sighing, she turned out the light and bypassed the bathroom to look in the spare bedroom, where she would be staying alone during the week and with Daniel on the weekends. When she flipped on the light, she gasped and stepped back. There had to be a bed in this room somewhere, but she couldn't see past the three tall dressers and the dozen or so tall tin cabinets and wardrobes huddled together, leaving only a narrow aisle.

Charlene groaned out loud.

There was no way she could get all this stuff up into the attic as Aunt Dorothy suggested. Dismayed, she closed her eyes for a moment to concentrate on positive thoughts. Unfortunately, they were as thin as Aunt Dorothy's bedspread.

Charlene let out another groan and opened her eyes. Cleaning the house would take hours and hours. She would probably be up half the night, which meant she could barely spare time to drive home to pack some clothes for herself, let alone think about spending her last night of freedom with her husband.

Worried that he might think she was overeager to be apart from him, she inspected the spare bedroom again to figure out the quickest way to make the room habitable.

If the wardrobes and cabinets were not too heavy, she might be able to shove them closer to the wall, along with one of the dressers. She opened one cabinet and found it stuffed with bags: grocery bags, shopping bags, plastic store bags, garbage bags and even a few small white bags from Sweet Stuff.

She tried one of the wardrobes. It held so many blouses there wasn't room for one more. Another cabinet was filled with recycled glass jars that her aunt had labeled for flour, sugar, pancake mix and more. Charlene opened one jar, saw the remains of several brown critters and promptly screwed the lid back on.

The other four wardrobes were packed with clothing, just like the first, and the remaining cabinets held a variety of rusted canned goods, laundry products, cleaning supplies, string, rubber bands and what looked like several years' worth of newspapers.

Charlene's first impulse was to pick up her cell phone to call and order a Dumpster; instead, she simply closed all the drawers and doors. She had heard that many people who had lived through the Great Depression in the 1930s never recovered from the deprivations of that era, and Aunt Dorothy's spare bedroom held proof that it was indeed true.

From what she was seeing Charlene suspected that Agnes Withers's concerns about Aunt Dorothy's competence were valid. Charlene was going to need to monitor her aunt much more closely than she had thought. She also had to do something to repair her troubled marriage, or she would spend the rest of her days with a heart as weak and broken as Aunt Dorothy's had been found to be.

Chapter Six

At six-thirty on Saturday morning, Ellie laced up her sneakers and tiptoed downstairs to the kitchen. She slipped the spare key into the waist pocket in her walking pants and zipped the pocket closed. Another pocket held her cell phone and a mini change purse. She tapped in the security code on the alarm pad, opened the back door then quickly reset the alarm and slipped outside.

Setting the house alarm reminded her that her cell phone was still programmed to vibrate. She hadn't used that mode much until her mother had gotten sick and Ellie had needed her cell phone on when she was teaching. Rather than resetting the cell phone now, she moved it into a smaller pocket so she could feel the vibration if someone called.

She drew in a huge gulp of crisp, fresh air, feeling her spirits lift with joyful thoughts of total freedom. For the next forty minutes or so, she would be completely alone with her thoughts on her first power walk since her mother became ill and moved in with her. Fortunately for both of them, their body clocks were as different as their personalities. Ellie liked to go to bed and get up early. Her mother liked to watch late-night TV and spend her mornings sleeping in. Once Ellie returned to work next Monday, she expected to see precious little of her mother. She hoped to build a more positive, loving relationship between them in the few hours they would have together.

Ellie stretched her muscles for a few minutes, then headed across her small backyard to the alley behind the house. As usual, the neighborhood was quiet at this hour. She quickly covered the two long blocks to the avenue and turned right toward the center of town. With virtually no traffic to worry about, she walked in the street close to the curb, avoiding the nuisance of going up and down the curbs at cross streets.

Block after block of residential homes, a mix of single-family Victorians, converted duplexes and World War II-era twin homes now called town houses soon gave way to the revitalized business district. New brick sidewalks had replaced cracked and broken concrete. Planters on each corner had recently been filled with fresh dirt and mulch, and sat waiting for volunteers to plant colorful flowers that would bloom from next month through the end of summer.

When a sparkle in the street caught her eye, Ellie smiled and stopped to pick up a dime. She started walking again as she slipped the coin into the mini change purse she carried for her funny money—change she found on the ground and had fun collecting in a cookie jar at home before donating it to a local charity. She had given nearly forty dollars to the new girls' crew team last year, but she hadn't yet decided on this year's recipient.

She kept her pace quick. When a pair of early-morning joggers passed her, she didn't feel a twinge of envy. Walking briskly was a good way to strengthen her post-menopausal bones and heart without adding stress on her knees.

She passed the town's newest restaurant, La Casita, and the ice cream parlor, Scoops, where a good number of her tenth-grade students would probably congregate tonight after the basketball game. With her heart and her feet hitting a steady rhythm, she passed other storefronts: The Deep End, an eclectic gift boutique; the unisex beauty salon; The Purrple Palace, a pet shop catering to felines. All the stores were new to the avenue.

When she spied Pretty Ladies, a hair salon that had survived in the small town's shopping district through the mall-building era and now thrived in the boom of the revival, she made a mental note to call later today. She needed to make a home appointment for her mother to have her hair done.

Growing traffic on the avenue in the heart of the business district forced Ellie onto the sidewalk in front of The Diner, where the air was heavy with the smell of sizzling bacon. Inside, seniors who shared her habit of rising early were taking advantage of the breakfast special and the owners' policy of encouraging the patrons to linger long after they finished eating.

Beyond The Diner, she stopped to pick up a penny, crossed the street and passed Sanderson Realty, the only real estate office in town. The closer she got to McAllister's Bakery—voted best of South Jersey for the past seven years—the harder she found it to concentrate on anything but sugared pastries.

She didn't slow her pace, but she did take several good whiffs of air, savoring the luscious aromas of butter, cinnamon and apples that drew the line of people waiting to enter. She deliberately didn't carry money with her on her walks so she wouldn't be tempted to stop and take home more calories than she would burn. She had another plan for where her calories would come from today.

To avoid the line outside the bakery, she returned to the street and hugged close to the parked cars until she reached the bank, which was the one-mile mark from her home. She used a pedestrian walkway to cross the street and start the return mile toward home. She had one destination in mind—Sweet Stuff.

Before the day ended, she needed to replenish her candy stash, at home and at work. Although it was way too early for the candy store to be open, she wanted to check the store's hours on Saturdays and see if they had been extended for the Easter holiday.

When she had to stop at the corner for a turning car, Ellie spied two quarters in the street and gleefully added them to her mini purse. Approaching the candy store, which shared an entryway with a recently opened health-food store, she was convinced this was the oddest pairing of businesses ever to grace the avenue.

At the door of Sweet Stuff, she read the sign listing the store's hours. Saturday, noon to five. She sighed. Charlene Butler had not extended the hours yet.

Disappointed, since her free time was so limited, Ellie turned away to resume her walk home. She had taken only a few steps before the sound of insistent tapping made her turn around. The rapping was coming from inside the candy store. Ellie looked closer and saw Charlene standing at the window, waving her back to Sweet Stuff.

Ellie met Charlene at the door.

"You're up early as usual, I see. Come on in." Charlene's smile came straight from the good spirit everyone in Welles-wood had come to know and love. Charlene was Ellie's favorite store owner on the avenue.

Ellie hesitated. "I only stopped to see if you'd extended your hours yet for the holiday. I had no idea you'd be here this early."

Charlene chuckled. "Neither did I. The high-school crew team ordered a whole slew of chocolate, oar-shaped taffies for their fund-raiser. I promised Ginger King I'd meet her here at nine to help finish them before she opened up for me. And since I haven't been in all week, I thought I'd come in extra early to catch up."

"Then I shouldn't interrupt you," Ellie said, remaining

outside. "I'll come back when you're officially open for business."

Charlene frowned for a moment before reaching behind the door to flip the Closed sign over. "There. For you, we're open, and don't think for a moment that I'm being patronizing. There are a couple of boxes I need to bring up from the basement, and I can't do it by myself. I should have known better than to have the delivery guys put them down there. Since you're here, I could really use your help before you pick out your candy."

Ellie chuckled, inhaling the gloriously decadent smell of chocolate as she stepped into the store.

Charlene shut the door and flipped the Closed sign back into place.

"You're one of the few people who doesn't lecture me about having a sweet tooth," Ellie said. "How has it been for business to have a health-food store open next door?"

Charlene grinned. "The owner, Andy Johnson, is nice enough, I suppose, and I can't argue with the idea that we have to take good care of our bodies. Heck, I stock low-calorie, dietetic treats here for anyone who needs them. I just prefer to celebrate my customers' lives with old-fashioned sweet stuff. It's as simple—and fun—as that."

"Hence the name of your shop," Ellie said. "Sweet Stuff."

Charlene's grin widened. "Exactly. I just try to make sure my customers don't overindulge. 'Seek moderation in all things.' That's what my pastor always says."

She led Ellie past the glass-fronted display cases filled with the usual variety of chocolates and a dazzling array of chocolate Easter specialties. "From the moderate amount of candy you buy, I'd guess you were a kid who could make a box of candy last through an entire movie."

"I usually saved some to take home, too," Ellie admitted, fully aware that she'd had the candy-stashing habit from an early age.

Charlene shook her head. "And I usually ate all my candy before the movie started, which might be why I haven't been able to find my waist since grammar school and you're so trim."

"Exercise helps me keep the weight off," Ellie said. "I started walking along the avenue every morning right after my husband died six years ago. I've found it's a great way to clear my mind and forget my troubles before the start of the day."

Charlene sighed and tugged her blouse back down over her hips. "I probably should take up walking. But I'm having a bit of a problem just squeezing in the time I need to be at the store and at home."

"I know you commute to Welleswood, but I don't know where you do live."

"Actually, I'll be living here in town for a while," Charlene confided, pausing to straighten a display of chocolate-covered Easter eggs. "Do you know my aunt, Dorothy Gibbs?"

Ellie nodded. "She's a darling. She lives over on Lady's Creek Drive, doesn't she?"

"Yes. I'm staying with her temporarily," Charlene replied. She explained about her aunt's recent hospitalization as she led Ellie toward the workroom and down the basement steps.

Ellie listened to the sad tale, and shook her head in sympathy. "I'm sorry. I hadn't heard your aunt was in the hospital, but I'm glad she's home now." She was surprised that she and Charlene hadn't bumped into each other at the hospital, but she assumed her mother's private room explained that. As they crossed the basement, Ellie told Charlene about her similar situation. "Caring for my mother is going to be a lot more difficult and more time-consuming than I ever expected," she finished, not mentioning anything about the added challenge of living day to day with constant criticism or the idea that if she had the support of a loving husband, as Charlene did, the challenge might be less difficult.

"I'm finding myself facing much the same with my aunt,"

Charlene offered. Then she pointed to two large cardboard boxes stacked against the wall. "The boxes aren't all that heavy. They're filled with little stuffed Easter animals, but as you can see, they're a bit unwieldy for me to handle by myself." She looked back at the staircase and shook her head. "I'm not even sure how the two of us are going to manage getting up those narrow steps with them."

Ellie eyed the boxes and studied the staircase for a moment. "Having four hands instead of two will help, I think. That's what I could have used raising my children—or trying to control twenty-five students in a classroom when I first started teaching. There were days I wished I'd been born an octopus."

Charlene chuckled. "I think I had a few days of my own like that. Still do, as a matter of fact."

Ellie bent to pick up an end of one box. "If you take the other side, I'll try backing up the steps, and you can direct me," she suggested.

Working together, they managed to get the first box upstairs with only a few stumbles—and lots of giggles along the way.

Before Ellie followed Charlene back to the basement for the second box, she set her cell phone, which had almost fallen out of her pocket, on a shelf near the worktable for safekeeping. "If you're going to be in Welleswood for a few weeks, will you be going back home on Sunday mornings for church?"

"I don't really want to be that far away from Aunt Dorothy, although the price of gas alone would be reason enough not to travel back and forth. I've really been feeling the pinch commuting lately," Charlene replied. With her back to the steps, she hoisted up the end of the second box. "I'll go first this time. I've got a bigger cushion to land on when I fall back and thump down on a step or two."

"You don't have a security camera anywhere recording us, I hope," Ellie teased as she grabbed the other side of the box.

"Me?" Charlene giggled and started walking backward

toward the steps. "Trust me, you're safe. Adding a dead bolt to the front and back doors was one big concession to store security."

"Careful," Ellie cried. "The bottom step—"

"Whoa!" Charlene tripped, plopped down on the third step and started giggling again as she struggled to shove the box away from her chest to get back to her feet. "That's it. Here's an idea. Unless you're directing me, there's no conversation until we get this box upstairs. Then I'll make us both a big mug of hot chocolate with whipped cream and some Belgian chocolate shavings that are so decadent you could almost swoon."

Ellie's mouth watered. "Okay, but first, let me invite you to come to church with me tomorrow. Services start at ten o'clock."

"I accept. Ready?"

Ellie adjusted her hands to get a better grip on the box, and nodded. This time they managed to get the box upstairs without either of them stumbling again.

"A job well done," Charlene murmured. "Thanks."

Ellie smiled. "You're welcome," she murmured.

Ellie had lost touch with a few friends after she was widowed—she just wasn't comfortable socializing any longer with couples, always being the fifth wheel. But she could certainly use a friend like Charlene, who would understand the hopes and fears she had about her mother and who would be in town without her husband, on weekdays, at least.

Maybe together, as friends, the two of them just might be able to help each other—to meet the challenge of caring for their elderly relatives and in other ways, too.

Chapter Seven

With her heart lighter and her tummy filled, Ellie headed home. She always made a point to finish the last mile of her power walk as strong and fast as she had begun, but after leaving Sweet Stuff, she had a good reason to slow her pace—the two white shopping bags she carried.

In one bag, she had enough candy to replenish her supply until the next semester. Included among the goodies were Necco wafers, her favorite. The other bag held a gift basket that Charlene had insisted on making for Ellie's mother, which contained one Easter bunny—from the assortment of stuffed animals that had been in a box they had carried upstairs—along with heart-healthy treats such as yogurt-covered raisins, fruit-flavored lozenges and salt-free carob-covered pretzels.

Ellie could still taste the scrumptious hot chocolate Charlene had made for them, and her sides were still aching from giggling so long and hard during her unexpected visit.

She was a block from home when she heard the whine of sirens. A few moments later emergency vehicles were whizzing by her. She cringed and turned her head away from the deafening sounds as the police car, fire truck and ambulance raced down the avenue, lights flashing.

Out of habit, she said a quick prayer for the unfortunate people who needed the emergency assistance. She also offered a prayer for the men and women who responded to any call for help.

Her ears were still hurting when she saw the police car turn onto her street. By the time the ambulance took the same left, she was running at top speed with the shopping bags slapping at her legs and her heart pounding in her chest.

"Please, no." She prayed that the emergency vehicles were not headed for her house. She charged down the alley behind her property. She was winded when she reached her backyard and, when she saw the lights flashing directly in front of her house, she grew frantic.

She didn't have time to notice that there was no sign of fire or smell of smoke. And it didn't fully register with her that all of the sirens were silent. She dropped the shopping bags and ran at full speed the moment she spied her mother standing in the crowd of people gathered across the street, wearing her winter coat draped over her green quilted robe and matching slippers.

Clutching her side, Ellie reached her mother and struggled to catch her breath as the fire truck and ambulance began backing up the narrow street.

"What happened? Are you all right?" Ellie managed to ask, searching her mother's face and form for any sign of injury or illness.

"I'm fine," her mother assured her, before turning to the two middle-aged men standing near her. "Thank you both. You were a great help. Now that my daughter is here, I'll let you get back to your families."

"Yes, thank you," Ellie murmured, and nodded to her neighbors, George Pullman and Elliot Welsh, who lived with their families in adjoining houses across the street. After being assured by both men that they were just a call away if she or her mother needed help, and as the crowd began to disperse, Ellie offered her arm to her mother.

"Please tell me what happened," she implored, and tried to prepare herself, because whatever it was, it was bound to be her fault, at least from her mother's perspective. Still, she wanted to hear her mother's side of it before she had to face the police officer, who was just coming around the side of her house carrying the two shopping bags she had dropped. "What happened?" she asked again.

Her mother's eyes flashed with irritation. "When I woke up, my room was stuffy. I guess it's just because the den is so small, and I'm used to a large bedroom. All I wanted to do was open the window for a little fresh air. Instead, I almost had a heart attack when the alarm started blasting. You could have warned me about the alarm on the windows, so all these poor people wouldn't have wasted their time coming out here making such a big commotion," she snapped as they crossed the street.

Ellie groaned. "You're right. I'm sorry. I guess I just assumed you knew the windows were included in the security system that I showed you yesterday," she apologized, although she was fairly certain she had specifically mentioned the windows. "Why didn't you just tell the alarm company what happened when they called the house?"

Her mother tilted her chin up. "I tried, but I couldn't remember the password, so they sent out the cavalry like I was some kind of an intruder who was stupid enough to answer the telephone, or simply an old woman who was too demented to understand what was happening to her."

Ellie frowned. "The alarm company should have called me," she said, reaching into her pocket and realizing it was empty. "I'm sorry. I was helping Charlene Butler in her store and accidentally left my cell phone there," she admitted.

When she saw the officer approaching, she held up her hand, motioning for him to wait a moment, and helped her mother back into the house. "I'm sorry about forgetting my phone, and I'm really sorry about the trouble you had with the password. I thought changing it to Daddy's name would make it easy for you to remember."

"As if I could rely on your father to do anything in an emergency." Her mother sniffed, slipped off her coat and handed it to Ellie. "I'm going to the kitchen to make a cup of that dreadful decaffeinated tea and try to forget this ever happened. You handle the police officer on your own. I've been embarrassed enough," she murmured, and walked away.

Embarrassed herself by the criticism, Ellie laid her mother's coat across the back of a chair and returned outside. Her morning went from bad to awful when she recognized the police officer: Bob Johnson, a former student. In his late thirties, he was a lot stockier now than he had been in tenth grade, but he had not been able to tame the cowlick that still stuck out from the top of his head.

"Thanks, Bob. I'm really sorry you had to come out here so unnecessarily this morning," she said as he handed her both shopping bags.

"No problem. I brushed off as much dirt from the bags as I could."

Ellie glanced at the bags for a moment and then smiled at him. "Good job. Thanks. Is there anything I have to do? Fill out a paper or a waiver or something?"

He grinned and patted his chest pocket. "All done. Got it right here. Spelled everything right, too," he added with a wink.

"I should expect you would," she replied. Spelling was never a problem for him. Turning in homework or projects on time had been his weakness. "How are Amy and the boys?"

He pulled out his cell phone, flipped it open and pulled up the picture gallery. "Amy's always great, but you know that," he said as he turned the cell phone so Ellie could see his wife's picture.

"I sure do," she murmured. Amy had graduated as valedictorian, earned her teaching degree in just three years, and now taught at a charter school in Philadelphia. She still wore her hair long and straight and looked nearly the same as she had in high school.

"The boys are catching up to me faster than I thought they would," Bob told her proudly, and clicked the viewer to enlarge the picture of them.

Ellie's eyes widened. "Those boys look like you put yourself through a copy machine three times!"

He laughed. "They're all in middle school now. The twins are in seventh grade. John's in sixth. They'll be heading up to the high school in a couple of years, so get ready. Unless you're planning to retire soon," he said as he stored the cell phone away.

"Not that soon," Ellie replied. In fact, she hoped she might spend the rest of her career as an administrator. It was a good possibility, as long as her current supervisor, Nate Pepperidge, finally retired this year, as rumors suggested he would. If she landed the job she had been dreaming about for most of her career, she would miss all three of Bob's sons in the classroom, but she wasn't ready to mention that possibility now.

Instead, she wrinkled her nose. "I don't suppose there's any chance the false alarm didn't go over the police scanner, is there?"

"Not even. My guess is that the students who don't find out about it over the weekend will know by the end of homeroom on Monday."

"You're right. They will."

"And they'll have a good time teasing you about it, too, unless what I've heard about you lately is wrong."

It was her turn to grin. "If you heard that I'm still a tough, no-nonsense teacher, you heard correctly. Unfortunately, I had to relinquish my title as the Cranky Queen of Corridor

Duty to Mrs. Josephs and Mrs. Snyder when I became head of the department."

His eyes twinkled. "I heard those two are so tough you might have put yourself through a copy machine twice when you trained them, too."

She laughed. "The Welleswood pipeline is alive and well, I see. Thanks again, Bob. I'll make sure there won't be another false alarm here."

Back in the house, she locked the front door but didn't rearm the security system. She hung her mother's coat up in the closet and carried the two shopping bags into the kitchen. Almost immediately, her tension melted away. She had repainted the kitchen last year, and the warm yellow walls made her feel as though she had her very own piece of the sun inside her home.

Her mother looked up for a moment from her seat at the round oak table, and used the palm of her hand to smooth the yellow-and-blue striped place mat under her mug of tea. "I never did understand the reason some people prefer these place mats. A properly ironed tablecloth looks so much nicer."

"Maybe it's because washing and ironing tablecloths takes too much work. Besides, a tablecloth would cover the top of the table, and the grain is really pretty," she pointed out, admiring the round table she had bought shortly after Joe died because she could not bear to eat a meal, especially breakfast, longing for him to be sitting at the head of the table.

"That may be true," her mother countered, "but you'll never be able to convince me that a home is ever as well cared for when a woman spends more time working outside of it than inside." She paused to take a sip of her tea. "Women seem to justify taking all sorts of shortcuts these days, and that's only one reason the divorce rate is so high."

Rather than provoke an argument by defending women who worked, Ellie pulled the gift basket from the shopping bag and set it on the table. "This is for you from Charlene Butler," she said, and tugged the lavender bow into place. After sliding the basket across the table to her mother, she put her own shopping bag on the table and sat down. "She sends her get-well wishes, too."

Eyes wide, her mother briefly fumbled with the bow before pulling the cellophane free. The moment she lifted out the tan cotton-tailed bunny that stood some twelve inches high, she brought the stuffed animal to her shoulder. "What a soft little sweetie," she murmured, stroking the fur with her fingers as if trying to calm a fussy baby. "I'm not going to be able to eat anything from Sweet Stuff. Not on my new diet. But this little bunny is just too dear."

Ellie removed the rest of the cellophane from her mother's basket. "Everything in here is quite suitable for your diet. Charlene's been stocking healthy items, including sugar-free candy, for a while now," she said, and then went on to share the news she had gotten about Miss Gibbs, as well as Charlene's temporary move to Welleswood to care for her aunt.

Her mother let out a sigh and tilted her head toward the bunny. "Poor Dorothy. I'd heard something about her being ill. She was about four years behind me in school, but I've known her for a good seventy-five years. What a sad life she's had."

"What makes you think her life has been sad?" Ellie asked.

"Back in our day, very few women chose to remain spinsters, but that's what Dorothy did. She never married and never had children. And she had her chances, too."

"Maybe she never met the right man," Ellie suggested, defending the elderly woman, since she was not here to defend herself.

"Maybe she was too fussy," her mother responded.

Ellie changed the subject to avoid an argument. "I'll let you sort through the goodies Charlene put into the basket for you while I unpack the other bag," she said.

Her mother tugged Ellie's bag down far enough to peek inside, and rolled her eyes. "Really, Ellie, one of these days you're going to regret fueling that sweet tooth of yours."

"If I haven't regretted it for sixty years, I think I might be safe," Ellie said, sliding the bag closer.

"That's what I thought when the doctor told me fifteen years ago to stop eating the way I did. Just look where that's put me." Her mother glanced around the room, frowning, as if being in Ellie's home was the worst place she could be.

Ellie swallowed hard, blinked back tears and left the kitchen to stash away her candy and to tuck this new hurt next to all the old ones before she walked back to Sweet Stuff to get her cell phone.

Chapter Eight

Charlene rose early again on Sunday to get a head start on the day. She showered quickly, as quietly as she could, and decided blow-drying her hair would be too noisy. Instead, she towel-dried her hair and pulled it back into a traditional ponytail, the way she had worn it since opening her store.

En route to the kitchen, in what was becoming a daily ritual, she stopped in the living room, picked yesterday's newspaper up off the floor and refolded it. She stuck it into the old mahogany magazine rack Aunt Dorothy used for her paper recyclables and remembered the days when she used to pick up after her little ones. Then, like now, walkways throughout the house had to be kept clear to minimize the risk of tripping and falling.

She continued through to the dining room, stopping in front of the small breakfront to retrieve the glass loaf pan that held all her aunt's medications, with the exception of the insulin that needed to be refrigerated. In the same way she had kept all medications out of her children's reach, Charlene had stored these pills out of sight to prevent her aunt from taking an accidental overdose.

She carried the pan with her into the kitchen. Fifteen

minutes later, she had her aunt's morning pills organized in a little glass dish at her place at the table, and her lunchtime and dinner dosages labeled and stored in plastic baggies. Charlene made a mental note to stop at the drugstore tomorrow to look at by-the-week pill organizers, although Aunt Dorothy had already insisted she had no need for one.

Aunt Dorothy's needs also required regular mealtimes, which meant Charlene could not eat on the run anymore. The meals had to be nutritious, well-balanced and consistent with the guidelines for her aunt's multiple medical problems. Hence, no more grabbing a handful of chocolates for herself and offering them to her aunt for dinner, too.

Surrounded by the hushed silence of early morning, broken only by the song of the birds outside, Charlene remembered how much she had enjoyed the solitude of the early morning when her children were little. As she peeled and diced vegetables for chicken stew in the Crock-Pot, she was convinced that in many ways, living with a sick, elderly person was not a whole lot different from living with a couple of toddlers.

There were great differences, though, she realized. A playpen could keep little ones from danger, but there was nothing to ensure a sick eighty-one-year-old woman would be safe if left unattended. And putting a toddler down for a nap was one thing; convincing a woman who had been independent and self-supporting for decades that she needed to rest in the middle of the day was quite another.

After living with her aunt for only two days, Charlene had learned that there was a thin line separating the need to respect an elderly adult's autonomy and the need to recognize when that adult needed to be told what to do and compelled to do it, if necessary.

To complicate matters, Aunt Dorothy had seemed to change since her stay in the hospital. Although she still had her marvelous sense of humor and still liked to flirt with men of any age, she seemed very content to have Charlene take care of her now, easily accepting dependency as she prepared to make the transition from this life to the next. Nonetheless, Charlene was determined to help her aunt make the most of what time she had left.

She placed the chicken in the Crock-Pot on top of the vegetables, added water, a dash of herbs and set the lid on top. Satisfied she had only to fix dumplings later this afternoon to complete the meal, she plugged in the Crock-Pot and turned the dial to Slow Cook.

She glanced at the red plastic clock over the stove and smiled. It was only seven-fifteen. She had plenty of time to tackle the preparations for the other two meals of the day before Ellie Waters picked her up for church at nine-thirty. By concentrating on her work, Charlene kept herself from wondering why Daniel had not called her—or if he had even missed her at all this weekend. She kept her stomach from growling with a mug of hot chocolate, without the whipped cream or chocolate shavings she had added when she had been with Ellie yesterday.

Within half an hour, she had a bowl of tuna salad with low-fat dressing and sugar-free, fat-free butterscotch pudding in the refrigerator, ready for lunch. She had just opened a package of English muffins when she heard the shuffle of her aunt's slippered footsteps. She looked up and smiled. "Good morning. You're up early today."

Aunt Dorothy waved in response. "Smells good! Chicken stew?" she asked as she slowly made her way to her seat at the chrome table. Her red plaid flannel robe was too big, making her look small and fragile, but her color was good, her curls were brushed and tamed, her eyes twinkled a bit and she was wearing perfume again.

"With dumplings," Charlene replied.

"My favorite!"

"Mine, too," Charlene said, but she didn't add that it was Daniel's favorite as well. "I don't think I've ever seen those red elephant earrings before, but I like them," she offered, changing the focus of her thoughts.

Aunt Dorothy blushed and tapped one of the dangling elephants with her fingertips. "I got these in 1965 at the World's Fair in New York."

Charlene chuckled as she carried the box with the glucose machine and testing strips over to her aunt. "You remember that?"

"Actually, I remember a whole lot more than that," she replied as she opened the box and started to lay out everything to test her blood sugar level. "Billy Martin, bless his soul, bought the earrings for me, and they weren't cheap, neither. They cost sixteen dollars, which was a respectable amount of money in those days. Not that I'd let a pair of earrings sway me, even ones as pretty as these."

She stopped talking to struggle with the small container of testing strips, and eventually got one out and laid it on the table.

"Sway you how?" Charlene asked, putting a cup of instant decaffeinated coffee into the microwave. She had found the appliance in its original box in the spare bedroom, just as she'd found the Crock-Pot.

Aunt Dorothy pricked her finger, caught a drop of blood with the test strip and slid it into the machine. "Billy and I had been keeping company for a couple of months by then." She smiled and shook her head. "Silly man. Like most of the other men I kept company with over the years, he wanted something he couldn't have and thought he could tempt me to give it to him."

"Aunt Dorothy!" Charlene clapped her hand to her mouth, shocked that her aunt would discuss such an intimate detail so openly.

"Don't be a prude, Charlene, and don't jump to conclusions. I'm from a whole different generation than the foolish young women today who break the Commandments, sleep with men and then act surprised when they move on to another fool. God didn't create women so they could have sex outside of marriage, and a man doesn't buy the cow if he gets the milk for free," she quipped, and paused to read the green numbers on the screen in front of her. "Write down one-eighty-seven in that book for me, will you please?"

Charlene recorded the number in the appropriate slot. Although it was a bit high, it was still within an acceptable range. "We need your weight, too," she reminded her aunt. She reached into a bottom cabinet and pulled out the new scale she had bought at the pharmacy. She set it on the floor near her aunt's chair, hoping her weight was also stable. Because her aunt's heart was not pumping blood properly, any sudden weight gain would be a warning that fluids were accumulating in her body, which could lead to a whole host of problems, including pneumonia.

Aunt Dorothy stood up and held on to Charlene's arm as she stepped on the scale. "One hundred and one, just like yesterday. I do like having a scale that just flashes the number, especially digits so large," she said with a grin.

Charlene helped her to sit back down before storing the scale away again. "So let me see if I have the story right. Billy Martin bought you earrings because he thought you'd sleep with him?"

Aunt Dorothy's eyes widened. "Not at all! The very first night he called asking me to go out with him, I made sure he knew I would never, ever sleep with a man who didn't put a wedding ring on my finger first. He just wanted me to break my rules. That's why he bought me the earrings and a pretty scarf and a box of German candy."

Although Charlene felt awkward discussing dating with her aunt, she was too curious to stop now. She heard the microwave ding, retrieved the cup of coffee and set it down in front of her aunt. "What rules?"

"My keeping-company rules," Aunt Dorothy replied, and wrapped her fingers around the steaming cup of coffee, waiting for it to cool.

"Dating rules," Charlene confirmed.

"Exactly. I had three, and I never broke them, no matter how good-looking the man happened to be or how many presents he gave me to try to sway my mind."

"Apparently I already know your first keeping-company rule. No sleeping together before marriage. What are the others?"

"Not sleeping together isn't my rule. It's one of God's," her aunt countered, and lifted her hands to count off her rules. "First," she said as she tapped the tip of one index finger against the other, "absolutely no kissing on the first date."

Charlene nodded. Her mother had pounded that rule, among others, into her head long before she had started dating. Not that she had always obeyed it. She clearly remembered kissing Daniel on their first date, but opted not to mention that to her aunt.

"Second," her aunt continued, "only two kisses per date. Two. Didn't matter if we went out to supper for an hour or two or if we spent the whole day together. Two was my limit."

"Why only two?"

"The same reason some people with a sweet tooth only have two pieces of candy a day—to satisfy the longing and avoid too much temptation. Which brings me to rule number three," her aunt replied matter-of-factly as she held up three fingers. "The third time a man asks you to break rule number one or two, he's out. Gone. It's over. Done. Kaput."

Charlene cocked her head. "How long did Billy Martin last?"

"Till Thanksgiving that year. But I had a new beau by Christmas," Aunt Dorothy said proudly. "I think I'll save John Hartman's story for another time, though. Are those English muffins I spied on the counter when I came in?"

"They are," Charlene said, and stood up. "Would you like one toasted?"

"Real dark, if you don't mind. I think there's some sugar-free crab apple jelly on the door in the refrigerator, but I need to take my needle first," she said, and started to get up.

Charlene gestured her back into her seat. "I'll get everything and toast the muffins. In the meantime, you need to take your pills."

Aunt Dorothy glanced at the mound of pills in the antique salt dish and frowned. "Half of those pills are big enough to choke a horse. The other half are so small I will hardly be able to pick them up. You'd think somebody at those drug companies would think about that, but they're all probably under thirty and wouldn't have a clue," she grumbled.

Charlene got a disposable hypodermic needle and an alcohol swab from the counter and laid them on the table before retrieving the bottle of insulin and the jelly from the refrigerator. Yesterday morning at this time she had been at Sweet Stuff, so this was her first chance to observe her aunt injecting insulin.

"I'm going to teach you how to do this, so watch closely," her aunt instructed. "There's nothing to it." She pulled the plastic cover off the needle and eased the tip into the bottle of insulin. "You just have to remember to fill the needle up to the line that's marked ten," she said, and pulled the plunger back to fill the syringe. Once she was satisfied she had the correct dosage, she pulled out the needle and handed it to Charlene.

Mindful of Agnes Withers's warning that her aunt was not able to see well enough to ensure she had the right dosage, Charlene checked carefully. Her heart dropped. "I think there's too much insulin in the syringe. Didn't you say you had to fill it up to the ten?"

"Yes, why?"

Charlene held the syringe closer to her aunt and pointed to the ten. "You've got it filled up too high. It's at fifteen—see?"

Aunt Dorothy leaned closer and squinted, without bothering to remove her glasses. "If you say so. It's hard to see because the insulin doesn't have a good dark color. I really ought to speak to the pharmacy. Maybe somebody there could add some food coloring or something to make the insulin easier to see."

"There's no harm done," Charlene murmured. She inserted the tip of the needle back into the bottle and extracted the excess insulin. "There. You're all set now," she said, and held the hypodermic needle out to her aunt.

Her aunt pulled back. "Go ahead. You do it."

Charlene blinked hard. "Do what?"

"Give me my injection," her aunt said, and pushed up the sleeve on her left arm.

"I—I don't know how."

Her aunt cleaned a spot on her upper arm with the alcohol swab. "Just shove it in. You can't hurt me."

Charlene's heart began to pound, but she took a deep breath, then gently inserted the needle and pressed firmly on the plunger.

"That was easy enough, wasn't it?" her aunt asked as Charlene removed the needle. "Just drop the whole thing into that plastic bottle over there, and you're done until tomorrow."

With her hands trembling, Charlene disposed of the needle. Assuming responsibility for this daily ritual had definitely not been part of her plans, but she clearly didn't have any other choice. In order to guarantee that her aunt injected the right amount of insulin every day, Charlene would have to fill the syringe for her.

"I've got some fresh tuna salad in the refrigerator for lunch. I shouldn't be home from church later than noon," she informed her aunt as she split an English muffin and popped both halves into the toaster.

"It's Fellowship Sunday. Stay for coffee and donuts. And don't worry about me. Annie and Madeline are coming over to stay with me while you're at church. Annie is a volunteer for the Outreach Ministry and visits with folks too old or too sick to go to church on Sunday anyway, and since Madeline is thinking about joining as a volunteer, too, she said she wanted to come along and pray with us here. Then we'll just visit together until you get home."

She pointed across the room toward the cabinets. "There should be a box of those small plastic baggies in that top drawer over there. Take one and stick it in your purse."

Charlene cocked a brow.

Her aunt moistened her lips. "I'd dearly love to have one of McAllister's raspberry-jelly donuts drenched with granulated sugar, not that powdery stuff. Bring me one home from church, will you?"

"You can't eat one of those jelly donuts," Charlene argued. "There's almost enough sugar in one of them to send me into diabetic shock, and I don't have diabetes! I thought you promised the doctors you wouldn't cheat on your diet."

"I said I'd try not to cheat so much," her aunt countered. She pouted for a moment, pulled a battered tissue from the pocket of her robe and wiped her nose. "Based on everything the doctors told me, I could die today or tomorrow or anytime in the next few months or so. Since the good Lord is really in charge, I've decided to accept the fact that He'll take me Home when He's good and ready, and not a moment before. So I'm going to use what time I have left enjoying things I like best. Today, I'm thinking that would be a raspberry-jelly donut from McAllister's."

Charlene shook her head. She was tempted to refuse her aunt's request, but she found it difficult to argue with her reasoning or her right to make these kinds of decisions for herself.

Reminded once again of the thin line separating her duty to see that her aunt followed her doctors' instructions and her obligation to respect her aunt's right to decide how she wanted to live the rest of her days, Charlene recognized the dilemma. But in this case, she was very sure about one thing: she was not ready to start bringing home treats from various functions in little plastic baggies.

Chapter Nine

Attending Sunday services in a new church with an unfamiliar minister did not feel nearly as odd to Charlene as sitting in a pew without Daniel at her side. Favorite prayers and the verses of Scripture that she had loved all her life helped to ease her discomfort. The welcome she had received from members of the congregation, as well as Ellie's companionship, also made her feel at home.

During the services, Charlene prayed for the wisdom to give Aunt Dorothy the best care, the courage to face the difficulties in her marriage and the insight to resolve them. She was still humming the closing hymn when she and Ellie left the church by the side door, both agreeing not to attend the coffee clutch.

"You like to sing," Ellie noted as they descended the steps.

Charlene felt a blush warm her cheeks and immediately stopped humming. "I hope I didn't get too carried away."

"Not at all. I always feel timid about singing," Ellie admitted.

"I think church is the one place I can sing my heart out. Since God gave me this pitiful voice, I figured He couldn't complain when I used it to praise Him," Charlene said. "Back home, folks are used to me singing off-key. I hope I didn't upset anyone here today."

Ellie laughed. "You weren't singing loud enough to drown out Mr. Owens. He almost barks his way through the hymns, and no one has the heart to complain," she said, and pointed to her right. "We can cut through the parking lot at Whitman Commons, or we can take the other path back to your aunt's house. Either way, we can carry our lights with us," she teased, referring to the closing hymn Charlene had been humming.

Charlene hesitated, trying to decide on a destination. "McAllister's would be in the other direction, right?"

Ellie nodded. "If you want something from the bakery, we should stay and join the others. They always have donuts from McAllister's on Fellowship Sunday here."

"Except that I'm not ready to be a bag lady," Charlene declared, and told Ellie about her aunt's request for a jelly donut in a plastic baggie. "Since you suggested walking together yesterday, I've thought about it, and hoped we could start today and walk to the bakeshop so I can buy some donuts for Aunt Dorothy and her friends. Unless you have to get right back to your mother."

"No. She's got her best friend, Phyllis Kennedy, with her for the morning. Actually, I could use the walk. I got up at five o'clock to grade papers before church, and I've still got two more sets to go, plus lesson plans to write. A good walk would be a nice way to grab a little time for myself. I could also use the company," she admitted as they headed off. "I don't know about you, but my light has gotten a whole lot dimmer lately."

"Mine, too," Charlene murmured, and increased her pace to keep up with Ellie.

"After spending so much time at the hospital, between trying to catch up on my schoolwork and taking care of my mother this weekend, I'm not sure if I'll have the energy to face eighty students tomorrow, although Monday is generally my easiest day. The kids are usually pretty sluggish on the first day of the week because they're recuperating from their busy weekends." She stopped at the corner. "Do you want to walk the avenue or stay on the side streets?"

"The side streets," Charlene replied. "I can get from my store to Aunt Dorothy's house, but I'm afraid I really don't know my way around Welleswood very well because I'm always in such a rush to get to work and home again. I should learn. Otherwise, if I do leave the avenue, I might walk in circles and never find my way."

"We'll turn here, then."

Side by side, they walked down Maple Avenue under a canopy of barren tree limbs, past stately homes much grander than Charlene's aunt's cottage or her own small house in Grand Mills, which sat on two isolated acres of wooded land.

"Did you ever think about taking care of your mother or father when they got old? I mean, before. When you were younger," she asked.

"Not very often," Ellie replied. "My mother and I are about as opposite as two people can be, and I spent most of my time growing up eager to be independent and move out. After my dad died awhile back, I did think about the possibility that I might need to care for my mother some day, but I usually set the idea aside, figuring I'd deal with it if and when I had to." She let out a long sigh. "I guess that time is now." She turned to Charlene. "What about you? Did you ever think you'd be caring for either of your parents one day?"

"I was only three when my father died," Charlene replied. "My mother died not long after I got married, so I never really thought about it."

They stopped at a cross street for a moment to let a Jeep filled with four teenagers go by. Charlene was also grateful for the chance to catch her breath before Ellie started them walking again.

"I got much closer to Aunt Dorothy once I opened the store here in Welleswood," Charlene went on. "But I'm ashamed to admit I didn't realize how her health had deteriorated until she was hospitalized."

"She's still incredibly active for a woman her age."

"And you walk incredibly fast," Charlene teased, struggling to keep up.

"Sorry. I forgot you're a newbie," Ellie replied, and slowed her pace.

"Better," Charlene said. "In the hospital, when the doctors told us Aunt Dorothy shouldn't live alone anymore, I couldn't bear the thought that she'd have to spend the rest of her days in a nursing home any more than she could. In a way, I think caring for her gives me the opportunity to do for her what I never had the chance to do for my mother because…because she didn't live long enough to get old."

Ellie looked at her and shook her head. "You're amazing."

"Not really," Charlene murmured. If she were amazing, Daniel would not be relieved to be living apart from her, and she would have known how to keep her marriage a happy one. She just didn't feel comfortable discussing her failures with Ellie. Not yet. "What are you going to do about your mother tomorrow when you go back to work?" she asked as they entered Welleswood Park.

Instead of following the asphalt walkways, Ellie set off directly across the grass, and Charlene had to be careful not to step on any of the spring crocuses that splashed the landscape with varying colors of purple and yellow. "I intend to pray a lot," Ellie said as they headed toward a gazebo facing the lake in the middle of the park. "After what happened yesterday with the alarm, I've also decided to take your advice and forget about using the security system while she's living with me."

"Welleswood is such a sweet little town, I'm still surprised by the fact that you have an alarm system at all."

"I had it installed after my husband died because I was scared to live alone. I never bothered to have it removed once

I got more accustomed to being by myself. Anyway, I've got my home phone programmed so all my mother has to do is hit one button and she'll reach my cell phone, which is never, ever going to be out of my possession again," she added.

Charlene winced. "I wish I'd noticed the cell phone before you left the store yesterday."

"Forgetting my cell phone was my fault, not yours," Ellie replied. "I have to make sure that I don't ever leave it anywhere again. We're not supposed to carry a cell phone in the classroom while teaching, but I don't think I have any other choice. I'll just make sure the ringer is off and it's set to Vibrate. In a real emergency, my mother will have to dial nine-one-one until the end of the week, when the Total Care system gets installed. Then she'll have an alert device to wear so that if she falls or is too sick to reach the phone when I'm not home, she can press a button to summon help."

Panting, Charlene nodded toward the gazebo just ahead. "Let's sit. I need just a minute to catch my breath, otherwise you'll be calling nine-one-one for me, and it won't be a false alarm," she teased.

"You'll be keeping up with me in no time," Ellie assured her as they walked straight to one of the benches built inside the gazebo. Honeysuckle vines and rhododendron bushes were just turning green, and although the fountain in the middle of the lake was still shut down, the springtime view was lovely. "We can sit, but just for a minute," she warned.

Charlene plopped down, opened her purse to get a tissue and wiped the sweat from her face. She looked around, did not see a trash can and stuck the rumpled tissue back into her purse. "I'm seriously thinking about buying a few shares in a company that makes tissues."

"Why tissues?"

"Now that old age is just around the corner for us baby boomers, the demand for tissues should absolutely skyrocket, if Aunt Dorothy is an example. She's gone through an entire box of tissues in two days. She keeps them in her pockets day and night and never remembers to throw them away. I did a load of laundry for her yesterday and made the mistake of not checking the pockets. I wound up with a tub full of wet clothes completely covered with itsy-bitsy, teeny pieces of tissue."

"Yuck!"

Charlene chuckled. "I thought for a minute they were tiny bugs gobbling up all the clothes. Unfortunately, I realized the pieces were pink and blue, and not brown, only *after* I'd sprayed the whole mess with an entire can of insect killer."

Ellie started giggling. "You did not."

Charlene grinned. "No, I didn't, but I made you laugh and I managed to keep us both sitting down for more than a minute."

"Let's go. Story time's over," Ellie announced, and slapped her knees. "McAllister's closes early on Sundays, so unless you intend to disappoint your aunt, we'd better get started again."

"How much farther?" Charlene asked.

"If we use the footbridge to cross the lake and take a shortcut, we have about a quarter mile. Ten minutes. Tops."

"And if we don't?"

"Maybe twice that."

Charlene raised her arm and pointed skyward. "To the footbridge!"

"Stop! I can't walk and laugh at the same time," Ellie protested.

Charlene smiled. "But you can talk and walk at the same time. While we're walking, I need you to tell me how to program my aunt's phone. Tomorrow when we meet again to walk, you can tell me how to get in touch with someone at that Total Care system."

Charlene returned to Aunt Dorothy's house with three small boxes the salesgirl at McAllister's had put into three plastic bags. After hanging up her coat, she stood in the living room for a moment and shook her head.

If she didn't know better, she would have guessed that the laughter in the kitchen was coming from a group of teenage girls rather than Aunt Dorothy and her elderly friends.

Invigorated by the fellowship she had found at church, as well as the friendship she was developing with Ellie Waters, Charlene carried her treats through the living and dining rooms with her light burning just a little brighter than it had been when she'd left the house this morning.

At the doorway to the kitchen, she ground to a halt. The laughter died instantly, and the three women seated at the chrome table stared back at her with their mouths agape and their eyes wide with guilt.

Annie Parker, her aunt's best friend, was sitting at one end of the table. With her sugar-white hair and her white polyester pantsuit, she looked like a plump marshmallow, and she was just as sweet. She blinked at Charlene with the innocence one might expect from someone eight years old, not eighty-one.

At the other end of the table, Madeline O'Rourke, at eighty, was the youngest of the trio. Her bright orange fingernails flashed as she toyed with her necklace of chartreuse beads. Her cheeks were covered with rouge, so Charlene couldn't tell if she was blushing or not.

Aunt Dorothy, on the other hand, was most definitely blushing, which added color to her pale features, but didn't hide her weariness.

The main focus of Charlene's interest, however, sat square in the middle of the table. Next to an open Bible, there was a large white cardboard box, with a logo identical to the one on the three boxes she was carrying.

"I didn't hear you come in," Aunt Dorothy said. She dabbed at her mouth with a tissue, but it was too late. Charlene had seen the raspberry jelly in the corner of her lips.

Madeline laughed nervously. "When the three of us get together, we're just a bunch of chatterboxes. We probably wouldn't hear Big Foot stomping through the house."

"That's not true, you know," Aunt Dorothy countered.

Madeline pouted. "Well, I wouldn't hear it, and I'm not ashamed to admit it."

"No, I wouldn't, either, but I meant Big Foot. It's not real. It's a myth or a legend or something."

Annie blinked her eyes hard, and frowned. "Are you sure, Dorothy? I always believed it was real, and I always felt sorry for the poor creature."

"What's real are those scrumptious donuts on the table," Charlene said as she walked closer and peeked into the box. "Let's see what's left. A couple of chocolate iced spinners, a cream donut and three sugar twists, but not a single jelly donut anywhere," she teased.

Aunt Dorothy tilted her chin up. "I only had one jelly donut."

Annie patted her stomach. "I had one, too. Then Dorothy and I ate a cream one. They're really my favorite. I would have enjoyed a second cream donut, but Madeline ate it."

Madeline huffed. "You had two and a half donuts, not two. I thought the vanilla iced spinners were your favorite. That's why I split one with you and gave you the half with the most cinnamon. If I'd known the cream one was your favorite, I wouldn't have eaten it."

Aunt Dorothy frowned at Madeline. "You know Annie's favorite donut is whatever she happens to fancy from one day to the next."

"Unlike a certain someone I know who hasn't changed her mind about her favorite since she started working," Annie said. "And we had to stop on every payday on our way home from work to buy one, too. I think they were only a nickel back then."

"Twists and fritters cost a nickel. The jelly donut I've always favored cost seven cents," Aunt Dorothy corrected her.

"Well, they all cost ninety cents apiece now," Madeline whined. "How fair is that for seniors like us who have to live on a fixed income?"

"Not fair at all," Charlene agreed, "which is why I'm going to wrap these up so you can take them home with you." She set her three bags on the counter, picked up the box and carried it back to the counter. "Do you have a preference? Or can I just split what's here and add them to what I bought for you?"

"But we brought them for Dorothy," Madeline protested.

Charlene cocked a brow. "Aunt Dorothy isn't supposed to eat donuts at all, let alone this many."

Madeline leaned toward Aunt Dorothy and lowered her voice to a whisper. "Is she always so bossy?"

Annie leaned forward, too. "She's not bossy. She's sweet. She's just trying to help keep Dorothy on her diet."

"Why?" Madeline countered, continuing the conversation as if Charlene could not hear them. "Dorothy hasn't kept to her diet for years."

Aunt Dorothy patted each of her friends' arms. "Make Charlene happy and take the donuts home. But take a good look first. There are three bags on the counter," she pointed out. "One for you both and one for me. And if I know my Charlene as well as I think I do, she's got a couple of jelly donuts in my bag."

When the three women looked over at the counter, Charlene pretended she hadn't heard a word.

"Just split the leftover donuts however you like," Aunt Dorothy said. "There's some plastic wrap and aluminum foil in the drawer."

Charlene made quick work of wrapping and labeling the leftover donuts, and added them to Annie's and Madeline's bags from McAllister's, fully aware that all three women were watching her carefully. She hesitated for a moment before she opened the bag she had brought home for Aunt Dorothy. "I'll wrap up each of your jelly donuts individually," she said.

Aunt Dorothy grinned at her friends. "See? I told you I know my Charlene."

"And I'm getting to know you," Charlene murmured to herself. She removed Aunt Dorothy's jelly donuts from the bag, wrapped them, labeled them and placed them on opposite sides of the freezer, tucked among other foods. She grinned. Even if Aunt Dorothy found one jelly donut, her sugar level might be down a bit by the time she found the other, which had purposely been mismarked.

Chapter Ten

If the first full weekend Ellie had spent living with her mother had tried and tested her patience, she was unexpectedly rewarded twofold on Monday morning.

First, her mother's closest friend, Phyllis Kennedy, showed up at Ellie's house to spend the whole day, easing Ellie's concerns about leaving her mother alone before the Total Care system was fully put in place later in the week.

Her second reward came at work.

She arrived at seven-thirty, went straight to the sign-in sheet, skimmed the other names and smiled. Even running late—she'd taken her morning walk a little slower for Charlene—she was still a Welleswood Wonk.

"And proud of it," she murmured, embracing the derogatory title given to her and five other experienced teachers who always reported to work early.

The name had been coined by a group of nontenured teachers who were referred to, in turn, as the Welleswood Wonders. The four young teachers had the arrogance to presume they already knew all there was to know about teaching. To add insult to injury, the Welleswood Wonders dressed like they were headed to an afternoon barbecue, wearing flip-flops and Capri pants, instead of to a professional day in the classroom.

Operating at full speed, Ellie turned to leave the office and nearly bumped into her supervisor.

"Mr. Pepperidge! I'm sorry. I didn't hear you come in." She backed up a step.

He glanced down at her over the rim of his half glasses. Half the faculty joked that those spectacles were super-glued to the end of his nose. Ellie was among the other half, who respected Nate Pepperidge as both a scholar and a gentleman, and she refused to link his name with a joke of any kind.

"Pace yourself, Eleanor," he said. "When the feet tread slowly, the heart beats steady and the soul listens gently to the universe." There was a hint of a twinkle in his eyes.

"Yes, sir."

"How's your mother?" he asked, his gaze gentle and concerned.

She shifted her briefcase. "Doing well, thank you. She's staying with me for a few weeks, but she's hoping to be in her own home by Easter."

He nodded. "Good. Stop by my office when you finish your last class. And bring your file."

She cocked a brow.

"Your personal file," he elaborated. "I'd like to make sure all your transcripts and certifications are in order before I write my recommendation. May I assume you're still interested in applying for my job?"

Her heart skipped a beat. "Are you going to retire this year?"

"Answering my question with a question of your own leaves me wondering if you want to answer the question at all," he reprimanded. He insisted on clarity in speech, and had done so for many years supervising students and teachers alike.

She straightened her shoulders. "Yes. I want to be the

supervisor of the language-arts department at Welleswood High School," she said confidently.

"Better. Precisely stated and on point." Then he looked around as if reassuring himself they were alone. "I'll be tendering my letter, expressing my wish to retire effective July first, to the principal this morning, but I would ask you to keep this information to yourself."

"Certainly," she promised, and hoped he couldn't hear how loudly her heart was pounding or see how her hands were trembling. "I'll be at your office by eleven forty-five with my personal file."

"Splendid," he replied, and stepped away to collect his mail.

Ellie walked out of the main office as slowly as she could, but the instant she rounded the corner, she started to speed-walk to her office. She shut the door behind her, tossed her purse on top of her desk, put her briefcase on the seat of her chair and raised her arms over her head.

"Yes! Yes! Yes!"

She whooped and did as much of a victory dance as she could in the cramped space until she was breathless.

Finally, after thirty-five years of teaching!

Finally, after seven years as department head!

Finally, after working hard all day and taking classes at night to get the certification she needed!

Finally, after waiting patiently, year after year, for the position to be open!

Finally, her career goal to become the department supervisor was within reach!

Finally!

"Calm down. Slow and steady," she told herself, repeating her supervisor's words. She paced the length of her narrow office, calmly and deliberately, breathing deeply as she tried to ground herself in reality instead of dreams.

Nate Pepperidge might be retiring at the end of the school

year, but that didn't mean she would automatically be appointed to fill his position. Granted, he was held in great esteem by everyone in the school community and the town. With his recommendation and her credentials, she had an excellent chance of landing the job she had coveted for years.

State law set strict guidelines for local school boards. All positions had to be posted and advertised before qualified applicants were interviewed. Only then could the position be filled. She had also been an educator long enough to know the maxim that seemed to prevail more often than not in most school districts: They would post and advertise every job, but no job would be posted before it was filled.

Mr. Pepperidge's plan to network on her behalf was in her favor. Realistically, she also knew that if a member of the school board or a local politician had a relative or friend who wanted the position, she would be history, and she would be long retired before the position would be open again.

Still, just the prospect of being able to apply for the position put a bounce in her step as she walked to her desk, eager to share her news. With a racing heart and trembling hands, she reached for the telephone and picked up the receiver. She glanced at the pictures of her family on the desk, and slowly set the receiver down.

She had no one to call.

Her late husband, Joe, was the one person she wanted to call. He was the one person who would have understood her elation and he would have jettisoned caution in favor of celebrating the opportunity she now had to fulfill her dreams.

But Joe was not here.

Not anymore.

She blinked back tears and glanced at the photographs of their children. Both Alex and Richard knew how much this opportunity meant to her, but the time difference made it too early to call them.

Just looking at her mother's picture was enough to dampen her spirits and squash the joy pumping through her veins. She fought a new wave of tears. Sharing her excitement with her mother was an invitation to heartbreak. Ellie knew that sad fact from experience.

Seven years ago, when she had been appointed as department head, she had foolishly called her mother to tell her about the promotion. Instead of offering her congratulations or expressing pride, her mother had pointed out every negative connected to the position. By the time Ellie had hung up, every bit of triumph she had felt had been extinguished.

She did not want to go through that again.

Not without Joe to help her as he had done then, and on many other occasions throughout their married life when her mother's criticisms had overshadowed her happiness.

"I have no one but You," she whispered, bowing her head and sharing her joy, as well as her fears, with the One who never let her walk alone and who would keep her light burning—her Heavenly Father.

"Homework. Homework. Homework. Tomorrow. One hundred percent. Right?" Ellie asked as the clock ticked off the final fifteen seconds of her last teaching period.

"Right!" the class cried in unison.

She frowned and looked at several boys sitting in the back of the room. "I couldn't hear all of you."

"Right!" The class called out louder, although three boys in the back still wore the same bored looks.

When the dismissal bell rang, she held her place in the front of the classroom and waited for two girls who had reflexively stood up without realizing everyone else was still seated, waiting for permission to leave.

"Sit down! That's not our bell. It's hers," Jeffrey Kirk

yelled at the two girls who seemed totally oblivious to anything but their conversation.

Katy Richards finally looked around and hit her seat hard. Kelly Meyers sat down again, too. "Sorry, Mrs. Waters," they mumbled.

Ellie grinned. "No problem, ladies. Don't forget, everyone. Try the extra-credit assignment tonight, too. And pick up any papers that have dropped on the floor on your way out. You're dismissed."

While the students filed out, Ellie did her customary desk check. She carried a spray bottle of cleaner in one hand and a plastic scrubber in the other as she walked up and down the rows of desks, looking for any scribbles on a desktop.

Relief that no one had mentioned the false alarm at her house on Saturday and that her cell phone had been quiet all morning was short-lived. No sooner had she spied the picture of a house, with a police car, fire truck and ambulance, all in a circle with a line drawn through it on one of the unassigned desks in the back of the classroom, than her cell phone started to vibrate.

She scrubbed the picture off with one hand and pulled out the cell phone with the other. She flipped it open without looking at the caller ID; there was only one person who would be calling her. "Mother? What's wrong?"

"Ellie, this is Phyllis Kennedy."

Ellie stopped scrubbing and felt her heart skip a beat. "Is my mother all right?"

"Rose started complaining about a pain in her arm almost as soon as you left this morning, and it just got worse by the hour."

Fearful that her mother was having another heart attack and horrified that both her mother and her friend had not called for an ambulance right away and had waited so long to call her, she rushed to the front of the room. "Tell her I'm on my way, but hang up right now and call nine-one-one," she ordered as she dropped her cleaning supplies into the bottom drawer in a file cabinet and kicked the drawer closed with her foot.

"We did that, dear. That's why I'm calling. We're in the emergency room at Cedar Grove Hospital, and I just stepped outside to call you—"

"Cedar Grove?" Ellie cried, her distress rising. "Why didn't they take her to Tilton General?"

"I'm not sure. The ambulance people said something about having to take her here. To be honest, I wasn't paying close attention. I was too worried about your mother, which is why I'm calling. They've taken her upstairs for some kind of test, and I don't think she'll be back for at least an hour. I'll be able to stay here with her until three o'clock or so, but I think she'd rather have you waiting here when she gets back. Is there any way you can leave school now?"

"Absolutely," Ellie told her.

"I'll meet you in the emergency room, then," Mrs. Kennedy said and hung up.

Ellie grabbed her briefcase, charged to her office to get her purse and stopped at the main office to tell the principal's secretary she was leaving.

All the while, she was praying nonstop for her mother and begging for more time to reconcile their differences, but she was halfway to the hospital before she realized she had forgotten all about her meeting with Nate Pepperidge.

Chapter Eleven

Different hospital. Different staff. Same routine.

After waiting in the emergency room at Cedar Grove Hospital for nearly six hours with her mother, Ellie listened to the harried emergency-room physician explain her diagnosis, which made no sense at all.

Ellie's skepticism could have been based on the fact that she had probably been married and had had both her children before Dr. Misty Graham had been born. On the other hand, Ellie simply found it highly unlikely that the pain in her mother's arm was totally unrelated to her heart condition.

"Fibromyalgia," Ellie repeated as she stood at her mother's bedside. "In other words, a muscle ache?"

"That's what she said," her mother murmured as she gently massaged her right forearm.

"It's not uncommon for something like this to come and go, especially in the elderly," the doctor explained. She gave the distinct impression that she felt Rose Hutchinson had wasted valuable emergency room time on a very minor ailment, raising Ellie's hackles.

The young doctor wrote a few prescriptions and handed them across the bed to Ellie. "Have the prescriptions filled first thing tomorrow. There's no rush, but you should follow up in a few days with your mother's primary-care physician," she said, then yawned and left the curtained cubicle.

"What time is it?" her mother asked.

As Ellie checked her watch, her stomach growled. "Just about seven o'clock," she replied. She had not eaten since breakfast.

"I feel a little foolish for wasting Phyllis's and your time on account of a little muscle spasm," her mother murmured. "Like the doctor said, I'll feel better in a day or two, so there's no need to call Dr. Stafford. I have an appointment with him in a couple of weeks. We'll mention this to him then."

Ellie suspected her mother very definitely needed to see Dr. Stafford, if only to confirm Dr. Graham's diagnosis, but she decided to save that argument for tomorrow after they had both gotten a good night's sleep.

"Old age holds a lot of surprises, Ellie, and most of them aren't good," her mother said sadly.

Ellie was surprised by her mother's candor and her soft demeanor. "At least you don't have to face them all by yourself," she replied. Instinctively, she braced herself for rejection.

Instead, her mother slipped her hand over Ellie's. "No. I don't," she said in a low voice, and blinked back tears as she tightened her hold.

"Here we go! You get to go home!" a nurse announced brightly as she bounced into the cubicle and shattered the most tender moment Ellie could remember having with her mother in a very long time.

Ellie swallowed the lump in her throat, turned her hand and gently squeezed her mother's hand. "I'll get the car from the lot and bring it as close to the entrance as I can."

"You can pull up right in the ambulances' bay. We'll have your mother waiting for you by the time you get here."

"Take my purse," her mother instructed.

"You sent it home with Phyllis," Ellie reminded her.

"Oh." Her mother shrugged. "Well, we'll have to stop at her house and get it then. I'll need my insurance card for you to take with you to the pharmacy first thing tomorrow morning."

"It won't be open when I'm going to work. It's too early. We can swing by Phyllis's now, on the way home, and drop off the prescriptions, too," Ellie suggested.

Exhausted, hungry and anxious to get her mother home, she left to get her car. She tried to set aside her skepticism about the doctor's diagnosis, for now.

Except this diagnosis involved her mother's life. Walking across the well-lit parking lot, Ellie shivered against the chill of an early March evening, and her determination to follow up with Dr. Stafford grew stronger with every step she took.

At eighty-five, her mother had grown up in an era when doctors were regarded as infallible; she typically accepted her doctors' words as law. Like many in her generation, she was also intimidated by all the recent technological revolutions in medicine.

Ellie, on the other hand, was a baby boomer who questioned everything, and she was comfortable living in a high-tech world.

She reached her car, clicked the remote to unlock it and slipped inside. If necessary, she decided she would take another day off and postpone her meeting with her supervisor. Whether her mother liked it or not, come morning, Ellie was making an appointment with Dr. Stafford.

She could live with her mother's criticism and complaining if the visit proved unnecessary, but she could not live with herself if she didn't follow her instincts that something other than an aching muscle was at the root of her mother's pain.

With that thought, she backed the car out of the parking spot and headed to collect her mother.

The following afternoon, Ellie left school at precisely three o'clock. Still glowing from her delayed meeting with Nate

Pepperidge, she had actually made it to her car and pulled out of the staff parking lot ahead of all the Welleswood Wonders, which would no doubt be fodder for gossip in the faculty room tomorrow morning.

She drove directly home and picked up her mother. Despite her mother's protests, Ellie had them at Dr. Stafford's office at three-thirty. By four o'clock, she and her mother were back in the car and headed straight for the emergency room at Tilton General Hospital.

Her mother leaned back in the passenger seat with her right arm resting on her lap and her eyes closed.

Ellie knew that her mother was not happy. For once, however, her ire was directed not at Ellie, but at Dr. Stafford.

"He's a stubborn, petulant man who thinks I have nothing better to do than rush from one emergency room to another," she whined without opening her eyes.

Ellie tried not to chuckle. "I seem to recall he just described you in the very same way."

Her mother opened one eye and glared at her. "You'd think he'd show a little respect for my age, if nothing else."

"He said he respected you," Ellie replied.

The other eye popped open. "Sure. After I gave him a piece of my mind."

"Which was right after he said you couldn't wait until Thursday to have the Doppler study done on your arm just because you wanted to go to the Shawl Ministry meeting on Wednesday night."

"Doctor Graham didn't say any such thing. She said all the tests came back fine and that I could do whatever I felt comfortable doing."

Ellie stopped at a pedestrian crossing to let a young mother with a stroller cross the avenue. "You can't knit with your arm hurting, anyway," Ellie countered.

"By Wednesday night, maybe it wouldn't be bothering me

so much. Even if it did, I'd like to go, just to thank everyone for giving me such a pretty lap shawl."

Ellie, preoccupied with her thoughts, didn't respond. She was deeply concerned. It was a very real possibility that Dr. Graham had indeed misdiagnosed her mother's pain as fibromyalgia instead of a life-threatening blood clot as Dr. Stafford suspected it was.

"I just got out of the hospital last Thursday," her mother went on, "then I was in at a different hospital on Monday. Now, less than twenty-four hours later, I'm heading back to the first one. That's ridiculous." Her mother blinked back tears. "At least Dr. Graham won't be at this hospital. She wouldn't be very happy to see me again."

Ellie reached over to lay her hand on her mother's shoulder. Slowly, without saying a word, her mother reached up with her left hand and held on tight—a gesture that gave Ellie the precious gift of hope that the love between them still ran deep.

Shaken by how quickly her mother had been rushed to surgery after Dr. Stafford's suspicions had been proved right, Ellie found her way to the hospital chapel shortly after nine o'clock that night.

Although the surgeon had told Ellie the surgery might last for several hours and she would not be able to see her mother until late tomorrow morning, Ellie refused to leave the hospital until she knew her mother had come through the surgery successfully.

Inside the tiny, dimly lit chapel, she knelt in a pew. She crossed her arms on the back of the pew in front of her and rested her forehead against them. With a deep sigh, she laid her fears and her troubles at the foot of her Savior and prayed that her mother would be allowed to stay on this earth awhile longer.

She did not say a single formal prayer, but let her heart speak, knowing He would hear her. In return, in the stillness,

He offered her the peace and the grace to accept His will for herself and her mother, along with the willingness to forgive a young, inexperienced, overtired doctor for her misdiagnosis.

Refreshed in spirit, Ellie left the chapel and went to find the waiting room reserved for family members waiting to hear about their loved ones' surgeries.

At this hour, she expected the elevator to be empty, but when the doors opened, there was someone inside who she recognized at once. Without hesitation, she stepped into the elevator and took the weeping woman into her arms.

Chapter Twelve

Charlene practically collapsed against Ellie. "I prayed and I prayed that no one would see me like this. But I'm so glad you're here," she managed to say, and hugged Ellie tight.

"Your Aunt Dorothy?" Ellie asked.

Charlene sniffled, let out a sigh and eased from Ellie's embrace. Swiping at her tears, she smiled. "She's back in the hospital and—"

The doors shut, interrupting her, and she groaned as the elevator started rising. "I think I've been riding in this elevator for ten minutes trying to get back down to the main lobby so I can go home. Because I've been crying, everything is so blurry I can't read the buttons clearly."

Ellie looked at the bank of buttons. "I think we're headed back up to the sixth floor at the moment."

"Great," Charlene grumbled. "Are you here with your mother?" She took out a tissue to wipe her face. "Never mind. Dumb question. Of course you are. What happened?"

"I'm afraid she's in surgery," Ellie replied.

The elevator stopped and the doors opened, again interrupting their conversation. But no one entered. Charlene poked her head out, didn't see anyone and ducked back inside. "All clear."

"I'll get you down to the main lobby," Ellie promised, and pushed a couple of the buttons. "All set. What brought your aunt back to the hospital?"

"She had another spell yesterday afternoon. Another ambulance ride and trip to the emergency room. Poor soul. She's having a rough time of it," Charlene said. She sighed and shook her head. "Fortunately, I had just gotten home from the store, so she wasn't alone. I'm so glad I'm having that Total Care system installed next week," she said as the elevator started to descend. "Aunt Dorothy has been stuck in the emergency room since yesterday. She's finally getting settled in the coronary care unit now because there wasn't a room for her anywhere else and the bed in the emergency room is needed. The doctors don't think she's had another heart attack, but we won't know for sure until tomorrow, when all the test results come back. She was having a terrible time breathing, but that's under control now. Did you say your mom had surgery?"

Ellie moistened her lips. "She had a blood clot in her forearm," she replied, and explained what had brought her to the hospital tonight.

Just as Ellie finished, the elevator stopped again. "I'm getting off here to wait to hear from the surgeon," she said, and tapped the one other lit button. "That's where you get off," she told her friend, and stepped out of the elevator.

"There isn't anyone waiting for me at home. Daniel drove down to the hospital to see Aunt Dorothy last night, but he had to get back for work in the morning, and he probably won't be back until the weekend. I'll sit and wait with you," Charlene offered.

Ellie shook her head. "You're exhausted. You don't need to stay with me. I'll be fine."

"You're right. I don't need to stay," Charlene said and stepped off the elevator. "I just want to stay—unless you'd rather be alone."

"No, but—"

Charlene hooked her arm through Ellie's and glanced around until she saw a sign for the waiting room. "Come on. Let's get to the waiting room, and you can tell me what you're going to do about that Dr. Graham over at Cedar Grove."

Ellie sighed as Charlene walked them both, arm-in-arm, with their purses swinging, down the empty corridor past quiet, dark offices. "At first I was tempted to drive straight to Cedar Grove and throttle the woman. Then I had second thoughts."

She opened the door to the waiting room. Inside the deserted room, Charlene took a plastic seat and Ellie plopped down next to her.

"What were your second thoughts, not that I'd blame you if you'd acted on your first impulse. The doctor made what could have been a deadly mistake!" Charlene said.

Ellie grinned. "I decided I'd wait until morning, get on the Internet and find the toughest malpractice attorney in the country."

"I think you'd have a good case."

"I know I do," Ellie replied. "I even had grand visions of personally tearing up that woman's medical license until I had a third idea that seemed even better."

Curious, Charlene turned to face Ellie. "Ninety-nine out of a hundred people would sue that doctor in a heartbeat, but you think there's a better idea than that?"

"It took me some time and lots of prayer to come up with it, but I think so," she murmured. "You'll probably think I'm being a little too optimistic, if not crazy."

"Try me," Charlene urged.

Ellie shrugged. "Dr. Graham spent at least ten or twelve years in school to become a doctor. She probably spent a fortune, too, and I wouldn't be surprised if she has school loans she'll be repaying for the next twenty years."

"True, but why would that matter? And why would you let that stop you from suing her?"

"She didn't choose medicine as her career because she wanted to hurt someone or put anyone's life at risk. Not deliberately," Ellie argued.

"That might be true," Charlene said, "but you can't take the risk that she might make the same mistake again. Someone else might not be as fortunate as your mother or have the sense to follow up with a second opinion."

"That's why I've decided to let Dr. Briggs, my mother's surgeon tonight, handle it," Ellie said. "Maybe if someone talks to Dr. Graham and shows her how she made the wrong diagnosis in a nonthreatening way, she won't make that mistake again. I think she'll also be less likely to dismiss complaints that elderly patients make in the future, too."

Charlene narrowed her gaze and stared at the woman sitting next to her. "You're amazing, Ellie," she proclaimed.

Ellie blushed and waved off the compliment. "Since we're both amazing women, how come we never got to be friends before now?"

Charlene chuckled. "I'm not sure, although I do think it's pretty pathetic that two amazing women like us are stuck in a hospital together at nearly eleven o'clock at night and there isn't a snack to be had," she said, glancing around the room. There was a counter along the far wall with a coffee machine that was empty, but nothing else.

"I missed dinner. What about you?" Charlene asked.

"Lunch and dinner, although I honestly haven't felt much like eating until now."

Charlene scowled. "Don't hospitals have vending machines anymore?"

Grinning, Ellie reached into her purse and came back up with a handful of goodies: two Mary Janes, a vanilla Turkish Taffy and a Sky Bar. "Take your pick."

Charlene's mouth began to water. "Let's split the Sky Bar, but I want the half with the peanut and fudge sections."

"Okay, but only if you crack the Turkish Taffy into bite-size pieces on that counter over there and have some with me," Ellie suggested.

Charlene took the vanilla candy and giggled. "I cracked one of these on my date's head once after he made the awful mistake of daring me to do it."

Ellie's eyes widened. "You did not!"

"I most certainly did."

"Did it work?" Ellie asked.

"Absolutely."

Ellie laughed so hard that Charlene was afraid a security guard might come running in to find out what was going on. "I guess that was the last time he asked you on a date," Ellie managed to say when she was finally able to draw a breath.

"No, he asked me for another date, but he told me later that he'd decided he was going to marry me, right then and there."

Ellie clapped her hand to her heart. "Daniel said he actually decided to marry you after you cracked a Turkish Taffy on his head?" There was total disbelief in her voice.

Charlene laughed out loud. "More or less. I should probably tell you that he was wearing a metal helmet at the time."

"A helmet? On a date?"

"And a full set of armor," Charlene elaborated. "He had taken me to a Renaissance festival and wanted to have his picture taken as a medieval knight. After he'd gotten into the costume, the photographer had some trouble with his camera. While he was trying to fix it, Daniel was getting hotter and hotter, so I offered some Turkish Taffy to take his mind off being so uncomfortable. I'm pretty sure the photographer was more surprised than Daniel was when I cracked it on the helmet. Daniel told me later that any girl who could be so goofy was bound to make life funny and interesting." Her voice dropped to almost a whisper as she remembered how things used to be between them before the passing years had proven Daniel wrong.

She carried the Turkish Taffy over to the counter, held it in her palm and smacked it against the countertop. She felt the tiny pieces through the plastic wrapper and sighed.

Like her dreams of a happy marriage, the solid taffy had splintered and broken.

Sharing stories and bits of candy, Charlene and Ellie waited together until nearly 4 a.m., when the surgeon appeared with good news: Rose Hutchinson's surgery had been successful.

In the parking lot with Ellie, Charlene took a couple of deep breaths of cool night air to rouse herself a bit. "I hate to break this to you now, but I'm definitely not going to be waiting on the corner for you in two hours for our walk."

Ellie groaned. "Good. You'd have been waiting there for a very long time because I've got to get a few hours of sleep before I go to work."

Charlene was surprised. "You're going to work?"

"Only for my morning classes, then I'm leaving," Ellie replied. "I don't want my students to walk into class and see the substitute teacher again. Besides, Dr. Briggs said I probably wouldn't be able to see my mother much before noon."

"Well, I'm taking the whole day off. I'm going to ask Ginger if she can work until five. If not, she can close the store at three when her grandson gets out of school. In any event, I'm heading back to the hospital around eleven."

"We could meet for lunch in the cafeteria. Say at one?" Ellie suggested.

"If I'm not there, you'll know I couldn't leave Aunt Dorothy."

"Same here. I'd like to stay with my mother as long as she's awake."

Charlene pointed ahead. "My car's right over there. I just wanted to say thank you."

Ellie cocked her head. "Shouldn't I be the one thanking you for staying with me most of the night?"

"That's what friends do, and that's why I wanted to thank you—for being my friend."

Ellie hugged her. Hard. "Somehow, we're both going to get through this. Together. Right?"

"Right," Charlene murmured, hoping her friendship with Ellie would not be the only blessing this new day would bring.

Chapter Thirteen

Charlene had not been this nervous since high school when she was getting ready for the prom.

On Friday afternoon, she closed up Sweet Stuff at exactly five o'clock, leaving half a dozen orders for gift baskets unfilled for tomorrow. The butterflies were fluttering in her stomach as she drove to Aunt Dorothy's house.

She bypassed the avenue, which was clogged with commuters and the first of the weekend diners drawn to Welleswood's new restaurants. After winding through Welles Park, she took several small side streets along the route Ellie had suggested that morning during their walk, and parked in the driveway under the carport at Aunt Dorothy's house.

She was anxious to get inside to see how Aunt Dorothy had fared on her first full day at home alone since being discharged from the hospital late yesterday afternoon. She also had less than an hour to get showered and changed before Daniel arrived for his first weekend visit.

She had only spoken to him twice—last Tuesday when she had called to tell him Aunt Dorothy had been moved out of the emergency room, and again on Wednesday, to let him know that her aunt had not suffered another heart attack and would be released in a day or so. Since then, they had played telephone tag, and in his final message, he had told her he would be coming to Aunt Dorothy's on Friday and hoped to be there by six.

Stepping into the living room, Charlene spied the top of Aunt Dorothy's gray head, resting on the arm of the sofa as she lay facing Agnes Withers, who was in a chair doing a cross-stitch. Charlene could smell the pork roast she had put into the Crock-Pot that morning.

Mrs. Withers looked up and smiled. "You're right on time, Charlene," she said, storing her stitchery in a canvas bag.

Aunt Dorothy turned her head, rose on one elbow and held up a necklace with a plastic pendant hanging from it. "Total Care came right at three o'clock today," she reported before lying down again.

Charlene went to the sofa and knelt next to her aunt. In a bright pink bathrobe, Aunt Dorothy was still pale and looked exhausted, but she was breathing easily again. "I feel better now that the system has been installed, don't you?" Charlene asked.

Her aunt nodded, adjusted the necklace with the signal button resting at her collar bone and laid her hand on Charlene's knee. "Mr. James said I could wear this necklace to bed at night, but I don't think I will. I'd probably set it off by accident. You're here at night if I need help."

"Mr. James was the nice man who installed the Total Care system, and he said she'd be better off wearing a bracelet instead of the necklace," Mrs. Withers interjected with a scowl.

Charlene furrowed her brow. "Why didn't you take the bracelet instead?"

"I never cared much for bracelets, and now that I've been in and out of the hospital and forced to wear those awful plastic identification strips, I like them even less."

Charlene smiled and patted her aunt's hand. "Then the necklace is a good choice."

"There's a machine in your aunt's bedroom that's hooked up to the telephone, and it can be activated from anywhere in the house," Mrs. Withers informed Charlene. "You'll need to check it every thirty days. All the information is in the paperwork that I put in your room," she added, and looped the straps on her canvas bag over her arm. "I'll call you tomorrow morning, Dorothy, to see what time you need me to come over," she said, and let herself out the front door.

Aunt Dorothy sighed, closed her eyes and folded her hands at her waist. "Agnes is a good soul and she means well, but I couldn't get much of a nap with her here. I'm just going to rest my eyes a spell while you get all gussied up for that handsome husband of yours. Even though it smells real good, I'm not real hungry, so don't hurry with dinner on my account."

Charlene stroked the top of her aunt's head and got a smile in return. "I won't be long, but I'd love to shower so I don't smell like chocolate."

Aunt Dorothy took a good long whiff. "You smell good to me, but you'll need to wear something that smells nicer to Daniel. Men don't seem to fancy chocolate like women do."

"I've never been much for wearing perfume," Charlene replied. In all truth, she usually relied on regular soap instead of scented body washes, too.

Aunt Dorothy opened one eye. "No toilet water? Ever?"

Charlene chuckled. "You're looking at me like I've just confessed to a serious sin."

"Not so serious. Just a little foolish. A little toilet water usually captures a man's interest," she murmured and shut her eyes. "Although I usually prefer to wear my Tabu, I've got all sorts of toilet water in the vanity in my bedroom. Pick one and wear it tonight. You'll see what I mean."

Charlene shrugged. "I guess it can't hurt," she replied. At this point in her relationship with Daniel, she was ready to try almost anything.

While her aunt dozed, Charlene showered and dressed in blue slacks and a flowered blouse. She blow-dried her hair and let it fall softly around her face rather than pulling it back. With barely ten minutes to spare, she went into her aunt's bedroom, turned on the light and sat in front of the vanity.

Unfortunately, she couldn't avoid seeing herself in the mirror. Her long, straight hair fell just below her shoulders, and she shook her head. Although the blond color was still attractive, the style was outdated. She should make an appointment for a cut, although she doubted she'd find any style as easy to manage as her ponytail. In the meantime, she opened the vanity drawers and found Aunt Dorothy's toilet water.

Sorting through the dusty bottles was like taking a museum tour. Lily of the Valley. Blue Midnight. Chantilly. And Tabu, of course.

Some of the bottles were empty; no doubt the contents had evaporated over the years. Others smelled like alcohol. Disappointed, she replaced the bottles, then saw an unopened fragrance gift set in one of the drawers. She took out a small blue bottle of perfume.

She sprayed a bit on the inside of her left wrist and held it up to her nose. It had a sweet, gentle scent.

Feeling adventurous, she sprayed both her wrists, and behind both her ears, adding a tiny spray at the hollow of her neck.

Then she bowed her head, closed her eyes, and prayed: *Father, we need Your guidance. Help Daniel and me to find our way back to one another again. Amen.*

Hearing the front door open, she swallowed the lump in her throat and rose from her seat. The moment she entered the living room, her throat tightened with emotion again. Aunt Dorothy was still lying on the sofa. Daniel was on one knee, pressing a kiss to her forehead. He held a large bouquet of carnations, wrapped in florist's paper.

Charlene knew this image of her husband would join many

others stored in her mind. And she knew, beyond any doubt, that she had loved this kind and gentle man from the moment she had met him. She'd loved him then. She loved him now. And she would love him forever.

When he stood up, he faced Charlene and put a finger to his lips. "She's sleeping," he whispered.

Charlene stepped toward him and he put his arm around her. As always, he bent for a kiss, then he quickly stole another, which was so unusual she felt her heart skip a beat. "You smell as good as these flowers," he murmured.

"Why don't we go into the kitchen so I can put them in water for Aunt Dorothy," she whispered.

He followed her. "There are two bouquets inside the wrapper," he told her. "One is for you."

She swallowed hard again, unable to recall the last time he had brought her flowers. "Thank you," she managed to say.

While she looked for vases, he lifted the lid on the Crock-Pot. "This smells great. New recipe?"

"I found it in the recipe book that came with the Crock-Pot. It's pork teriyaki. Hungry?"

He patted his stomach. "Starving. I'm not much for cooking for myself. How's Aunt Dorothy doing, really?"

Charlene, feeling a brief stab of regret for not being at home to cook for him, washed out two dusty vases and unwrapped the flowers as she answered. "She's very weak and very tired, but the doctors say she's doing as well as can be expected."

"But she didn't have a heart attack?" he asked, pulling out a piece of pork and nibbling at it.

"Not this time. Her lungs were starting to fill with fluid, but they've got that under control again," she replied as she arranged one bouquet of pastel carnations. "Every time I ask how long she might have, I get the same answer."

He put the lid back on the Crock-Pot. "What's that?"

"The doctors say that Aunt Dorothy is eighty-one years old, and to make every moment count."

He sighed. "That's probably pretty good advice."

"But they won't say how much those moments will add up to, although no one seems to think I should worry beyond the next few months." Blinking back tears, she finished the other arrangement.

"Does Aunt Dorothy say anything about it?" he asked, taking a step closer to her.

"One minute she says she's ready for the Lord to take her Home, but in the next breath, she's talking about going to sunrise services on Easter morning or celebrating her eighty-second birthday in September," she replied. "I talked to the kids this week. They each said they'd try to come soon. Since neither can be here for Easter, they're going to try to figure out another weekend that works for them both."

He reached out and touched a carnation. "So you'll need to stay here with her…"

She turned to face him. "I can't leave her. She needs help bathing and dressing. She's not up to cooking for herself, and she certainly doesn't have the strength for housework. I'm not certain how long I'll need to be here, but I promised her I wouldn't force her to go into a nursing home."

"We both promised her," he said softly, and his blue eyes filled with compassion. "If she's here with us, we'll take her to Easter sunrise services, get Greg and Bonnie here for a weekend together, and we'll plan on throwing a birthday party for Aunt Dorothy in September. In the meantime, whatever else she wants or whatever it is that she needs, we'll see that she has it."

Charlene dropped her gaze. Touched by his support and his commitment to family, she also realized they were having a real conversation together, the way they used to. "Daniel, I—"

A knock at the back door interrupted her and ruined the intimate moment.

When Daniel opened the door, Agnes Withers tiptoed into the kitchen. "I didn't want Dorothy to know I came back, so I waited until I saw the light in the kitchen," she explained in a whisper. She glanced at the flowers on the counter before looking directly at Charlene. "I think you should have Dorothy's hearing checked, but remember not to tattle on me."

Charlene held back a sigh. Aunt Dorothy might be failing, but her hearing seemed just fine. "Aunt Dorothy had a full examination at the hospital," she said, hoping that would satisfy the woman.

"Well, she can't hear like she used to. I tried watching television with her today, and she made me put the sound up so high, I got a headache and turned it off."

Charlene stifled a grin. There was nothing wrong with Aunt Dorothy's tactics, either.

Mrs. Withers tilted her chin up. "I hope you can do something so I don't miss any of my shows when I'm here," she said before she turned and smiled at Daniel. "Those carnations are quite pretty. You must have brought them."

"As a matter of fact, I stopped on my way here to get them," he confirmed. When he caught Charlene's gaze, she answered his unspoken question with a quick nod.

"I brought one bouquet for Aunt Dorothy, but the other one is for you—for being such a good neighbor."

Charlene handed him one of the vases, which he held in one hand while taking Agnes Withers's arm with the other. "Why don't you let me carry these back to your house for you?"

The elderly woman blushed and blinked hard several times. "For me? Really?"

"Consider it a token of appreciation for your help," Charlene said. "Now that Daniel is here for the weekend, he'll be helping Aunt Dorothy when I'm at the store tomorrow afternoon, so you can just relax at home."

"It's no bother. Really. I don't mind coming over to stay with Dorothy," Mrs. Withers argued as Daniel led her to the back door.

"I'd really like to spend time with Aunt Dorothy since I can't be here all week," he informed her, ushering her out. He turned to give Charlene a wink before he shut the door, an unexpected gesture that suddenly, sweetly opened the door to her heart.

Smiling, she left the kitchen and went straight to the vanity in Aunt Dorothy's bedroom to take possession of that bottle of perfume.

Chapter Fourteen

Aunt Dorothy presided over breakfast the following morning, wearing a green-and-yellow striped housecoat. On the collar, she had tucked a pink carnation from her bouquet. Instead of Tabu, however, she was wearing Lily of the Valley.

She polished off the last of her oatmeal and took a sip of decaffeinated coffee. "I think we should celebrate the three of us being together," she said, looking directly at Daniel. "Be a sweetheart and get a treat for us from the freezer that we can share for dessert."

He cocked his head. "The freezer? Please don't tell me you want ice cream for dessert. It's barely eight o'clock in the morning."

"And the last I checked, you had already eaten the jelly donut from McAllister's," Charlene said, feeling smug that she had successfully hidden the second jelly donut by mislabeling it as creamed spinach.

Unfortunately, she had been less successful recapturing the tenderness between herself and her husband after he'd returned from escorting Mrs. Withers home last night. They had not had any time alone together to talk, since he had gone to bed early and was still asleep when she'd gone out earlier to meet Ellie for their walk.

For now, however, Charlene was satisfied that taking care of Aunt Dorothy was bringing them closer, although they still had a long way to go.

Aunt Dorothy ignored Charlene's comment and smiled coyly at Daniel. "If you check the right side of the freezer, I believe you'll find a foil package marked 'creamed spinach.'"

He grimaced, but got up from his seat. "I take back what I said. Maybe ice cream would be a better choice for dessert, after all."

"Not really," Charlene mumbled, recognizing that Aunt Dorothy was on to her.

Her aunt looked at her and grinned. "Just bring it over here to me."

"How long did it take you to figure it out?" Charlene asked, surprised that her aunt had not already consumed the donut.

Aunt Dorothy chuckled. "I figured it out before I went to bed that first night. I knew you'd brought me two jelly donuts because I watched you wrap them up. I only found one later, so I started rooting through the other packages. I don't favor creamed spinach, which made me suspect you'd played a bit of a trick on me."

Charlene cringed. "I'll have to plead guilty, but I only meant to keep you from eating too much sugar."

Aunt Dorothy patted Charlene's hand. "In a way, I suppose you did. I can't tell you how many times I wanted to tell you I'd discovered your little trick, but I was having too much fun."

Charlene sighed, grateful that her aunt found the whole affair amusing.

Bemused, Daniel put the frozen package on the table and sat down again. "That's really a jelly donut?"

Grinning, Aunt Dorothy peeled away the silver foil. Sure

enough, one of McAllister's donuts sat in the center—a fat, sugar-crusted donut with cream in the middle.

Charlene leaned forward and stared at the frozen confection. "That's…that's not the jelly donut I wrapped up for you!"

Aunt Dorothy beamed with triumph. "Nope. That's one of the cream donuts Annie brought me last week, and I just couldn't resist having a little fun with you. I so enjoyed that jelly donut you wrapped up for me the morning Annie came to see me, but I had even more fun watching you check that freezer every time you opened it to get something out, and think you'd gotten the best of me."

Charlene shook her head. Balancing her aunt's rights with her own responsibilities as caregiver was so hard. Occasionally allowing her aunt to make her own decisions about what she ate, however, seemed not only fair, but right. "I'm sorry. I was only trying to—"

"Don't be sorry," her aunt insisted as she pushed the donut toward Daniel. "Slice that up for us into three pieces, Daniel. It's frozen hard. You're so much stronger than either of us, I'm sure you'll manage slicing it without any effort at all," she said coyly before she turned back to Charlene. "Playing that little game with you made me remember how much fun your mother and I used to have teasing each other. You may not look much like her, but you have her great sense of humor. You truly are your mother's daughter, Charlene."

Charlene blinked hard. Her mother had died only months after Charlene and Daniel had been married, and Charlene welcomed a chance to hear and talk about her. "You teased each other by playing tricks on one another?"

"All the time," Aunt Dorothy replied, and placed a piece of donut in front of each of them. "Try this frozen. To my mind, it's the best way to eat a cream donut."

Daniel tried a bite and shrugged. "It's okay, but I'm not a

good judge. I don't really favor sweets, but I think I like the cream better when it's soft and gooey."

"You try it, Charlene," Aunt Dorothy urged as she nibbled her own piece.

Charlene took a tiny bite and then another. "It tastes even sweeter this way. I like it," she declared and polished off the last bite.

"That's just what your mother said when I convinced her to try one frozen. Of course, she didn't always agree with me, especially when I outwitted her in one of our little games."

"Tell us about one of those games," Daniel urged and leaned back in his chair.

Aunt Dorothy thought for a moment, and smiled. "Marie and I both had a sweet tooth, even as youngsters, you know."

Charlene grinned. "I'm afraid it's genetic, Daniel."

"As I was saying," Aunt Dorothy continued, "Marie and I both loved our sweets, but we also loved our toilet water."

"I remember that about her. She always smelled real good, like you do," Daniel put in and looked at Charlene almost shyly.

"That definitely wasn't genetic," Charlene said. Judging by the look in Daniel's gaze, however, she hoped wearing a light scent could be an acquired habit.

"Father used to bring us each a bottle of toilet water now and then, and we'd trade back and forth," Aunt Dorothy reminisced. "One time Marie gave me a bottle of Tabu. In return, I gave her half a bottle of Evening in Paris."

"Half a bottle?" Daniel asked.

"Well, the bottle of Evening in Paris was twice the size of the Tabu. We always tried to keep things even, so when that happened, we'd pour the toilet water into tiny glass bottles we had for our baby dolls and label the scent. As a matter of fact, I still have most of them stored up in the attic," she explained before popping the last bite of donut into her mouth.

"So how did you tease her that time?" Charlene asked.

"That was easy. I waited until she fell asleep one night, switched bottles with her and changed the labels. The next time she got all fixed up to go out with Gary Nelson, she doused herself real good with Tabu," she admitted and started laughing again. "Marie tried washing it off, but she still smelled like Tabu when he came calling. I think he must have liked that scent a whole lot better than Evening in Paris, too."

"Really?" Daniel asked. "Why?"

"It's the only thing that explains why he stopped by one day when Marie was at the library and asked if he could keep company with me instead of my sister."

"You didn't say he could, did you?" Charlene asked.

Aunt Dorothy's gaze hardened. "All I gave him was a good tonguelashing! There isn't a man who has ever walked this earth who would have been worth hurting my sister. Blood's thicker than water—or in this case, toilet water."

She turned and looked directly at Daniel. "Not all men have the same good heart you do, Daniel. I know you're not blood, but you're as good to me as any son or nephew could be, sharing your wife with me during the week to take care of me and coming down here yourself on weekends to help me. I won't forget you, either. After I'm gone, you and Charlene will both share everything I own."

Daniel blushed, adding a rosy hue to his tanned features. "We're family. Let's hope we have lots of time to enjoy together."

The elderly woman sighed and glanced from Daniel to Charlene. "I know what the doctors say and I know what this old body of mine is telling me, too, but I also know the good Lord will take me Home when He's good and ready. When He does, I pity you both," she said with a hint of a smile on her lips. "You're going to have a mess of a time cleaning all my junk out of this house after I'm gone, and don't think for a minute you took care of most of it in that spare bedroom. There's a whole lot more in that attic," she warned.

Charlene chuckled, grateful her aunt had used her sense of humor to lighten the sad mood after talking about her death. "We could always sort through some things while I'm here," she offered.

"There's not much I care to see again right now, other than a good view of the creek behind my house," her aunt replied.

"Which I'm ready to tackle today," Daniel said as he rose from his seat.

When he started to clear the table, Aunt Dorothy shooed him away by waving her hand. "Charlene can take care of the kitchen. I need those muscles of yours outside."

He leaned down and pressed a kiss to the top of her head. "Then I'll get started right away." He grabbed his coat and headed out the back door.

After he left, Aunt Dorothy rose from the table. "While you clean up, I'm going to get a few things from my bedroom. Meet me in the living room when you're finished. And don't dawdle. I'm thinking I might need a bit of a nap this morning, but you're right. I should probably show you some things before I do, just in case I'm still napping when you have to leave to open the store today."

Curious, Charlene watched her aunt walk slowly from the kitchen and through the dining room. Once she had the dishes washed and the table wiped clean, she joined her aunt in the living room.

Aunt Dorothy was lying on the sofa with her head propped by a bed pillow and the black lap shawl with a purple fringe covering her legs. In addition to the tissue box and a plastic flower arrangement, her aunt had placed an old, square candy tin on the coffee table.

Aunt Dorothy scooted over on the sofa and patted the edge of the cushion by her side. "Sit with me and open that tin."

Charlene did as she was told. Cautiously, she lifted the lid and glanced inside. Neatly lined up in a single layer were tiny cardboard jewelry boxes. Some had turned golden brown with age. Many carried the names of jewelry stores Charlene recognized, although most of them had closed down years ago.

"I've got a whole drawerful of costume jewelry I don't think is worth much to anyone but me, but I keep what little I do have that's valuable or important to me in that tin," her aunt explained. "There's not much there, but once I'm gone, these will all belong to you. You can pass them down to Bonnie and your grandchildren someday. It's the least I can do to thank you for taking good care of me."

Charlene blinked back tears. "I don't expect—"

"I know you don't," her aunt argued. "And I'm afraid I'm being just a little selfish about this."

"Selfish? You don't have a selfish bone in your body," Charlene countered.

"We all have a touch of selfishness now and then," her aunt cautioned. "I was hoping I could tell you about the jewelry. Each piece has a story, you know, and if I don't tell them to you, those stories will die with me. I'm hoping you'd like to hear them," she whispered."

"Of course I would," Charlene said, then glanced down at her lap, counted the tiny boxes and put the tin back on the coffee table. "I think I should probably write down the stories, though. Would that be all right? I'm afraid I might never remember them all."

Aunt Dorothy removed her glasses, put them on the coffee table, folded her hands on her lap and closed her eyes. "There's paper and a pencil in the kitchen."

Charlene found a notepad and a pencil in one of the junk drawers quickly enough, and paused for just a moment to peek out the kitchen window. She couldn't see Daniel, but she could hear the snapping of tree limbs, and assumed he had started to trim.

By the time she got back to the living room, Aunt Dorothy

was asleep and snoring. Loudly. "Apparently, you really did need that nap," she mumbled, and adjusted the lap shawl.

Although tempted to take a peek inside one of the jewelry boxes, Charlene merely laid the notepad and pencil down next to the candy tin. She returned to the kitchen again to get tonight's supper into the Crock-Pot, hoping Aunt Dorothy would wake before Charlene had to leave to open the store at noon. If not, she might hear more about the stories tonight after supper.

She glanced at the kitchen clock when she finished making the pot roast. It was only nine-fifteen, and she had more than two hours before she needed to leave. In Grand Mills on a weekend with Daniel, she would have kept busy with laundry or other chores. Living here, however, she was loath to do anything that might disturb her aunt's sleep.

Then she remembered an important project that needed her attention—a project dear to her heart.

She tiptoed back to the spare bedroom, grabbed a coat and a pair of gloves and went straight outside to the backyard. The air was colder than usual for March, but the sun was bright and warmed the top of her head. She wasn't sure if Daniel wanted her help, and the look of surprise on his face when she found him tying up branches he had cut told her he hadn't expected to see her at all.

He stopped working. "Is something wrong with Aunt Dorothy?"

"I thought you could use an extra pair of hands," she replied and waited for him to send her back into the house.

He narrowed his gaze. "You'll probably wind up ruining your good gloves if you help."

"I have other pairs of gloves," she said, quite sure now that this was the only man she ever wanted—and she was determined to win him back.

He shrugged and tossed her the ball of twine he had been using.

Naturally, she missed it and had to use her feet to clear away last fall's leaves to find it again. When she did, she turned around and found him still watching her, and the smile on his face gave her hope that he might want to salvage their marriage as much as she did.

Chapter Fifteen

Nearly two weeks after her mother's emergency surgery, Ellie was sitting behind the desk in her classroom long after the school day had officially ended. She waved off the two students she had held for detention for the past half hour with a smile, satisfied she had been able to help them resolve the argument that had exploded during class earlier in the day.

"I'm really sorry I disrupted your class today," Harry offered.

"Me, too, Mrs. Waters," Peter added before the two of them grabbed their backpacks and headed home together, apparently friends again.

Both pleased and relieved that she had been able to help the two boys settle their differences, she reached for her briefcase, wondering why she had never seemed to have the same success resolving the differences between herself and her mother. Humbled by the lesson in forgiveness she had just learned from her students, she pulled the cell phone from her briefcase to call both of her sons before heading home.

"I need to go home. Today."

Ellie heard her mother's terse pronouncement the moment she stepped into the house from work. With a briefcase full of papers to be graded in one hand and her keys and purse in the other, she kicked the front door closed with her foot. By habit, she turned to disarm the security system, then remembered she was no longer arming it for fear her mother might set off another false alarm.

She had no idea what could have happened during the day to make her mother so determined to leave today. When they had talked about the subject last night, they'd agreed that her mother was still too weak to live on her own.

Now Ellie found her mother sitting in the upholstered rocking chair next to the aquarium. She was wearing her spring tweed coat and matching hat. Her suitcase was on the floor next to the chair. With her gaze hard and her lips pursed, she was clearly a woman with her mind set on what she wanted to do.

Ellie spied one of her water turtles swimming leisurely about the calm water in the aquarium, and took a deep breath. She resisted the urge to argue with her mother's demand. She set down her briefcase and drew in another deep breath as she stored her keys in her purse.

Before she could pose a single question, however, her mother glanced at the clock on top of the television and frowned. "You're usually home by three-thirty. I've been waiting for over half an hour. Why are you so late today?"

"I'm sorry. I didn't know you were waiting for me. I had a few things to do after school," she replied without going into any detail. "Did you have any problems today?"

"Phyllis stopped to see me earlier. She offered to run me home, but I told her she had done enough for me already and that you wouldn't mind taking me home. Unless you've got too many papers to grade again," she added.

Ellie dropped down on the sofa. "I always have too many papers to grade, but I can save them until later. I took some fish out of the freezer this morning. Are you sure you need to go home right now, before supper?"

Her mother scowled. "You know I'll be too tired after supper to do much of anything."

Ellie tried a different approach. "Did I do something to make you upset with me today?"

"Other than the fact that you're late getting home from work and you didn't bother to call me to let me know, you weren't here all day, so I rather doubt it. Now, if we don't leave soon," her mother cautioned, "I'll be so overheated from sitting here wearing my coat, I'll be bound to catch a chill when we do leave. If it's too inconvenient for you to take me home, just say so. I'll call a cab. I need to go home, Ellie. It's as simple as that."

"You need to go or you want to go?" Ellie questioned.

"Both," her mother replied. "You may not care about the way you dress, but I certainly do. I've been wearing the same clothes for weeks now, and I wasn't all that thrilled with what you picked out for me, anyway. I need to get more."

"Oh," Ellie said and tried not to be hurt by her mother's criticism. "Maybe I misunderstood. When you said you needed to go home today, I didn't realize you meant you just wanted to go home to pack more clothes."

"Why else would I have my suitcase ready?"

"The suitcase is empty?"

Her mother rolled her eyes. "I couldn't carry it out here if it were full, could I? Neither could Phyllis, which is really why I didn't want to have her run me home. I didn't want to hurt her feelings by telling her she wouldn't be strong enough to carry the suitcase once it was packed."

Smiling, Ellie stood up, grateful she had cleared up the misunderstanding before it escalated into an unnecessary battle of wills. She grabbed the keys from her purse. "You're right. If we leave now, we'll be home well before dark and before you start to tire," she said, helping her mother from her chair and grabbing the suitcase.

As they walked to the front door together, Ellie's spirit was refreshed and the light of her faith was burning just a bit brighter, with hope they might resolve their differences one day after all.

While her mother sat on the edge of her bed giving directions, Ellie padded back and forth from her mother's closet to the suitcase. She had already filled it with a dozen perfectly coordinated outfits, but there was not a single pair of slacks in any of them.

Ellie was not really surprised. She had never seen her mother wearing slacks, not even during last year's bitterly cold winter.

"That should be enough for now. I don't need anything else from the closet," her mother said as she refolded the last blouse Ellie had given her. "Since there's room, I think I'll take one of the quilts from the hope chest at the end of my bed. I'm not used to sitting around so much, and I'm always getting a chill. The lap shawl from my friends at the Shawl Ministry keeps my legs warm enough, but it's not long enough to keep my shoulders warm, too. If I move it up to my shoulders, my legs get cold."

"You might be surprised by how much warmer you'd be if you tried wearing a pair of slacks in the winter," Ellie said. After she turned out the light inside the closet, she closed the door and lifted the lid of the hope chest. She was so startled to see the little pink quilt covered with tiny green turtles in between two old blankets, she barely heard her mother's response.

She pulled out the quilt and lifted it to her face, remembering all the stuffed animals, mostly turtles, that had been heaped on top of this quilt when she was a small child.

A sentimental keepsake from her childhood was not something Ellie expected to discover among her mother's things. She swallowed the lump in her throat and handed the quilt to her mother. "I can't believe you held on to this quilt all these years," she whispered. She wondered what other treasures her mother might have saved.

Her mother folded the quilt into quarters, laid it in the suitcase and smoothed the fabric with the palm of her hand. "I made this quilt for you, not that I had much choice."

Ellie closed the hope chest and sat down on top of it. "You made it? I don't think I ever knew that."

"You were only two years old when we put your crib away and you started sleeping in the youth bed, but you knew your own mind, even then. I made the mistake of taking you with me to Mendlekoff's to pick out a little quilt for your big-girl bed, but you'd have none of them."

"I don't remember that, either."

Her mother frowned, although Ellie thought she detected a gleam of amusement in her mother's eyes for a moment. "I'm certain the salesclerk who waited on us still remembers, if she's still alive. You made such a scene I didn't go back to that store for a good long while."

Ellie cringed and flexed her right foot. "Then I assume the stomping foot was there," she ventured, vividly recalling how she used to stomp her foot to get her own way as a child, only to blame the foot itself, as if it had a will of its own, when she was reprimanded.

"That and a whole bucket of tears. I should have known not to even try to get you to choose something you clearly didn't want. They had lovely little-girl quilts with baby dolls or teddy bears on them. But no, you had your mind set on turtles, so off we went to Woolworth's to search for fabric."

She paused and shook her head. "I was convinced once I showed you there wasn't any fabric available with turtles on it, I could go back to Mendlekoff's, apologize and buy one of the ready-made quilts," she recounted, then looked at the quilt again and smiled. "You spied that turtle fabric before I did.

Once I saw how happy it made you, I knew I had to make a quilt for you, although I had no idea your fascination with turtles would last so long."

Touched by the memory her mother had shared, as well as her mother's willingness to please the little girl Ellie had once been, Ellie smiled. "I've loved turtles for as long as I can remember, although I'm not sure why."

Her mother sighed. "Neither am I. I thought collecting turtles was a phase you'd outgrow, but I guess I was wrong about that, too. Just how many turtles do you have in those aquariums of yours?"

"Five water turtles, plus the two land turtles."

"I shouldn't be surprised. Your father encouraged you by finding that baby box turtle on his way home from work and bringing it home. After I refused to have it in the house, he made a place for it in one of the window wells, where you could care for it outside without worrying that it would run away."

Ellie grinned. "That I remember. I kept Myrtle the turtle for the entire summer."

"And you had the sense to let her go in the fall to hibernate."

"But only after I painted my initials on her shell. Remember? Miss Dillon lived a few blocks away. All the kids used to call her the turtle lady because she always had a few turtles for pets in her backyard. She knew everything about turtles. She gave me the idea, as I recall. I searched and searched for that turtle in the spring, but I never did find it. Miss Dillon let me play with her turtles, instead, but it wasn't the same as having Myrtle back."

"Miss Dillon was a strange one," her mother noted. "But even she had the sense to keep her turtles outside. Why you insist on having turtles as pets now, in the house, no less, is beyond me. I suppose it's better than having a dog or a cat, but all pets are a nuisance," she grumbled.

Instead of defending pets, Ellie probed deeper. "Did you ever have a pet growing up?"

Without replying, her mother got up and walked over to her jewelry box on her bureau. "I need to get a few pieces to match my outfits," she said, ignoring Ellie's question.

"Did you ever have a pet?" Ellie repeated as her mother sorted through her jewelry.

Her mother paused and held very still for a moment. Ellie saw her mother's pained expression reflected in the mirror. "When I was eight, I had a dog, a German shepherd mix of some kind. His name was Duke, but he got too big for the house," she said before rooting through the jewelry box and laying a silver necklace on the bureau.

"Oh," Ellie breathed, with a glimmer of understanding of why her mother had never wanted her to have pets. "Did you have to give Duke away?" she asked, watching her mother's face closely.

Her mother pursed her lips for a moment, as though she was trying to keep them from trembling. "He... My father was waiting for me when I got home from school one day, but Duke was gone. My father told me he had taken Duke out to a friend of his who lived on a farm." She paused, cleared her throat and closed her jewelry box. Tilting her chin up, she carried several sets of earrings and necklaces back to the suitcase and laid them on top of Ellie's old quilt.

"Did you ever get a chance to visit Duke?"

Her mother closed the lid on the suitcase. "No. My father said Duke was happy on the farm with his new family and probably wouldn't remember us, anyway. I just need to get a few things from the bathroom. If you could carry my suitcase out to the living room, I'll meet you there. Remember to turn out the light when you leave," her mother said, and walked out of the bedroom.

Ellie sat on the hope chest for a moment. With only limited memories of her grandfather, she had no basis to attempt to understand what he had done. Instead, she grieved for the little girl her mother had been. A little girl who had loved her dog, only to have him sent away forever. And she had never even had the chance to say goodbye.

She stood up and hoisted the suitcase from the bed. Now filled with her mother's things, the suitcase was very heavy, but Ellie's steps were quick. She turned out the light, but the gentle beacon of new understanding shone in her heart. She hoped she would find many more opportunities to learn about her mother.

Ellie sat at the kitchen table, watching her mother serve herself. Since the incision on her mother's arm was nearly healed, Ellie hadn't had to help her with her meals for several days now.

Tonight's menu of broiled flounder, steamed peas and brown rice would have required little assistance anyhow. There was no salt or butter on the table and no cream sauce for the peas. Ellie was proud of herself for sticking to the dietary guidelines for her mother's heart condition.

When her mother finished taking a small serving of everything, she set down her fork and wrinkled her nose. "Supper doesn't look any more appetizing tonight than last night, I'm afraid."

"It's nutritious and it's hot," Ellie replied, thinking about how she might be up until midnight grading papers due to the hours spent on the errand to her mother's house for clothes, and then in the kitchen preparing the meal.

"This flounder has no flavor at all." Her mother frowned as she chewed it. "Frying it in a bit of garlic butter might have helped."

Ellie slid a saucer of fresh lemon wedges toward her mother. "Butter is off your diet, remember?"

"You remind me so often, I'm not likely to forget," her mother snapped. "I suppose I'm not allowed to have any cream sauce for my peas or gravy for the rice. It looks dry."

Ellie flinched. "I sprinkled some seasoning on the peas and some paprika on top of the flounder to add a little zip, but you might try squeezing a little lemon juice on them," she suggested and helped herself to a serving of all the dishes. She tasted each and reached for some lemon. "You're right. This way of cooking is going to take some getting used to, but I'm only trying to help you follow your doctors' orders," she added.

She tried to remain positive and not whine about following the diet herself. In all likelihood, if her mother had not been here she would not have bothered to cook for herself tonight and would simply have nibbled on cheese and crackers while she graded her papers.

"I wonder what those doctors are having for dinner tonight," her mother grumbled, ignoring the lemon slices as she tried another bite of fish.

"I have no idea, but they don't have heart trouble, as far as I know," Ellie countered, struggling to hold on to a little patience.

"Maybe not, but it seems to me that if I don't have all that much time left, like they seem to think, I'd rather not spend it eating food that may as well be cardboard for all the flavor it has. I know you might have to cook a bit differently for me, but you might think about stopping and asking me what I'd like to have for lunch or supper once in a while. I had also hoped you might at least have taken a few days off to spend at home with me, since it's very clear you're far too selfish to consider retiring. Instead, you just insist on planning everything around your schedule and what you want, including what I should or shouldn't do."

Stung, Ellie put down her fork and blinked back tears. Being called selfish hurt. A lot. Between working all day, seeing to her mother's needs at home and meeting all her other obligations, the forty minutes she spent walking in the morning with Charlene was the only time Ellie made for herself anymore.

Granted, she did plan the meals without consulting her mother, and she did have to make time at night to do her work, but given that there were only twenty-four hours in a day, Ellie had to be extremely organized to make everything work.

"We've talked about this before. I'm just not ready to retire yet, but I'm trying to help you the best I can," she managed. "I've taken off more time in the past month to help you when you were in the hospital than I took off in the past five years. I can't be away because I feel like it. My students need me in the classroom, and I have responsibilities to my colleagues," she explained, relieved that she still hadn't told her mother about her hopes to become the next language-arts supervisor.

Her mother took the napkin from her lap, laid it on the table and rose from her seat. "That you're always so worried about work should tell you something."

"It tells me I'm trying to be conscientious about my career. At the same time, I'm trying to be conscientious about my responsibilities to you," Ellie said, defending herself.

"No, Ellie. You're putting your students and your friends at work ahead of me. Ahead of family. But I have to admit, I'm not surprised. You did the same thing to your husband and your children when you decided your career was more important than they were, when you didn't really have to work at all. Now that I've gotten sick, you won't stay home, either. But then, I'm only your mother," she whispered sadly. She turned and walked out of the kitchen, leaving her words to echo deep in Ellie's troubled heart.

Chapter Sixteen

Bright and early on Wednesday, Charlene handed the nickel she had found lying in the street to Ellie, who was waiting for her on the corner for their morning walk. "I'm sorry I'm a few minutes late. Here. Add this to your funny money."

Ellie smiled and slipped the coin into her pocket, but her gaze was as cloudy as the sky overhead, which offered little hope of spring sunshine today. "Thanks. Would you mind if we just followed the walking path in the park today instead of taking our usual route along the avenue? I've got so much on my mind, I'm bound to miss a curb or something and trip."

"Sure," Charlene replied, and nodded toward her right. "I think I know the way, but just holler if I make a wrong turn."

"Welles Park is smack in the middle of the town. Unless you walk around in circles, you can't help but find it."

"I've gone round and round in circles without getting anywhere more often in the past few weeks than I care to admit," Charlene chuckled. "I no sooner fill all the orders for Easter gift baskets before I've got twice as many new orders to fill. Ginger King is helping out nearly full-time, and I've hired a couple of high school girls to work after school, too.

They wait on the customers while Ginger and I focus on making up the baskets, but I'm still way behind."

She paused while they waited for a utility truck to rumble by. "I'm either going to have to stop taking orders, or risk disappointing my customers later when I have to call and explain I just don't have the time to fill their orders. Unless I can grow a couple of extra arms—"

"Like an octopus?" Ellie teased. "I know the feeling, remember?"

Charlene grinned as they followed a curve to where the street forked. "I've been searching for an octopus mold in supply catalogues. I haven't found one yet, but don't be surprised if you see a chocolate octopus in Sweet Stuff the next time you come in to replenish your stash."

This time, Ellie's smile reached her eyes. "Would that be before or after you've filled all those gift-basket orders?"

"Funny, funny," Charlene said. She spied a penny and snatched it up. "Here." She handed over the coin. "A penny for your thoughts. You're the most organized woman I know. Have you got any brilliant ideas about how I can survive the Easter crush and not disappoint my customers? Keep in mind that it's too late to hire anyone who I would trust to work on the baskets and that I have to be careful not to work too many hours away from Aunt Dorothy, plus I really don't want to abandon my husband the entire weekend since that's the only time he's here." She didn't mention how she was enjoying spending time working with Daniel to clear out Aunt Dorothy's backyard. Their reconnection was too new, fragile and private to discuss.

At Park Avenue, Charlene turned right.

"Correct street, wrong direction," Ellie said as she walked left.

Charlene turned and hurried her pace to catch up. "I thought you said I couldn't help but find the park unless I walked in circles."

"You'll find the park that way, too, but only after you reach the dead end at Lady's Creek Drive and realize you've made a wrong turn."

"I've been doing a lot of that lately, too," Charlene admitted, surprised that she was able to keep up with Ellie without panting now that they'd been walking together for a few weeks.

"You're not alone," Ellie replied. "Making wrong turns has become a frequent occurrence in my life lately, too."

Charlene glanced at Ellie and saw the same frustration that stared back at Charlene in the mirror every morning. "How's your mother doing?" she asked.

Ellie didn't answer right away, but her pace slacked off a bit. "Physically, she's about the same. The incision on her arm is healing well, but I'm having a hard time trying to balance how much I should do for her against what she should do for herself."

She paused to tug up the hood on her jacket. "Like you said, I've always been pretty organized, but now, trying to care for my mother means I have to be more organized than ever. Just making it from one day to the next, meeting my obligations at work and seeing that all my mother's needs are met is overwhelming."

She turned to look at Charlene. "Maybe I could ask you a question. Your aunt must have a special diet she has to follow, doesn't she?"

Charlene almost snorted. "She's diabetic and she has chronic heart failure. Her diet is pretty rigid, not that she follows it faithfully every day," she admitted and shared the jelly donut story as they entered the park and started walking along the asphalt path around the perimeter.

Ellie furrowed her brow. "So you pretty much try to get her to follow her diet, but let her cheat whenever she wants to? Aren't you afraid she'll get sick again…or she'll…she'll…"

"That she'll die?" Charlene finished the sentence without hesitation.

She stopped walking and Ellie halted, too.

Charlene shoved her hands in her pockets to keep them warm while she and Ellie were standing still. "I've had to think about Aunt Dorothy dying for weeks now. Every time I see her sleeping late in the morning or taking a nap on the sofa, I have to check to make sure she's still breathing. I'm scared to death that I'll find her one day…gone."

Ellie glanced down at the path. "I do that, too."

"It's probably pretty normal," Charlene said. "I used to do the same thing when I had my babies. It's just odd now, because of the reversal of roles with my aunt."

"So true," Ellie whispered before she started them walking again.

Charlene let out a sigh. "I know it's hard for me and you, but I can only imagine how difficult it must be for my aunt and your mother to know that they have a terminal illness and their time here on earth is about to end. But I'm trying to look at it this way—we're all born to die. We just don't know when that will be. How we live each day we're given here is what's important. It's not when we die that matters—not as much as how we approach our death." She was grateful for the opportunity to give voice to her thoughts with someone who might truly understand them.

"My father and my husband both died very suddenly and unexpectedly," Ellie said. "Watching my mother face an illness that could last for days or weeks or months before she dies is much different, and I'm struggling with what's right to do. And she seems confused. Most of the time, she's making plans or talking about what she'd like to do when she's back in her own home again. Other times, all she talks about is how she wants to spend her last days with me."

"I'm struggling, too," Charlene replied, "but Aunt Dorothy is teaching me that if we live each day like it's our last, then we can embrace our death. We don't have to be afraid because we know there's a glorious eternal life waiting for us."

Ellie nodded. "So if that means your aunt wants a jelly donut today, you'll buy her one and watch her enjoy it without a single morsel of guilt?"

"No, I'm not saying that. I'd argue with her. To eat recklessly or to stop taking her medications is dangerous. I'm just saying that I have to remind myself that she isn't a child. As an adult, she should be able to control how she lives until the final moment. I know I'd feel pretty awful if I denied her request for a simple treat and found her gone the next day."

"Which is how I'd feel if my mother passed away and I hadn't fixed her that special meal she wanted or let her have her say over what she did or didn't do," Ellie said and looked up at the sky. "This is so, so hard for me."

Charlene put her arm around Ellie as they walked. "I know. But you're not alone—"

The rest of her words were lost as she tripped over something lying on the path and pitched forward. She tried to pull her arm off Ellie's shoulder, but ended up yanking her friend off balance, too.

Somehow, Ellie managed to plant her feet and brace herself, keeping Charlene on her feet as well. "Hey! We were walking here in the park so I wouldn't trip."

Charlene pressed her hand to her heart and felt it pounding. "It's a good thing you're steady on your feet, or I'd have pulled you down with me. Are you okay?"

"I'm fine. How about you?"

"Just feeling pretty clumsy." She looked behind her, saw a small branch lying on the path and shook her head. "As long as we're both okay. I guess we'd better finish our walk, or you're going to be late for work."

Ellie shrugged. "I've got time to go on a little farther." She pulled out the penny Charlene had given her earlier and grinned.

"I also owe you my thoughts on how to help get you through the Easter rush. Otherwise, I have to give this back to you."

Charlene grinned. "Shall we try walking just a little slower so I can walk, talk and listen at the same time?"

Ellie put the penny back into her pocket. "Sure. It's probably safer that way."

Together, they started down the path again, but at a slower pace. "From what you told me, you and Ginger are the only ones who are working on the gift baskets," Ellie prompted.

"That's right. I'm pretty fussy about how they're done. Ginger is good at it, but I'd rather keep the high school girls working the counter."

"You did post a deadline for customers to place their orders, didn't you?" Ellie asked as the path curved toward the center of the park.

"Oops. No, I didn't think of that."

Ellie laughed. "Post one today. Since you're already backed up, you might want to make the deadline for this Friday. That way you'll have the weekend and all of next week to get them done."

"Actually, I plan to close the store next Wednesday. I know that most of the other candy stores in the area will be operating straight through the day before Easter, but I found in the past that working that close to Easter really distracted me from the holiness of the holiday. This year, I especially want to have those days at home with Aunt Dorothy."

"All the more reason to make the deadline this Friday," Ellie said. "I'll be able to come in on Saturday for a few hours early in the morning to help you before you open up at noon. I'm pretty good with making bows and stuff."

Charlene shook her head. "Absolutely not. You have enough to do as it is. Aunt Dorothy offered to help me, too, but I didn't want to hurt her feelings. She wouldn't be able to handle the cellophane or tie the bows."

"What about your husband? Would he help?"

Charlene looked at Ellie and grimaced. "Daniel? You're kidding, right?"

"Not really," Ellie replied with a laugh. "If you set up some kind of assembly line, maybe he and Aunt Dorothy could fill the baskets while we add the finishing touches. As a matter of fact, my mother has been telling me she'd like to get out of the house for a few hours this weekend. She could certainly sit and fill baskets with chocolates or stuffed animals just as easily as she sits at home knitting. Besides, it might do her good to visit with your aunt for a little while. They grew up here together, you know."

"No, I didn't, but—"

Ellie hooked her arm with Charlene's. "But what? You're too proud to let people help you?"

"Maybe," Charlene murmured.

"Then get over it," Ellie ordered. "We're friends now, right?"

"Right," Charlene replied with a smile that came straight from her heart.

"Friends and family help one another, so instead of arguing with me, let's talk about how we can make this work. Oh, but you should know that I happened to mention your incredible hot chocolate to my mother, and I have a feeling she'll want some herself."

"So will Aunt Dorothy. I'm afraid it's a bit heavy in sugar and fat for their diets, but I could make something else for them."

"Why don't we let them both choose?" Ellie replied.

Charlene chuckled. "Sure, although I think we both know what they'll pick. Is eight o'clock too early?"

Chapter Seventeen

Sometimes one good idea inspires another.

After mulling over Ellie's suggestion of an assembly line and deciding it was a good one, Charlene found herself considering more new ideas.

When she was drying the breakfast dishes, she paused to glance out the kitchen window, thinking about the possibility of Daniel helping her in the store. He had made good progress clearing the backyard, but he still had a great deal of work to do to keep his promise to give Aunt Dorothy a clear view of the creek by Easter. The overhead skies threatened rain at some point today, and the forecast for the weekend was still undetermined. But whether or not Daniel could work outside this weekend, Charlene would fine-tune her plan for the assembly line before mentioning it to him—or to Aunt Dorothy, for that matter.

Charlene also decided to call and make an appointment for a haircut. She'd put it off too long, and Ellie's recent trim had inspired her.

She was drying a saucer when Aunt Dorothy entered the kitchen carrying the old candy tin containing her jewelry. "Let those dishes go for now. They'll air-dry just fine. If we don't make time for me to show you this jewelry, we never will."

Charlene winced. She had been so busy, she hadn't had the opportunity to sit down with Aunt Dorothy again for a jewelry-and-story session. "I'm sorry. With Easter so close, it's been a little hectic for me," she apologized. Reluctant to put her aunt off yet again, she gave up any hope of getting to work early today.

Aunt Dorothy chuckled. "Maybe you've been busy, but all I've had to do is worry about convincing Agnes Withers that I'm not dead yet, so she shouldn't be so worried about who is getting what after I'm finally good and gone from this world." She set the tin on the kitchen table and sat down.

Charlene grabbed a pencil and a notepad from a junk drawer and took a seat next to her aunt. "I'm ready," she announced, ready to see what kind of jewelry her aunt had saved in the tin.

Aunt Dorothy lifted the lid and set it aside. She took out an old cardboard box held together with blue rubber bands. Inside, there was a faded maroon velvet box, which she snapped open to reveal a tiny gold ring with a square amethyst stone centered between two diamond chips.

Charlene smiled immediately. "I recognize that ring. You used to wear it all the time."

"It's my birthstone. Your mother gave it to me when I stood up for her at her wedding. Thanks to these old knobby knuckles of mine, it doesn't fit anymore." Her gaze softened, as if she traveled back in her mind's eye to glimpse at the past for a moment before she packed the ring away, tucking in the note Charlene had quickly scribbled to explain the ring's significance.

The next few boxes held a fourteen-karat-gold cross with a diamond chip in the center, which had been given to Aunt Dorothy on her sixteenth birthday by her parents; a dented gold locket containing a lock of Aunt Dorothy's baby hair; and a chunky gold ring studded with opals that a former old neighbor had bequeathed to Aunt Dorothy in her will.

"I saved the best for last," Aunt Dorothy proclaimed, slowly, almost reverently lifting out the final box.

Yellowed as all the others were, this box was larger by half and was held together with a faded green ribbon.

Charlene leaned forward in her chair. She expected to see a bracelet of some kind, but when her aunt finally removed the cardboard lid, she was surprised to see three diamond engagement rings, side by side, sparkling brilliantly as Aunt Dorothy tilted the box to catch the morning light.

"They're lovely," Charlene murmured, impressed by the antique settings as well as the diamonds themselves.

"They are lovely. And they're a big part of the history of the women in our family, which is why I wanted you to know the stories behind them. One day, I hope you'll pass them on to Bonnie," her aunt replied. One by one, she laid the rings on the table. "These were my mother's engagement rings," she said, pointing to the two closest to her. "The other one belonged to her mother."

"Then these were my grandmother's and my great-grand-mother's engagement rings," Charlene clarified.

"That's right."

Charlene picked up her great-grandmother's ring, a symbol of commitment that represented the hopes and dreams of a young couple from so long ago. Although she had never known her great-grandparents, this ring created a tangible connection to them, just as her mother's engagement ring, which Charlene kept stored in her jewelry box at home, did. "I don't think I've ever known my great-grandmother's name."

"It was Anna Hughes," Aunt Dorothy told her. "She was an Altman by birth, but she was married to Jack Hughes for fifty-seven years. They were both gone by the time I was nine or ten years old. I do remember she always wore a hat, and he had a big mole on the lobe of one of his ears. It's funny what a child remembers about people, isn't it?"

Charlene gently set the ring back on the table and studied the other two rings that had belonged to her grandmother. Although the diamonds in both rings were identical in size, perhaps half a karat, the settings were very distinct—one gold and the other platinum. "I don't think I ever knew that Grandmother Phillips was married twice."

"As you know only too well, Charlene, war always makes lots of widows and orphans. When your father died in Korea, it wasn't the first time a woman in our family became a war widow."

Charlene nodded and swallowed the lump in her throat.

"My mother married for the first time when she was seventeen," Aunt Dorothy continued, and pointed to the gold ring. "Her husband, John Gibbs, was killed in France during World War I. After the war, she married his brother, Jake, who was your mother's and my father. This is the engagement ring he gave her," Aunt Dorothy said, pointing to the platinum ring.

"She married brothers?" Charlene asked.

"That wasn't uncommon back in those days. I worked with a girl once who married brothers, but she was a floozy. Seems she forgot to divorce the first brother before she married the second," she said and laughed. "There was enough gossip in the factory about Flossie Decker and the Birmingham brothers to fuel the assembly line for months!"

"I imagine there would be." Charlene chuckled as she wrote a brief note about each of the three rings. After folding it into quarters, she tucked it into the black box underneath the velvet. "There. Now I won't forget what you've told me."

"Before I put these rings away, why don't you let me see yours?" Aunt Dorothy asked.

Charlene slid her engagement ring from her finger. When

she held it out, her aunt took it and laid it on the table next to the other rings. "Knowing who owned what ring is nice, Charlene, but not as important as the men who gave them to the women they loved as a symbol of commitment—a promise, fulfilled through marriage, to love and honor each other," she said softly. "Do you still have your mother's engagement ring?"

"Yes. It's at home."

"Well, if we laid her ring right here," she said, pointing, "there'd be four generations of our family represented here. Four generations of women who spent their lives keeping the promises they made. I'm pretty sure it wasn't always easy. But every time I think I'm not strong enough to do something I need to do, I like to take these rings out and remind myself that I come from a long line of very strong women. So do you."

Moved by her aunt's words, Charlene slipped her engagement ring back on her finger with a renewed awareness of the commitment she and Daniel had pledged to each other so many years ago. Before she could thank her aunt, the back door opened, filling the kitchen with a blast of damp, chilly air.

When Charlene turned, startled, to face the door, her eyes widened. "Daniel! What on earth are you doing here?"

Grinning, he nudged the door behind him closed before he set a brown cardboard box on the counter. "I came home from work yesterday and decided to use a couple of my vacation days to work here in the yard. I thought I'd surprise you both," he said and planted a kiss on top of Aunt Dorothy's head. "How's my best girl?" he asked before walking over to Charlene and pecking her cheek.

"I'm feeling better now that you're here. I can't say I've ever been fond of surprises, but you could change a girl's mind about almost anything," her aunt said coyly.

"It looks like I've interrupted the two of you," he said as her aunt discreetly put the three engagement rings away again before gathering up the rest of the boxes and storing them in the candy tin.

"You're about the best interruption I've had in ten years," Aunt Dorothy teased. "We were finished, anyway," she said and handed the tin to Charlene. "If you wouldn't mind, you could put this back in my room now."

Disappointed to end her conversation with her aunt, yet very pleased with her husband's unexpected arrival, Charlene picked up the candy tin and got up from her seat. "Have you had breakfast?" she asked Daniel.

"Hours ago. I wanted to get a full day of work in today."

"It's a shame you didn't wait until tomorrow," she said, glancing out the kitchen window at the gray skies again. "It looks like it's going to rain."

"I've taken care of that, too," he replied, and nodded toward the cardboard box on the counter. "I picked up some earth-friendly cleaning products. I found an old concrete birdbath in the brush at back, but it's covered with grime and algae. I thought I'd clear out more brush until it rains, then I'll move to the carport to tackle the birdbath. According to the clerk at the hardware store, I should be able to clean it up almost as good as new."

Aunt Dorothy clapped her hands together. "I was hoping that old birdbath was still out there, although I'm sure it's in deplorable condition. You're such a considerate man to want to fix it up for me."

Charlene nodded. "Daniel is probably the kindest man I've ever known," she said, offering him a compliment of her own. Telling Daniel how much she admired him or appreciated the little things he did for her was something she used to do a lot, and he had been just as open with his compliments to her. She was not sure how or why they had stopped doing that. But she certainly liked the way he smiled back at her right now.

"Did you happen to find anything else out there in the yard?" Aunt Dorothy asked.

He leaned back against the counter. "No. Why? What else is out there?"

"I used to have a concrete bench by the edge of the creek, but it's probably gone. Either kids shoved it in the creek or it just caved in by itself after a heavy rain."

"It might still turn up," Daniel said before turning to lift a small, covered aluminum pan from the cardboard box. He placed it on the table in front of Aunt Dorothy, who beamed up at him.

"For me?"

"For you. I was hoping I'd get here in time for your breakfast, since you usually sleep late, but I see from the dishes drying on the counter that you've already eaten. You can save these for tomorrow."

"That depends on what they are," she suggested.

"I'm not sure what you like, other than jelly donuts, but I think you'll like these."

Without waiting for another invitation, she peeled back the corner of the lid and peeked inside. The aroma of bananas filled the air.

"Banana griddle cakes!" Aunt Dorothy cried. She picked up one of the silver-dollar-size treats, devoured it in two bites and took another.

Charlene chuckled. "I better get a plate."

Daniel urged her to take a seat. "Relax. I'll get one for each of us."

"These are delicious," Aunt Dorothy managed to say between bites. "I remember you made these once before. I believe it was for your birthday, Charlene. You turned forty-one that year, I think."

Impressed by her aunt's amazing memory, Charlene invited her own memories to surface. During the years they had been raising a family, Daniel had not cooked very much.

The kitchen had always been her domain. But he had commandeered it on special occasions, such as their birthdays, usually making Charlene and the children their favorite breakfast. Once Greg and Bonnie had grown up and moved away, the tradition had faded to a memory that Charlene had almost forgotten until now.

Like his father, Greg loved creamed beef on burnt toast, of all things. Bonnie favored homemade waffles with blueberry syrup, while Charlene's favorite breakfast was banana pancakes.

She wondered now if Daniel had made them today to please her as much as to please Aunt Dorothy.

When he laid a plate in front of her, she placed her hand atop his and glanced at her engagement and wedding rings. Thinking of the women in her family, she prayed that she might find the strength to keep the promises her rings represented, too.

When she looked up at her husband, she found what she was hoping for in his eyes. In his own quiet, gentle way, he reassured her that the promises he had made when they married were still important to him, too.

Chapter Eighteen

As it turned out, not every surprise Charlene would have that day would be so heartwarming.

Despite her plans for an early start, she did not pull out of Aunt Dorothy's driveway until nearly ten o'clock, a good hour and a half behind schedule. But she drove to the shop without an ounce of regret.

Softly humming a hymn in thanksgiving for the blessings this day had already brought, she cut through Welles Park. Lured by the tranquility and beauty that surrounded her, she gave in to the urge to pull into a parking space at the edge of the lake, to be alone with her thoughts before she started a very busy workday.

She had barely shifted the car from Drive to Park before the gray clouds overhead parted to reveal a patch of blue the same color as her husband's eyes. Rays of sunshine dappled the green grass and danced across the surface of the lake.

This display of nature reminded her that God was all-present and the source of all strength. He was here, watching over her. She folded her hands on her lap and closed her eyes. *Thank you, Father God, for helping me and loving me,* she prayed. She also asked him for strength and guidance for Aunt Dorothy, Daniel and herself in the days and weeks ahead.

When her heart was filled with peace and hope, she ended her prayer, backed out of the parking space and continued her drive to work. Unfortunately, she missed the turn that would have taken her to the alley where she had a parking spot directly behind her shop. But she was too content at the moment to be upset by anything so trivial, and proceeded straight ahead, to circle the block.

She sat for a couple of minutes at the corner, waiting to turn. As she had feared, traffic on the avenue was very heavy. After a gracious driver waved her on, she urged the car into the slow-moving line of cars, and spied a police officer a block ahead who was directing traffic off Welles Avenue.

"Not a detour. Not now," she groaned, envisioning driving through clogged side streets and losing more time. The avenue was occasionally closed for town events, but as far as she knew, nothing was scheduled for today. She opened her window and leaned out to get a better view, but she didn't see any barricades stretching across the street behind the officer, which meant that something unexpected must have happened.

As she got closer, she recognized the officer as young Joe Karpinski, better known as Officer Joe to the children he befriended on his bike patrol. He stopped in at Sweet Stuff frequently to check on things, and she never let him leave without some wrapped candy to pass along to the children he met on his beat.

Moving at a crawl, she pulled over a little when she reached him and lowered her window. "Did I forget some kind of event in town today?"

"Not today," he replied as he bent down and looked in. "Mrs. Butler! I just heard over the scanner that the dispatcher is trying to reach you."

Instinctively, she pressed harder on the brake, fearing that Aunt Dorothy had taken ill in the short time that had passed since Charlene had left. She felt the blood drain from her face.

She must have looked like she was going to pass out,

because Officer Joe reached into the car and placed his hand on her shoulder. "No one's badly hurt, but I'm afraid I can't say the same about your store."

She pulled in a huge gulp of air. "My store? This—this is about my store?" she asked, recovering slightly from panic mode and realizing that if Aunt Dorothy had taken ill, Daniel would have called and the police department would not have had to detour traffic along the avenue.

"Yes, it is. I didn't mean to alarm you. I forgot about your aunt being so sick," he said.

"What happened at the store?"

"Apparently one of the residents from the Towers, who probably should have turned in his driver's license long before now, tried to avoid hitting a squirrel, stepped on the gas pedal instead of the brake and lost control of his car. Unfortunately, he ended up driving right through your storefront window. Good thing you don't open early, or you might have been inside."

Her heart skipped a beat. If she hadn't stopped at the lake to pray, she could have been there when that poor soul had had his accident. Quickly, she said a silent double prayer— to thank Him for keeping her safe and for the man who had driven into her shop.

"Was the driver hurt?" she asked.

"Nothing serious, but they just took him to Tilton General to make sure," he said. "Give me a second. I'll let the dispatcher know you're on your way, and clear out some of this traffic so you can turn and go straight down the avenue. You won't be able to park near your store, though. We've got the whole block shut off from traffic."

The moment he left her, her cell phone rang. She fumbled in her purse, finally found the phone and flipped it open without looking at the screen to see who was calling. "Hello?"

"Charlene? This is Aunt Dorothy. The police called—"

"Yes, I know. Is Daniel there?"

"He asked me to call you and let you know he'd meet you at the store. How bad is it?"

"I'm not sure yet. I'm still a good distance away, but I've got to go now. The police are redirecting traffic so I can drive around the detour. I'll call you when I know more."

"Be careful."

"I will," she promised, and closed the phone.

With visions of her pretty little shop reduced to nothing but a broken dream, she followed Officer Joe's directions, turning and heading down the avenue.

She parked the car and walked to a wooden barricade a couple of storefronts away from Sweet Stuff. Two fire trucks and several patrol cars were parked in the center of the street in front of the shop. A tow truck had just begun pulling the car out of her store, beeping loudly as it backed out to the street again.

Broken glass and smashed brick crunched underneath both sets of tires. The sound of glass falling from the store window to the brick walkway shattered Charlene's nerves. Blinking back tears, she trembled from head to toe until she felt a strong arm wrap around her shoulders.

When she looked up, Daniel was smiling down at her with tears in his eyes. "When the police called, I was afraid I'd lost you. I thought for sure you would have been inside when the car rammed into the shop. I wanted to believe it when I was told you weren't there, but I really wasn't convinced you were all right until I spied you standing here."

She leaned into his embrace and felt him trembling, too, as she wrapped her arm around his waist. "I would have been inside, but I stopped in the park to say a prayer by the lake," she murmured, and sighed, recalling how they used to pray together at home nearly every day. "We used to pray together," she whispered.

He tightened his arm around her. "We still can," he said,

his voice husky with emotion. He held her for a few moments before letting go. "It—it looks like they're asking everyone to move farther back, and there's a police officer headed our way. Are you feeling up to checking out the damage now, or would you rather wait? It might be better if I take you home—"

"No," she insisted, and straightened her back. "I'd rather see the damage now." She looked up at him. "I'm glad you're here. I'm not sure I could do this alone."

Ben Jenkins, a police officer who was also her customer, approached them wearing a pained expression. "I'm real sorry about your store, Mrs. Butler. I can take you up there now to get a closer look, but you'll have to wait to get inside until an engineer checks for any structural damage. We'll set up a smaller barricade and have an officer on duty here until then, so you don't have to worry about anything."

"Like making sure I haven't lost my entire supply of pistachio fudge?" she asked dryly.

He grinned. "That'd be the first thing I'd check."

After introducing the two men, Charlene took Daniel's hand as they walked down the middle of the street and around the emergency vehicles to approach her shop. She wondered how long it had been since they had held hands like this. Who had stopped reaching for the other first? It didn't matter, she decided—not now when this felt so good, and so right.

She was surprised that the adjoining health-food store wasn't damaged at all, but the gaping hole in the window of her store was just as jagged and huge as she'd feared it would be. A single piece of stained glass hung precariously from one section of the window. The other pieces were gone, along with the pink lace curtains—save for a strip of torn lace that had caught on one of the broken points of glass. Smashed and broken gift baskets that had once lined the bottom ledge were scattered about the floor of the shop, like peanut shells that littered the stands after a ball game.

Seeing the destruction, she felt her heart fill with grief. Looking beyond the window into the shop, she saw that the vintage candy on the hutch had flown everywhere, although the hutch itself seemed to be intact. Unfortunately, she couldn't say the same for the glass cases that held her chocolates. What appeared to be several large, tin ceiling tiles, which must have been dislodged by the force of the car hitting the building, had made a direct landing on the cases, shattering the glass and showering the candy with splinters, making it a total loss.

Curiously enough, her front door had escaped any damage. The pink-and-white Closed sign was still hanging straight, and the sign listing her store hours was also in place. She turned to address Ben Jenkins, who had remained at her side. "Would it be all right if my husband and I went in through the back door? I'd like to check my workroom and get the cash from the register, if that's possible."

The officer grimaced. "Maybe a little later. We're expecting someone from the utility company to arrive here soon to check the gas line first before we let anyone on either side of this block open for business. Like I said, we'll have an officer here until everything is checked out, so don't worry about the contents. In the meantime, you might want to get somebody over here this afternoon to board up the window."

"I can handle the window," Daniel said. "Will you call us when it's all clear to go inside so I can get started on it?"

The officer nodded. "Someone will. Absolutely."

Charlene heard the men continue talking, but she didn't register what they were saying. The shock of seeing Sweet Stuff destroyed was too great, and she was consumed by thoughts of having to disappoint the many customers who were counting on her candy for their Easter celebrations.

"We'd better go. I need to get a few sheets of plywood," Daniel urged, pulling her back from her thoughts as the officer left. "I'll drive you back to Aunt Dorothy's first. We can get your car later." He led her to the brick sidewalk on the other side of the street, where police officers were attempting to disperse a crowd of onlookers.

Andy Johnson, the owner of the health-food store, made his way out of the crowd and rushed toward her. "Mrs. Butler!"

Charlene stopped and let go of Daniel's hand to take the white shopping bag that Mr. Johnson held out to her. "I'm so sorry about your store, but I can't tell you how relieved I am that you weren't there. While the EMTs were helping poor Stanley Murphy to the ambulance, I managed to slip inside your store. I dumped the contents of your cash register into the first bag I could find. You are planning to reopen, aren't you?" he asked, finally stopping to draw a breath as he wiped the sweat that had beaded up on top of his bald head.

"I—I imagine I will," she replied, hopeful that insurance would cover most, if not all, of the damage. Touched that he would think of her welfare when they'd barely spoken more than a couple of words to each other in the short time since he'd opened his store, she managed to offer him a smile.

"A lot will depend on what the engineers have to say," Daniel interjected, and then introduced himself. "Now, if you'll excuse us, I have some plywood to buy. I'm concerned about getting the window boarded up before it rains, and I'd like to take my wife home first."

"No!" Mr. Johnson said quickly. "I mean, don't buy any plywood. I've got a couple of sheets in the basement, along with all the tools you'll need." He took out his business card and handed it to Daniel. "Once you hear from the police that the building is safe, call me. I'm going to stay as close as they'll let me to watch over things, anyway. I'll meet you back here. I'm sure there are a couple of other folks who'd like to help you, and we could have the store boarded up in no time."

"Thank you. You're very kind," Charlene said.

"Thank you," Daniel echoed. "I'd be grateful for your help."

"I'll wait to hear from you, then," Andy Johnson said, then turned and walked away.

When Charlene heard the ring of a nearby cell phone, she realized she must have left her purse in her car. "I promised to call Aunt Dorothy when I got to the store, but I forgot. And my cell phone is in my purse in my car. It's just a block down the street, this way," she said, pointing straight ahead.

Daniel pulled out his cell phone and handed it to her. "My car is closer. Use my phone," he said, and then reached for her hand again.

She smiled, squeezed his hand and held on tight.

Chapter Nineteen

Only minutes after she'd finished teaching her last class, Ellie picked up her mail in the main office, then hurried down the hall, to escape to the relative peace and quiet of her own office.

When she turned the final corner, eager to slip inside her own space before anyone came out of the faculty room across the hall to delay her, she spied three students who should have been in class gathered around an open locker. She stopped, raised a brow and stared at them.

A red-faced Alicia Conners, a student in Ellie's second-period honors class, nudged the locker closed with her knee. "Mrs. Waters is here," she croaked, and scurried off with her two girlfriends following on her heels.

"Rank and reputation have their benefits," Ellie murmured to herself, rather pleased that she'd only had to show her displeasure to get the students moving to class. She turned to enter her office when Meghan Vincent-Douglass, one of the youngest teachers in the school and a Welleswood Wonder, came out of the faculty room.

A first-year mathematics teacher, Meghan had an Ivy League graduate degree, a Barbie doll figure and a condescending attitude that irritated a lot of people.

"Oh, there you are," Meghan crooned as she clicked her way over to Ellie in stiletto heels more suitable for a formal affair than the classroom. "Bless your heart. Don't you look so professional and so dedicated again today."

Ellie bristled, but she kept a smile pasted on her face. "Hello, Meghan," she replied, and reached for the doorknob to make her exit before losing valuable time listening to the young woman's usual prattle about how she wanted to bring Welleswood High School out of the Dark Ages, a term that historians had abandoned years ago.

"I'm just on my way to see Tommy Murphy's guidance counselor, Mr. Grant," Meghan said in a low voice, forcing Ellie to pause and listen. "That poor sweet boy is bound to be very upset about what happened, and I'd like to make sure he gets all the support we can offer him."

Ellie had taught Tommy last year. Although she would scarcely have described the teenager as a "poor sweet boy," she was concerned about what might have happened to him that required the intervention of his guidance counselor. "Why? What happened?"

"Haven't you heard?"

"Obviously not," Ellie replied.

"I shouldn't be surprised," Meghan said, patting Ellie's arm. "You're much too busy taking such good care of your students and the members of your department to spend any time at all in the faculty room."

Sighing, Ellie decided not to argue. "What happened?" she asked again, directing their conversation back to the point.

Meghan's gaze grew troubled. "Poor dear. His grandfather, I mean. He had an automobile accident not half an hour ago, right in the middle of town."

"Was he badly hurt?" Ellie asked, loath to admit that Meghan was right to get the counselor involved, because Tommy would be very upset if anything had happened to his grandfather.

"From what we understand, he's only shaken up by the whole experience. They took him to the hospital by ambulance, just to be on the safe side."

"That's good news," Ellie replied. She had known Tommy's grandfather, the elderly Stanley Murphy, for many years. He and his wife, Margaret, had lived up the street from Ellie's mother until a few years ago, when they had sold their home and moved into the high-rise for senior citizens.

Ellie was surprised, however, that the news about the poor man's accident had spread to the faculty room so quickly, and she worried that Tommy might also have heard about it, since it was hard to enforce the school rule requiring students to keep their cell phones turned off during the school day. "How did you find out about the accident so soon?"

"Actually, I only heard about it just now in the faculty room. Mrs. Anderson was talking about it. Apparently Mr. Elliott's cousin was having a late breakfast at The Diner when the accident happened and sent a text message to him with all the details. He told Mrs. Anderson, since they teach in adjoining classrooms, and she told the rest of us. Naturally, I thought at once about helping Tommy."

"I'm sure Mr. Grant will appreciate your interest and make sure Tommy knows his grandfather wasn't hurt," Ellie said.

"I'm more concerned that the other students don't tease Tommy about it," the younger teacher said. "The latest research tells us that it's better to address all forms of intimidation, including teasing, rather than ignore it."

"I'm not sure we have to worry about the students teasing Tommy about his grandfather simply because he had an accident on the avenue," she countered, not bothering to add that there weren't many students in the entire school who would dare to tease Tommy about anything.

"The accident is only the half of it. The poor soul plowed right through the plate-glass window into Sweet Stuff,"

Meghan said, shaking her head. "Half the students here stop there on their way home to buy candy, when they would be much better off walking right next door for some unsalted nuts or naturally dried fruit. That's one of the reasons I've been trying to get more active in the PTA," she explained earnestly. "I honestly think we should make a real effort to convince the candy-store owner to either stop selling candy to the students after school or at least limit what they buy. Sugar causes all sorts of health—"

"I'm sure they'll be glad to have the benefit of your insight," Ellie said, too worried about Charlene to care if she was being abrupt with Meghan. "If you'll excuse me, I'd like to go inside and make a few calls to make sure the store's owner wasn't hurt in the accident."

Meghan sniffed. "You don't have to bother. She's fine. At least, that's what Mrs. Anderson said, although there were quite a few teachers concerned about their orders for Easter candy, as much as I was."

Ellie narrowed her gaze. "You ordered something from Sweet Stuff?"

"Of course not. I ordered some special treats from Natural Wonders for Easter, but Mrs. Callow said she had gotten another text message from her son-in-law, who was having his hair cut at the time. He rushed out of the barber shop when the accident occurred, and sent a text message that Sweet Stuff was pretty damaged, but Natural Wonders seemed to be just fine. So my order should be, too," she explained. "I'd love to keep chatting, but I really do need to get to Mr. Grant before this period ends," she said, then turned and clicked her way down the hall.

Ellie opened the door and slipped into her office, convinced that new technology, like cell phones, had added as many troubles as it had offered benefits.

Concerned about Charlene, Ellie was reaching for the

phone when she had second thoughts. Charlene was probably preoccupied with more pressing matters than talking to Ellie. She had to be devastated by the damage to her shop. Ellie didn't know if any stock remained to fill the Easter-basket orders now, but she did know that Charlene needed prayers more than she needed a telephone call.

After pausing to pray for Charlene, as well as for poor Stanley Murphy and his family, Ellie started sorting the paperwork from her mailbox. She found a note from her supervisor asking to meet with her tomorrow at one o'clock. She added the appointment to her calendar, hoping Nate Pepperidge might have some news about how soon his position would be posted and interviews might begin.

By working straight through lunch, Ellie finished grading all the quizzes half an hour after the end of her official workday. She selected a package of Necco wafers from the candy stash in her bottom drawer, opened it, removed all the chocolate ones—which she set up on her desk like a stack of coins—and put the rest away. She finished one wafer before calling home to check on her mother and ask if she wanted Ellie to pick up anything at the store for supper on the way home. It was a sincere effort on her part to consider her mother's wishes for the menu.

Her mother answered the telephone on the first ring.

"Mother?"

"Ellie, I'm glad you called. I was just writing you a note. Phyllis Kennedy is here, and she's taking me with her to visit with Stanley Murphy. He's just back from the hospital. Poor dear. He and Margaret are both very upset, as you might expect. Phyllis made a tuna casserole for them to have for supper. She thought it would be nice if I went along with her, so she was kind enough to pick up dessert from McAllister's for me to take to them. We were neighbors with the Murphys for years, if you recall. I suppose you heard what happened today on the avenue."

"I did," Ellie replied, swallowing her concerns that her mother was going out on a social call for the first time since taking ill. "I'm sure they'll both be happy to see you. Will you be back in time for supper?"

"Probably not. Phyllis made a huge casserole. She seems to think we'll be staying to eat with them, but I'm sure I'll be home by seven. If that changes, I'll call you, but don't wait on my account. If you're hungry, go ahead and make something for yourself to eat. Something nutritious. Not a handful of candy," she added and hung up.

Ellie stared at the receiver for a moment before placing it back in the cradle. "Not bad. Not bad at all," she murmured, easily dismissing the barb at the end of her conversation in favor of appreciating how she and her mother had talked to one another civilly. Inspired by her mother's plans to visit her friend, Ellie made a few quick calls before leaving work, on behalf of a friend of her own.

The meal she ordered from The Diner to be delivered to her home later was not homemade, like Phyllis Kennedy's tuna casserole, but she ordered a dessert from McAllister's to be delivered, as well—a German chocolate cake—and her intentions were just as well-founded. She suspected she might find Charlene at Sweet Stuff, trying to find a way to fill her Easter-basket orders, in spite of the setback she had suffered—and she was unlikely to be thinking about supper. If she wasn't there, Ellie would deliver the meal to Charlene's aunt's house with an offer to help however she could, because that's what friends did for each other.

And that was one lesson Ellie had learned long ago from the most important person in her life: her mother.

Chapter Twenty

Ellie finally arrived near the scene of this morning's accident shortly after four o'clock, wearing old jeans and heavy shoes, with a pair of thick work gloves in the pocket of her jacket. She was ready to help Charlene, whether that meant working to clean up the shop or simply sitting and listening to a friend who must be at her wit's end, if not completely devastated, by what had happened.

With dinner in one shopping bag and dessert in another, Ellie walked along the brick sidewalk. The moment she saw the plywood across the window of the candy store she caught her breath.

Although she had expected to find the storefront boarded up, she had not anticipated the degree of sadness she would feel or the heaviness that filled her heart when she got close enough to see Sweet Stuff awkwardly spray-painted in large pink-and-white letters on the rough wood. She paused to read the brief and soulful message painted under the name: *Trust and Believe.*

Moved by her friend's faith, Ellie swallowed hard. She tried not to question why Mr. Murphy had accidentally driven into Sweet Stuff, out of all the shops on the avenue. This tiny store offered so much more than scrumptious chocolates or nostalgic candy. It inspired memories of long ago and created new memories for the children who stopped here on their way home from school.

Sweet Stuff was the one place on the avenue where you could stop, without a penny in your pocket or with your spirits low, and leave minutes later with a handful of candy and a smile in your heart. Even now, the store continued to inspire and touch anyone who drove by, with the simple message of hope, courage and faith painted on the plywood.

When Sweet Stuff had first opened, many residents of the small town had been quick to criticize Charlene for abruptly closing the store in the middle of the day for a "chocolate emergency," which meant she had left to deliver a sweet treat to someone who needed a friendly ear or a hug of encouragement. Everyone had quickly learned, however, that if they waited for a bit or came back later, Charlene would reward their patience by adding a little bit extra to their order, free of charge.

Ellie tightened her hold on the shopping bags and approached the entry to the store. Surprisingly, she found the glass door intact. Unfortunately, her view inside was blocked by a pink-and-white gingham curtain. The Closed sign was hanging inside the door, but the sign listing Charlene's hours was missing.

Stymied for a moment, Ellie set down one of her shopping bags and knocked. If Charlene was here, she would answer. Ellie knew her well enough to be sure Charlene would not turn anyone away, even now, although Ellie had no idea how much stock had been ruined by Mr. Murphy's mishap.

After waiting for a few moments, she reached out to knock a second time, when the door opened.

"Ellie! I knew you'd come," Charlene said, glancing at the bag on her stoop and the bag in Ellie's hand. She swung the door open wider. "I sure hope you have something in one of those bags for supper. I'm so hungry I could eat my way through three pounds of chocolate-covered pretzels, which I don't have at the moment."

Though her words were typical Charlene, upbeat and humorous, Ellie detected the sorrow and strain in her friend's voice. She could also tell by the puffiness around Charlene's eyes that her friend had done a fair bit of crying today.

Ellie picked up the bag on the stoop and handed it over. "I had a feeling you'd be too busy to stop and eat, and too tired and upset to cook when you got home. Since today is Wednesday, the special at The Diner is stuffed pork chops, so I got a couple of orders for you and your aunt. I wasn't sure if either of you liked them, so I asked for a meatloaf platter and a chicken pot pie, as well. You probably have enough food to last for a couple of dinners, even if your husband is here, too," she said, assuming that Charlene's husband would want to be here, under the circumstances.

"Daniel is here. He decided to surprise Aunt Dorothy and me by taking a few vacation days so he could finish up clearing out her yard. He got here early this morning, which turned out to be both a surprise and a blessing, considering what happened," she replied as she took hold of the bag.

Her eyes filled with tears, which she blinked away. Smiling, she lifted up the bag to inhale the delicious aromas. "Ah, this smells great, great, great. Daniel should probably be finishing up in about an hour, so I'll try to hold off eating all of this before I meet him back at Aunt Dorothy's. He had a few errands to run, including meeting with our insurance agent, Jack Meloni, to take care of all the paperwork, so all I'll have to do is sign," she said, eyeing the bag Ellie was carrying. "Come on in."

Ellie handed the second bag to Charlene as she entered the store, and laughed when she saw her friend's eyes widen. "Yes, it's a McAllister's bag. No, it's not donuts, which probably won't make your aunt very happy, but yes, what's inside is luscious and decadent and loaded with enough sugar and chocolate to satisfy both of you," she teased.

Ellie sobered the moment she saw that the store was empty, totally, the stock gone and the display cases nowhere in sight.

The counter was gone, too, along with the cash register. Even a few of the antique tin ceiling tiles were missing, and the planked floorboards had been swept so clean of all debris, Ellie could not see a single dust ball.

If Charlene hadn't been standing right there, Ellie might have suspected she had entered the wrong store. She looked at Charlene and cocked her head. "What happened to all your…your stuff?" she asked.

Charlene's bottom lip trembled. "I—I think I've asked myself the same question a hundred times today. What's happened to my store and my candy and my cases and my…my stuff?" she whispered, sniffling back a tear. "It's gone, Ellie. All of it. Gone."

"Gone? You mean stored away somewhere?"

"I wish I did," Charlene replied. "When Daniel and I got here this morning, right after the accident, we weren't allowed inside because the authorities had to make sure the structure of the building hadn't been compromised and the gas line wasn't raptured. I'd seen enough to suspect that I might have to close down for a few days to clear away the debris, but I was more worried that Daniel would get the window boarded up before it started to rain."

She paused, looked around the empty store again and sighed. "As it turned out, the rain didn't amount to much more than a drizzle, and we got a call within an hour or so that we could come back. But…but once I was inside again, I realized that the glass from the storefront window had shattered and sent splinters flying everywhere. I found bits of glass in the fur of the stuffed animals and in the weave of the gift baskets."

She glanced up at the ceiling for a moment and shook her head. "When a couple of the tin ceiling tiles fell, the glass in the display cases broke and shards rained down on every bit of candy inside. At least the storeroom survived," she said, brightening a bit. "Come on back. I unplugged the telephone so I wouldn't be constantly interrupted. I needed to make a list of what I had stored in the basement so I could try to figure out a thing or two," she said, and started walking toward the back of the store.

Ellie followed along behind her friend, their footsteps echoing across the wooden floor. "Now that I've seen it, I'm afraid I still don't believe it," she said, amazed at how quickly the store had reverted back to the empty space that had languished here for a number of months after the pet store had closed.

"I don't think I quite believe it yet myself," Charlene replied, and placed the two shopping bags on the worktable.

"What did you do with everything, and how on earth did you get it all cleared away?" Ellie asked as she removed her jacket. The workroom itself, which was protected by a wall that separated it from the main store, was intact and looked much the same as it had the last time Ellie had been here. Even the two boxes of stuffed animals she'd helped Charlene carry up from the basement were still in the corner.

Charlene walked over to the small kitchen, past the machine that melted the chocolate, and opened a cabinet. "I turned into an octopus, or at least that's how it felt," she said as she took some paper plates from the cabinet.

"You had lots of help?" Ellie asked, finding it impossible to believe that in the space of five or six hours, her friend had gotten enough help to clean out the entire store.

Charlene carried the plates back to the worktable, along with a knife and a couple of plastic forks. "If I ever, ever doubted the wisdom of opening my store in a small town, where the only person I knew was my Aunt Dorothy, I found out today that this is the best place in the whole world I could have chosen," she murmured. "Sam Watkins, the president of the Welleswood Business Association, galvanized an entire crew of people, who had this store cleaned out in a matter of hours. Even the mayor helped, sending over some municipal workers, who showed up with trucks and hauled everything away. Ginger King, bless her heart, called her friend, Lisa Williams, the head of the Women's Auxiliary, who called some of the other members, and showed up with lunch for everyone. I think there might have been twenty or thirty people here to help me at one time or another, including some men who helped Daniel board up the window. Aunt Dorothy's friends, Annie Parker and Madeline O'Rourke, even went over to the house to spend the day so I wouldn't worry about her."

"Well," Ellie said. "I would imagine that most of those people have either been at the receiving end of one of your 'chocolate emergencies,' or know someone who has. Small-town life has its quirks and its problems, for sure, but when trouble hits, there isn't a better place to be than right here in Welleswood."

"True," Charlene agreed firmly. She opened the bag from McAllister's and set the cake box at the end of the worktable. She glanced at Ellie as she cut the string. "Don't even bother telling me I should eat my dinner first. I've got to have a piece of this cake, and you do, too."

Ellie chuckled. "I do?"

"Never eat chocolate alone. That's one of my rules, so I can't have a piece of this unless you do," Charlene insisted.

"I'm not sure I like that rule, since I usually eat alone. Or I used to, before my mother came to live with me. And she doesn't favor chocolate or sweets as much as I do."

"Then you fall under rule number two, which is never, ever let a friend eat chocolate alone," she quipped, then opened the box, lifted out the cake and placed it on the table.

The two friends looked at the cake for a moment as if it were a work of art. A full three layers high, the top of the cake was smothered in caramel-colored custard thick with coconut, which oozed and drizzled down the dark-chocolate icing covering the cake on all sides. Inside, as Ellie knew from experience, each layer contained more of the same custard and coconut.

Judging by the look on Charlene's face, Ellie was quite certain her friend's mouth was watering as much as hers was. She grinned and handed Charlene the knife, "When my mother told me she wouldn't be home for dinner tonight, she told me to fix something nutritious, and not to eat a handful of candy for dinner. I didn't exactly tell her I would, but I don't think she'd be very pleased if she found out I decided to eat a piece of McAllister's German chocolate cake for dinner instead."

"This isn't dinner. It's a snack," Charlene argued. She cut a piece of cake thick enough to serve three people, put it on a plate and handed it to Ellie. "Did you say your mother went out for dinner? So soon?"

Ellie shrugged. "The doctor said she could do whatever she felt up to," she replied. She felt awkward telling Charlene where her mother had gone, but she didn't want to hide the fact that her mother was visiting Mr. Murphy. "Actually, she's in good hands. She's with her friend, Phyllis Kennedy. They took dinner to the Murphys, but I don't expect she'll be there much past seven." She watched Charlene closely to see how she would react.

Charlene paused, holding her knife in the air above the cake, and let out a sigh. "Poor Mr. Murphy," she said softly. "I wasn't thinking very kind thoughts about him earlier today. I think I was numb at first, and once I got back to Aunt Dorothy's house and reality set in, I got angry, because no one had made Mr. Murphy, a man well into his eighties, turn in his driver's license. And I got angrier still because it was my shop he rammed, when it could very well have been any of the others. Not exactly thoughts worthy of a woman who claims to be a good Christian, were they?" she asked, and cut an equally thick slice of cake for herself.

"They sound like a very normal reaction to a very stressful situation," Ellie reassured her friend.

"Fortunately, I didn't stay angry for very long," Charlene went on. "I got depressed, instead, thinking about the people who will be disappointed because I won't be able to fill all their Easter orders. Then I got more depressed, when I realized I was only being selfish."

She paused and shook her head. "When I really thought about how many people could have been hurt if Mr. Murphy had plowed into The Diner, or one of the other businesses, I realized that I had to trust God to be in control, and believe that He would use this whole event for His own purpose." She glanced away. "I'm not sure yet what that purpose might be. I am certain I'll backslide a bit, and get frustrated dealing with the insurance company and with all the calls I'll have to make to my customers, canceling their orders, but I'll try hard not to do that for very long. That's why I had Daniel paint that message on the plywood. It's mostly for me," she admitted.

She took a bite of cake, sighed with pleasure and looked up at Ellie. "Delicious! This helps. A lot."

"It's supposed to," Ellie replied. "That's rule number three."

"Rule number three? Since when do you make the rules about chocolate? I'm the one who has the candy store, such as it is."

"I don't make the rules about chocolate. I'm just learning them," Ellie replied. "But they're easy enough to figure out. Since rule number one says you can't eat chocolate alone, and rule number two says you can never let a friend eat chocolate alone, then rule number three obviously states that when a friend is in trouble, bring chocolate and offer to help in any way you can."

"I like the way you think." Charlene took another bite of

cake. "Since you offered, maybe you could stay while I make a little something up for Mr. Murphy. I don't have much candy left, only what's here in the workroom, but I've got more baskets in the basement, and some stuffed animals right here. He must be terribly distressed by what happened today, and embarrassed, too. I hate to think he'll be upset again every time he goes by my store, once it reopens. I'm sure I can make up a basket for him, just to let him know there are no hard feelings. Since he might feel awkward if I drop it off, maybe you could do that for me."

Ellie grinned and snagged a forkful of coconut custard from the cake on her plate. "Which brings us to rule number four."

"Which is?"

"There isn't a problem you can't solve or a hurt you can't forgive with faith and a little bit of chocolate," Ellie proclaimed, inspired by the spirit and loving wisdom of this woman who had become her friend.

Chapter Twenty-One

Impossible. Unquestionably and undeniably impossible.

With that depressing thought, Charlene drove home from her pitifully empty store, surrendering any hope of filling the seventy-eight orders for Easter gift baskets she had taken as of yesterday. True, she had plenty of stuffed animals and baskets downstairs, but she had only enough undamaged candy to fill half a dozen baskets, at most.

Even if she managed, miraculously, to order the candy she needed, it wouldn't arrive until the middle of next week, not nearly soon enough to fill the baskets, let alone get them wrapped in cellophane and topped with a bow before Easter.

Trying to focus on the gratitude she felt for Daniel's support and the help from so many townspeople today, as well as Ellie's visit, Charlene pulled into the driveway of Aunt Dorothy's house. Since Daniel's car was not here, she assumed his errands were taking longer than expected, and she was relieved to see Madeline's car parked in front of the house, which meant she and Annie were still here with Aunt Dorothy.

She held her purse with one hand, and with the other, she grabbed the shopping bags holding dinner, and what was left of dessert.

She was halfway to the front door when Agnes Withers came charging across the lawn, headed directly for her.

"Yoo-hoo! Charlene! Wait a moment."

Charlene stopped and gritted her teeth. After the day she had had, chatting with Agnes Withers didn't even make the bottom of her to-do list, which included making seventy-eight calls to customers to explain that she would not be able to fill their orders, and sitting down with Aunt Dorothy, to relate everything that had happened at the store today after the accident.

The elderly neighbor was huffing and puffing by the time she reached Charlene. She paused, pressing her hand to her heart until she caught her breath. "I heard what happened and I just had to tell you in person how bad I feel."

"Thank you. I appreciate your concern."

"Dorothy was quite upset, too. I came right over the minute I heard, of course. I offered to stay with her for the day, but once her two friends arrived, I left. I didn't want you to think that I'd abandoned her."

"Not at all. I'm sure you had enough to do at home to keep you busy," Charlene replied, shifting her bags from one hand to the other.

"I hope you don't mind, but once I got home, I spread the word that Dorothy shouldn't be disturbed. After that, I couldn't get a bit of my housework done. My phone was ringing all day, but at least Dorothy didn't have to be bothered. I won't keep you long, but I promised Janie Lewis that I'd check with you the minute you got home. Emma Mitchell and Janie were chatting in the social room at the Towers, and Emma said she had heard from Derek Eldridge, the custodian, that you were closing down the store permanently and that you were going to sue Mr. Murphy for driving into your store and destroying it."

Charlene dismissed all the names Mrs. Withers tossed into the conversation simply because she didn't know any of them. She could only imagine the gossip that had spread through the Towers today, especially since she had heard more than one person refer to the social room there as the Gossip Garden.

"Please tell your friends that I'm hoping to reopen Sweet Stuff, although I really haven't any idea how soon that will be," she replied, wanting to dispel the false information before the rumors spread any further. "I'm very sure, however, that I have no plans to sue Mr. Murphy. My store is well-insured," she added politely, but firmly.

Mrs. Withers pulled her head back and batted her eyes. "Really?"

"Really," Charlene replied.

"I'm sure the Murphys will be relieved to know that. I did hear that Stanley got a ticket for reckless driving, though, and his son is pretty set on making sure his father doesn't drive again."

"If you'll excuse me, I'd better get inside and see Aunt Dorothy." Charlene attempted to escape without commenting on Mr. Murphy's driving issues, if only to avoid planting any additional seeds of new information that would sprout in the Gossip Garden and flower as a misquote.

"I hope Dorothy isn't overtired. I told her friends not to stay long so she could take her naps, but they've been here the entire day," Mrs. Withers remarked, frowning as she glanced over at Madeline's car. "Some people just don't listen."

"Thanks for helping out today," Charlene said, and resolutely headed for the front door. Once she was inside the living room, she set her purse and bags down long enough to remove her coat and lay it across the back of a chair. Neither Aunt Dorothy nor her friends were in the living room, but Charlene could hear voices and laughter coming from the kitchen.

She smiled. Remembering the day she had found the three of them feasting on donuts from McAllister's, she carried the bags through the living room and dining room. Just like last time, she stopped abruptly the moment she reached the archway, looked inside the kitchen and blinked hard.

Annie and Madeline stood on either side of Aunt Dorothy, who was sitting at the table with her eyes closed while her friends attended to her.

The tabletop looked like the makeup counter in a department store, although far messier. The entire surface was littered with cotton balls, cosmetics squares, Aunt Dorothy's abandoned eyeglasses and all sorts of makeup, including lipstick, blush, face powder, eyeliner and mascara. The air was thick with the distinctive smell of fresh nail polish.

Aunt Dorothy had her hands resting on the table, palms down, with her fingernails sporting a shiny coat of bright orange polish that looked like it could be used as reflective paint by a highway-construction crew. Around her neck, in addition to her Total Care necklace, she wore a pendant featuring the head of an elephant with bright orange eyes the same vibrant color as her nails.

Annie was applying matching lipstick to Aunt Dorothy's lips, while Madeline worked at blending blue and green eye shadow above Aunt Dorothy's eyes.

"You look younger already," Annie said.

"Not too young, I hope. He likes mature women, so I hear," Aunt Dorothy said.

"He likes all kinds of women," Madeline countered, and burst out laughing again. "He kept company with Connie Wilson a few years back and complained that she was too old for him."

"Connie wasn't even seventy then," Annie countered.

"Keep your eyes closed for another minute, Dorothy," Madeline ordered, and leaned back to look at her handiwork. "I want to make sure the color is right. What do you think, Annie?"

Annie nodded. "Nice. But don't forget that after Connie died, he started keeping company with Carol Gillerman, who was only sixty-one. Why on earth you told that man when he called on the phone that he could stop to see you tomorrow, Dorothy, is beyond me. You haven't been home from the hospital for all that long, you know."

Growing uncomfortable observing the three friends, Charlene cleared her throat. "Hi, ladies. Having fun?" she asked, entering the kitchen before she got caught eavesdropping, and embarrassed herself. "Did I hear somebody say that someone was coming by tomorrow?"

Aunt Dorothy opened her eyes and grinned sheepishly before donning her glasses again. She looked as if she were made up for a part in a play. "Max Duncan is coming to see me tomorrow."

Annie beamed. "He wants to start calling on Dorothy."

Madeline's grin was just as wide. "Which means he'll probably want to keep company with her. He did say he wouldn't come until Dorothy had her afternoon nap, though, which was very considerate."

"Or convenient. At eighty-five, he probably needs a nap as much as Dorothy does," Annie quipped.

Charlene held back a groan and put her bags on top of the counter.

Aunt Dorothy patted the chair next to her. "Sit a spell, Charlene. We've been thinking about you all day."

"Most of the day," Annie corrected. "We all took a couple of catnaps to make sure Dorothy didn't overdo it, just because we were here."

Madeline cleared the table in front of the chair next to Aunt Dorothy. "Having a manicure always makes a woman feel better. I've got plenty of nail polish. Would you like me to do your nails for you?"

"I'd better not," Charlene replied as she slid into the chair. "I don't have time to let them dry."

"Daniel stopped back to check on me in between errands about an hour ago. He told us all about your store," Aunt

Dorothy reported. Her gaze grew tearful as she patted Charlene's hand. "I'm so sorry. I know how much you loved Sweet Stuff."

"Is there anything we can do to help?" Madeline asked.

"We've got lots of time on our hands," Anne added.

"You've both helped a lot already, just by being here today," Charlene told them. "You could stay for supper, though. Ellie Waters dropped off enough food from The Diner for all of us. Did Daniel say when he'd be back?"

Aunt Dorothy shrugged. "I thought he'd be home by now."

While the women debated whether or not to stay for supper, Charlene grabbed her cell phone from her purse and called her husband. He answered on the fifth ring. "How close are you to coming home?" she asked.

He laughed. "About four steps from the back door. I've got my hands full, though, so if I drop the phone, don't be surprised. I could use some help."

"I'll get the door," she said and hung up. "Daniel's home," she explained as she got up and hurried to open the door. She found him standing with the cell phone scrunched between his head and his shoulder. He had two shopping bags in one hand, while tucked in the crook of his other arm was a twenty-five-pound bag of bird seed, which was sliding down. She stepped outside, grabbed hold of the bag, and shifted it out of the way to let him inside.

"Thanks. I was afraid I'd drop it and end up with bird seed spilled everywhere but in the feeders I just set up. Just set it down for now, but don't say anything to Aunt Dorothy. I want her to be surprised," he whispered, and pecked her cheek as he passed her.

She eased the bag to the ground, followed him inside and shut the door.

"I brought enough supper for everyone," he announced as he walked into the kitchen and over to the table.

Annie and Madeline scrambled to clear the table.

Aunt Dorothy turned her head to smile at him. "What a dear, sweet man you are."

"And you look especially lovely," he said, pressing a kiss to the top of her head and setting the bags on the table. "I wasn't sure what everyone liked, but I figured I couldn't go wrong with pasta."

Laughing, Charlene added her bags with the food from The Diner to the table. "Pasta isn't the only thing on the menu. We have meatloaf, stuffed pork chops and chicken pot pie, too. My friend, Ellie, dropped these off for us," she explained.

Aunt Dorothy clapped her hands. "I love a smorgasbord. And I have lots of baggies for leftovers so you can take some home with you, too," she said to her two friends. She looked around the table at everyone and smiled. "Isn't having supper together just the best way to end the day?"

Charlene nodded. Aunt Dorothy was right. Again. The best way to recover from the losses she'd suffered today and to recharge for the daunting task of starting over again was to surround herself with good food, lots of conversation and laughter, caring friends and a loving family.

Everything else, including making those seventy-eight calls, could wait until tomorrow.

Chapter Twenty-Two

The following morning, Charlene woke early after a fitful sleep. She met Ellie for their usual morning walk at six-thirty and was back at the house by seven-fifteen. Both Aunt Dorothy and Daniel were still asleep, so she showered and changed quietly, trying not to wake them. At eight o'clock, Daniel got up, skipped breakfast and went outside to work in the yard.

By eight-thirty, Charlene was returning to her aunt's bedroom every ten minutes to reassure herself that the frail elderly woman was still breathing.

Finally, a little after nine o'clock, Aunt Dorothy got out of bed. Acting a bit lethargic, considering she'd had a good thirteen hours in bed, and looking unusually pale, Aunt Dorothy complained of feeling a little dizzy, and she was unsteady on her feet.

Charlene helped her aunt change her nightgown and took a fresh housecoat out of the closet for her aunt to wear. Charlene also stayed very close as her aunt walked out to the kitchen for their pre-breakfast morning ritual of glucose testing, insulin injection, weigh-in and pills.

Aunt Dorothy's sugar level was higher than yesterday, although still within normal range. But she had gained three pounds overnight. Charlene added that number to the daily log. Only time would reveal if the weight gain was a warning that she was beginning to accumulate fluids again or the result of eating an amazing portion of last night's smorgasbord.

Already fearful that her aunt might be on the verge of another episode that could land her back in the hospital, Charlene grew even more concerned when her aunt asked her to call Max Duncan to tell him not to stop by today since she was not feeling up to par.

By late afternoon, after a dreary but rain-free day, Daniel was still in the backyard, trying to make good use of the waning daylight. Charlene was in the living room watching her aunt nap yet again, still worried about the shallowness of Aunt Dorothy's breathing. When the telephone rang, Charlene bolted to the kitchen to answer it.

"Hi, Charlene. Andy Johnson here. I'm sorry to have to bother you at home, but we've got a bit of a problem here."

Charlene closed her eyes for a moment and took a deep breath. She had all the problems she could handle right now, including how she might manage to make her calls to her customers when her aunt obviously needed her attention. "What kind of problem?" she asked, trying to keep her voice loud enough for him to hear her, yet low enough to keep from disturbing her aunt.

"Like I promised, I've been taking in some deliveries for you, but there've been so many today, I'm about out of room. I know things are probably pretty hectic for you right now, but is there any possibility you could come over and move these boxes into your own store?"

Charlene furrowed her brow. When she had accepted his offer to take in her mail and any deliveries that might come, she really hadn't expected there would be more than a few supply catalogues or bills, and she wasn't expecting any deliveries for the simple reason that she hadn't ordered anything from her suppliers. Everything she needed for Easter, as well as Mother's Day, had been delivered weeks ago.

"You've got that much?" she asked, hoping he was exaggerating the situation.

"Seven boxes. No, make that eight. I forgot to count the one that just got dropped off."

Thoroughly confused, she shook her head. "I can't imagine what they'd be for. Did you check the mailing labels? Are you sure they're mine?"

"Every box has Sweet Stuff written on it."

"All right. I'm really sorry you've been bothered—"

"No bother. I just need to clear a path to the cash register for my customers and all the folks stopping by to find out if you'll be reopening for Easter."

"I'll be over as soon as I can. Give me half an hour. Maybe a little more."

"Great," he replied, and hung up.

"Great," she repeated, and hung up, too. Still confounded by having so many boxes delivered when she couldn't remember ordering anything, she had yet another problem to solve before she could leave. With Aunt Dorothy feeling so poorly she simply couldn't, in all good conscience, leave her alone in the house. She hesitated to ask Daniel to stop working since he had already lost a whole day yesterday. She didn't want to call on either Annie or Madeline again, either, for fear Aunt Dorothy would overdo it. Ellie would probably be home from school by now, but she needed to stay with her mother.

Charlene sighed and shook her head. Agnes Withers was probably the only option she had, but she was reluctant to ask the next-door neighbor, especially without asking her aunt first. She turned away from the telephone to walk back to the living room, but immediately flinched and halted her steps, startled to see Aunt Dorothy walking toward her.

Heart pounding, Charlene managed a smile. "Mercy! I didn't hear you coming."

Aunt Dorothy stopped and looked down at the hospital slippers she wore on her feet. "I'm sorry. I guess these don't squeak like my slippers do. I brought so many pairs of these socks home from the hospital that I thought I might as well use them," she said while walking toward the table a bit more steadily than she had all day.

She sat down, smoothed the collar on her purple housecoat and untangled the corded necklace she still wore faithfully, which had gotten caught on the white enamel elephant pinned to her housecoat. "Did I hear the telephone ring?"

Pleased that her aunt was looking and acting quite a bit better than earlier, Charlene explained the call from Andy Johnson, as well as her dilemma. "I feel awful imposing on him, so I really don't want to keep him waiting, if I can help it."

"Don't worry about me. I'm feeling a whole lot better now that I've slept most of my day away. Take Daniel with you and let him help you with the boxes. The yard has waited this long, so another day or two won't matter. I'll just sit here a spell, have a cup of tea while you're both gone and give Annie a call. If I have a problem, I'll hang up and call you on your cell phone. I have my necklace right here, too." She smiled as she held up the Total Care pendant she could press to summon help.

"Are you sure? Maybe it'd be better if Daniel stayed here. I could probably move the boxes myself, if Andy is too busy. But I'll fix your tea for you before I go," Charlene said. She filled a mug with water, added a tea bag, slid the mug into the microwave and set the timer.

"Every man likes to be needed, and I'd venture to say that every man *needs* to be needed," Aunt Dorothy countered. "It might be better all around if you asked Daniel to help you once in a while instead of being so independent all the time, especially when it comes to that store of yours."

Stung by her aunt's gentle reprimand, which was as unexpected as it was uncharacteristic, Charlene swallowed hard.

"Sit down. Talk to me. Andy Johnson can wait a bit," her aunt instructed.

Charlene sat down opposite her aunt.

"You've been good to me, Charlene, and I'm grateful for everything you're doing to help me," her aunt said. "Now you can take what I'm going to say with a grain of spilled salt and toss it right over your shoulder if you want to, but I've got something that needs to be said, because days like this remind me I might not have too many days left."

Charlene nodded. Although she wasn't sure where her aunt was going, she had a feeling this conversation was not going to be as lighthearted as their talks usually were. She was relieved, however, to know she hadn't been overreacting today, and she was moved by her aunt's ability to talk openly about her death.

Aunt Dorothy folded her hands together and laid them on top of the table. The bright orange nail polish was the only reminder of yesterday's makeover session. Her expression grew serious. "When you moved in here to take care of me, and Daniel came down on weekends, I noticed that you two didn't seem as happy with each other as you used to, although you both try to hide it pretty well." She drew in a shaky breath. "I'm probably to blame for that, since I was the one who encouraged you to open that store of yours here in Welleswood. And I—I wanted you to know I never would have encouraged you to do that if I thought for one minute that running that store would put a strain on your marriage."

Charlene glanced away, troubled that her aunt seemed to be taking responsibility for the distance in Charlene's marriage—an estrangement Charlene had thought was undetected. Obviously, she had been mistaken. She needed to reassure her aunt that she was not to blame, although Charlene felt very awkward discussing these problems.

"It's not your fault," Charlene whispered, drawing in a long breath and looking directly at her aunt. "Ever since the children left, things between Daniel and me have been…different. I thought we just needed a little time to adjust, and with Daniel working all the time, frankly, I needed something to do. Something meaningful. If I hadn't opened my store here, I would have opened it somewhere else."

Her aunt's gaze was steady, if not piercing. "Do you love that man? Really love him?"

Charlene blinked hard. "Yes. Of course, I do," she insisted without hesitation.

Aunt Dorothy cocked her head. "Do you think he still loves you?"

"I—I guess so. Yes, I do," she replied with more confidence—confidence that had somehow grown since coming to stay with Aunt Dorothy.

"Then stop dillydallying around, and get his attention again, even if that means shutting down your store for good," her aunt instructed. Her eyes began to twinkle. "Flatter him. Wear some toilet water. Cut your hair and fix it pretty, like you used to do before you opened that store. And learn how to flirt a little, too."

Charlene gasped with surprise at receiving pointers from her aunt on how she might win back her husband's devotion. "Flirt? With Daniel?"

Her aunt shrugged. "Why not? But all the flirting in the world won't keep him interested unless you have something in common, something you love to share together as much as you loved raising your children. And don't think it's taking care of me now, because I'm not going to be here forever. And if you think you can't do it, then remember those rings I showed you. You come from a long line of strong women, Charlene. Do what you have to do, just like I'm certain they did."

Flustered by her aunt's candor, as well as her advice,

Charlene didn't know what to say. At that moment, however, the microwave dinged, and Daniel came in through the back door, giving Charlene a double excuse to avoid responding to her aunt, and to end their conversation.

When Charlene got up from the table to get the mug of tea, Aunt Dorothy turned and smiled at Daniel. "There you are. Were your ears ringing?"

He laughed as he brushed the dirt from his jacket. "No, why?"

"We were just talking about you. Andy Johnson called. Apparently, there were a lot of boxes that got delivered today for Sweet Stuff, and Charlene needs your help getting them out of his way," she said before turning her back to him again. Glancing in Charlene's direction, she lifted her brows and batted her lashes, as if urging Charlene to do the same.

Charlene caught a chuckle before it escaped, and thought about imitating her aunt for less than half a heartbeat. But she smiled at her husband, instead. "It wouldn't take too long, but if you're too busy in the yard…"

"No, I'm done working outside for today," he said before walking toward Aunt Dorothy. "Take a look," he urged her, and helped her out of her seat and over to the kitchen window, where Charlene joined them. "What do you think?"

His blue eyes sparkled and his smile was proud, reminding Charlene of how he'd looked the day he'd finished building the fort for their son in their backyard in Grand Mills. Warmed by the memory, she looked out the window, and heard Aunt Dorothy gasp with surprise.

"The birdbath is done! And look, Charlene. There are feeders for the birds, too."

"I see them," Charlene replied, equally surprised and impressed by the transformation of the area just outside the window. Freshly trimmed bushes and trees now created a natural backdrop for a small alcove, where a pair of double shepherd's hooks held wooden bird feeders. In the center of the alcove, the cleaned and restored birdbath rested on a concrete pedestal.

"With all the wild-bird seed out there now, you should have plenty of birds to watch this year, right from here. I should have the rest of the yard trimmed back, and a walking path cleared out so you can see right through to the creek, by Easter," he informed her. "I haven't found it yet, but I'll keep looking for that bench you mentioned."

"Thank you. Thank you," Aunt Dorothy whispered, then turned and kissed his cheek. "I think I'll just stand here and watch for a while, just to see if the birds will find the feeders. You two go ahead."

Charlene dragged a kitchen chair over and set it next to her aunt. "If you sit down, you can still see just as well, and you won't get as tired. Your tea is ready, too."

"I think I'll wait awhile for my tea. Just set it on the counter for me," her aunt replied. She sat down, but kept her gaze focused on the window.

"Did you want us to stop and pick anything up while we're out?" Daniel asked.

"If you wouldn't mind, I need a couple of boxes of tissue. Charlene knows what brand I like."

"Fair enough," Daniel replied, and nodded to Charlene. "I'll get the car and meet you out front."

"I just need to grab a jacket," Charlene said before he slipped out the door. "We won't be long," Charlene promised her aunt. As she was heading out of the kitchen, she heard her aunt call out to her, and turned around. "Yes?"

"Splash a little toilet water on before you go, and don't forget to make a fuss over Daniel for helping you."

Charlene laughed and hurried to get her jacket. But she did pause long enough to dab a little perfume behind her ears before she left the house.

Chapter Twenty-Three

Charlene stared at the seven plain brown cardboard boxes that Daniel had carried into her showroom from next door. The largest was big enough to hold a television; the smallest was maybe the size of a toaster. There was nothing written on any of the cartons, except the name of her store. They had to have been hand delivered, although Andy Johnson had offered no information about who might have dropped them off.

When Daniel set the last box down, he shook his head in answer to her question about whether Andy had revealed anything regarding this one. "Not really," Daniel reported. "His best guess is that you volunteered to serve on some committee that was collecting donated items and just forgot about it."

"Volunteer? At the busiest time of the year for me? No way," Charlene replied, and stepped closer to the boxes to study the handwriting again. "Some of these boxes look like they came from the same place. See? Look, the handwriting is the same," she said, pointing.

Daniel pushed the two boxes labeled in orange marker together while she picked up the smallest box, which had been addressed in turquoise ink. They organized the boxes into four groups. "Now what?" he asked.

"I guess we open them."

Growing excited, Charlene hesitated, just like she did on Christmas morning when deciding which gift to open first. "This one," she said, and pointed to a small box sitting by itself.

After Daniel sliced through the packing tape with a knife, she lifted the flaps and immediately caught the aroma of chocolate. Inside, on top of individually wrapped chocolate chicks and bunnies, she found a handwritten note. Her fingers trembled as she opened it and read out loud:

> *Dear Charlene, we were so sorry to hear the news about your store and the losses you suffered. Please share these with your customers and try to enjoy the holiday, too. Sincerely, Ronnie and Lonnie Calder, Twin Treats.*

"What's Twin Treats?" Daniel asked.

Overwhelmed by the twin sisters' thoughtfulness and generosity, she blinked back tears. "It's a little candy store in Mount Ephraim, just a few miles from here," she replied and shook her head. "I met them at the candy convention last year, but we never did get together again like we said we would. I can't believe they did this for me. From what they told me, their store doesn't do nearly the business I do at Sweet Stuff. They must have sent half of their inventory to me."

"Then they didn't send any of the other boxes?" he asked.

"I don't think so. Let's open the others to see if there's more candy and other notes," she suggested.

Excited now, she worked in tandem with her husband. Once he opened a box, she checked inside for a note while he moved on to the next. When they were finished, she was almost dazed by the assortment of Easter candy that filled each box. She looked at the two notes in her hand and the one Daniel held. She couldn't imagine how word had spread and how these caring people had responded so quickly. All the notes contained messages similar to the Calder sisters', and Charlene's heart filled with awe and gratitude.

"One note is from Joe and Hazel Welsh. They own Aunt Celia's Chocolate Boutique in Philadelphia. The other note is from Janice Mueller. Her candy store is in Collmont. Here. Take a look at these while I read the note you have," she suggested.

"It's from somebody named Lisa or Linda something. I can't make out the signature. Maybe you can," he said.

Charlene glanced at the signature and recognized it immediately. "It's Lisa Ashe. The first time I went to the candy convention, Lisa took me under her wing. We've been friendly ever since, although I haven't spoken to her in six weeks," she explained.

While Daniel read the notes she had handed to him, she read Lisa's message:

> *I hope you don't mind, but the instant I heard what happened to your store, I sent out an e-mail to a few good people like you who add joy and pleasure to their customers' lives with a bit of candy and with friendship. I hope this chocolate will help make Easter very special for you and your customers. Call me!*
> *Lisa Ashe*

While Charlene wiped away more tears, Daniel finished reading the other notes and handed them back to her. "All this candy came from your competitors?" he asked.

Pressing the notes to her heart, she nodded. "Selling candy can be very competitive, but for the most part, many of the small store owners I've met feel a lot like I do about their stores, although I'm sure they probably turn a greater profit at year's end than I do. We offer more than candy to our customers," she explained, hoping he would understand. "Some folks who stop into Sweet Stuff just need a place to warm up from the cold outside, or want someone to listen to their problems. Other folks are just plain lonely, and stop to chat or taste a piece of chocolate they've never tried before. Sweet Stuff is about celebrating the happy moments in people's lives, or reaching out to someone who is grieving. It's about loving and caring for people we know and trying to be just as loving and caring to people we don't."

He gazed at her so tenderly, her heart skipped a beat. "I always thought your store was just a hobby," he murmured. "I never knew that you ran the store less like a business and more like a…a ministry."

"I never thought you were interested in my store, so I never told you," she said quietly.

"But I should have known," he said, clearing his throat and glancing at the boxes. "I think you have enough candy now to be able to fill all your orders. Your friends have really saved the day for you."

"I wish I could say you were right. I hate to disappoint the well-meaning people who donated all this candy, but I still just don't think it's possible to fill my orders. I'd need a full day just to get all this candy sorted and organized, and I'd need another day or two to call the seventy-eight customers who placed orders to ask them to choose what they want from the candy I now have available. Even if I set up some kind of assembly line and get people to help me fill the baskets, which I was already considering, I'd still have to wrap them up and call the customers back to tell them to come and pick up their orders. And with Aunt Dorothy feeling poorly again today, I'm not certain if I want to abandon her right now," she replied, hoping she didn't sound like she was whining. "I'm afraid this is one problem I can't solve, even with other people helping me."

"When you put it that way, probably not," he said, and

narrowed his gaze for a moment. "Maybe you should look at solving your problem from a different perspective."

She cocked a brow. "Such as?"

He held up both hands. "I'm just a plain country boy, not a businessman, so don't get too hopeful, but I can't help comparing your situation with a problem Jake Edison had years ago when I was a kid. He had an apple orchard not far from my parents' farm."

"I own a store and sell chocolates. He had an orchard and sold apples. What could we have in common that might help me right now?" she asked.

"I'm positive I told you about him before," he said. "Right at harvest time, Jake took a spill from his tractor, landed on his head and spent the next couple of weeks in the hospital in a coma before he finally woke up again. Sound familiar?"

Charlene rolled her eyes. "No, not really. But if you're telling me to curl up on the couch and sleep away the next couple of weeks, you can forget it. Unless you want to handle everything like I assume Jake's wife had to do for her spouse."

He grinned. "I'm up to the challenge, but if my idea works, it will only take a couple of days, not weeks. And you can forget the couch idea. I'd need a little help, assuming you're game in the first place."

"You're serious?"

"Absolutely."

"Why?" she asked. "Why now? You've never seemed interested in my store before."

"Why now?" he repeated, and let out a sigh before he caught her gaze and held it. "Because...because I don't want to lose you. Because I'm beginning to realize that unless we find something we can enjoy together, we might never be happy again, the way we used to be. For starters, that could be working together to get your customers taken care of."

Her heart trembled, but before she could respond to him,

he continued. "Maybe you're right," he whispered, his voice thick with emotion. "Maybe it did take this accident, along with Aunt Dorothy becoming ill, to make me realize that I'd been so busy working extra hours, trying to fill the emptiness in my life after the kids left, that I forgot what was most important to me."

Tears blurred Charlene's vision, and a lump in her throat made it almost impossible for her to breathe, let alone speak. To hear him talk about their problems and his hopes to resolve them was an answer to her prayers.

"You, Charlene," he whispered. "Our marriage. That's what matters most to me. Unless…unless it's too late."

She eased into his embrace, laid her cheek against his chest and listened to the beat of his heart. "I love you," she whispered. "It's not too late. I made mistakes, too. Lots of them. I've missed the kids, too, and I thought opening the store and taking care of my customers would be enough, but it isn't. I need more. I—I need you," she managed before dissolving into tears.

He held her tight and rocked her for several long minutes. "Where do we go from here?" he asked when she finally stopped weeping.

"Before or after we get my customers' orders filled?" she teased, before starting to cry again or deciding being held in his loving arms was all that mattered.

He hugged her hard. "After."

"What's your plan?"

He grinned. "Do you trust me?"

"Completely."

"Good. Let's lock up for now. We'll call Aunt Dorothy and tell her we're headed home once we make a quick stop at Tim Fallon's. You know where his store is, right?"

"Sure. It's only a few blocks away, but—"

"Good. We can walk down to see him together."

"How do you know Tim?" she asked as she riffled through her purse to find her cell phone.

"He was one of the guys who helped me board up the storefront window. He wasn't thrilled that I spray-painted the name of the store on the plywood, though, let alone that little message," Daniel explained as he stood by the door waiting for her.

"Since he owns a print shop, I guess he wasn't," she said, grabbing hold of her cell phone and tapping in Aunt Dorothy's number. "Why do we need to see Tim? And just exactly what is this plan you've come up with?"

"I'll explain on the way."

"The line's busy," she said, and closed the cell phone. "I'll try again in a few minutes, but if she's talking to Annie Parker, she'll probably still be on the phone when we get home."

"At least she won't be wearing that awful makeup," he teased and stepped outside.

Chuckling, she lifted her keys out of her purse, paused and handed them to him. "You should probably have a set of keys of your own. The hardware store isn't far. We could get a set made for you," she suggested.

"Good idea," he said, then locked up the door and handed the keys back to her.

After stepping back inside Natural Wonders to thank Andy Johnson again for handling the unexpected deliveries, Charlene walked down the brick sidewalk, hand-in-hand with her husband. As usual, rush-hour traffic clogged the avenue, with cars stopping at pedestrian crossings on every block to let groups of shoppers cross from one side of the avenue to the other. Charlene was stopped several times by well-wishers, who offered their support.

"You're a bit of a celebrity," Daniel teased.

She laughed. "Not really, but it's nice to be in a small town where people know one another and really seem to care. Are you getting claustrophobic yet?" she asked, knowing how much he preferred the solitude of the pinelands and their rural home.

"Not yet. Aunt Dorothy's house is so secluded, when I'm working out in the yard I almost forget where I am."

"Until you're on the avenue."

"True. But except for the traffic right now, it's not so bad," he admitted. "Oh, before we both forget, is there anywhere along the avenue where we could get those tissues for Aunt Dorothy?" he asked when they stopped to wait at a red light.

Charlene laughed. "The last time I checked, which was only a few days ago, she still had a dozen boxes stored in one of those cupboards in our bedroom. I'll get two boxes from there."

"I hope you're not going to start hoarding things when you get older," he said, urging her to walk again when the light turned green.

"Only you," she whispered. "Only you."

Chapter Twenty-Four

For students and teachers alike, weekends offered freedom from the rigid structure of the school environment, where a dress code controlled what they wore and a series of bells dictated when the day would start, when each class would begin and end, when to eat and when to go home.

On the final weekend before Easter, Ellie chose a pair of comfortable jeans and a matching jacket to wear on Saturday. She didn't have any bells to regulate her activities today, but she did have a long list of chores and errands to do, papers to grade and lesson plans to write, which left her little time for much else, including her morning walk.

Determined to keep her promise to Charlene to include a stop at Sweet Stuff, where her friend was having a rather unusual open house, she had three loads of laundry finished, two very clean bathrooms and breakfast made by the time her mother got up at eight o'clock. Ellie spent the next two hours taking her mother to the lab for blood work so that Doctor Stafford and the cardiologist would both have the results in hand for her mother's appointments next week. She even managed to go online to get her bills paid and leave another message for each of her sons, to ask if they had been able to come up with a weekend when they could both come home to see their grandmother.

Alert to the dangers of identity theft, yet another consequence of modern technology, she reviewed all her accounts to make sure there hadn't been any unauthorized withdrawals. While logging off, she mentally added the considerable amount she and her late husband had saved for retirement in a variety of portfolios, where she had also invested the proceeds of his life insurance.

If she considered the generous pension she would receive at retirement, which included lifetime medical benefits, she had no doubt she would be very well set financially as a retiree.

She shut down her laptop and tried to close her mind to any thoughts of retirement that tempted her to dream about the luxury of having the free time she didn't have now. Once she retired, she could increase her volunteer role with the ministries at church. Once she retired, she would have much more time to take care of her mother, if necessary, and spend time with her. Once she retired, she would not have to schedule her visits to her children and grandchildren around the school calendar, either, or spend part of every weekend on schoolwork.

"No retirement. Not yet," she murmured, and walked out of her home office, determined to retire only after she had achieved the objective she had set for herself many years ago: to become department supervisor. With that goal well within reach, she had no intention of letting it slip away now.

When she got back downstairs, she found her mother in the living room, standing by the aquarium and watching the turtles. "Would you like to feed them this morning?" she asked, surprised that her mother would pay any mind to Ellie's pets, since she was so opposed to them.

Her mother sniffed. "Certainly not. I was just checking to make sure they were all accounted for, so I wouldn't have to worry about finding one crawling about."

Ellie laughed. "The box turtles are still hibernating. These are water turtles. They prefer the water, but if they want to crawl about, it won't be on the living room floor. There's plenty of room in the aquarium for them to rest on the mulch or the jetty, which is where most of them are right now. Besides, they can't climb up the glass," she added before she opened the storage cabinet under the aquarium to get the cylinder of turtle food. Before she got the lid off, the three turtles had scooted back into the water and swum toward her.

"They must recognize you," her mother said, surprise in her voice.

"They're hungry. They'd swim over to anyone who had the food," Ellie replied. When she sprinkled the pellets into the water, the turtles immediately dove and bobbed for their breakfast, battling one another for each morsel.

"The littlest one doesn't stand much of a chance to get any food," her mother noted.

"That's Gizmo. It's practically doubled in size since it hatched."

"Hatched? Where?"

Ellie pointed to the far corner in the section filled with mulch. "Right there. When I found the shell, too, I told Amy Flynn, the biology teacher at school. She had me bring the shell and the baby turtle to school so she could show her students." She was happy to be having a civil conversation with her mother. She was also pleased by her mother's steady recovery, in spite of her setback and the surgery on her arm. She suspected her mother might even try to get both of her doctors to agree next week that she was well enough to live back in her own home, although Ellie doubted that would be encouraged.

Ellie stored the turtle food back inside the cabinet. "I have some errands to run this morning, and I promised Charlene that I'd stop at her open house today. Since I'll be housebound most of the afternoon with paperwork for school, would you like to come with me this morning?"

"I'm not up for gallivanting. Since the weather turned fair, I was hoping we might take a ride today, maybe to the shore and have lunch in one of those nice little restaurants facing the ocean. But I see you're too busy," her mother murmured.

"It's hard for me to get all my errands done during the week," Ellie explained, but didn't mention that she had even less time now that she had to come directly home every day to be with her mother.

"Of course it is. If you had the sense to realize that you'd be better off at home than at work every day, like Phyllis's daughter, you wouldn't have that problem. Obviously, you do what you want to do, so go on. Take care of your errands. I've got some magazines I can read to keep me occupied."

Ellie felt too guilty to argue or to defend her decision to continue working. "If I work late enough tonight and set some work aside until Monday, I could free up tomorrow. What about it? We could go to the early service and drive to the shore afterward. One of the teachers at school mentioned a new restaurant. It's right on the water and it's only open on weekends during the off-season, but it's supposed to have a fabulous brunch. I don't remember the name of the restaurant or where it is exactly, but I could call her at home and find out."

"It sounds like Ocean's Gate, a new restaurant in Brigantine. Phyllis had brunch there with her daughter a couple of weeks ago. I suppose tomorrow will have to do, but I won't count on it, just in case you don't get your work done," her mother said, and started to walk away.

Ellie was tempted to call her mother back and try to convince her that their plans for tomorrow were not tentative, but she sensed it was better to let the matter drop. "I'll be back in time to make lunch," she promised, then grabbed her purse and headed out the door.

* * *

Ellie finally found a parking spot two blocks from Sweet Stuff. As usual on Saturday, the business district hummed with activity, and she was surprised not to see a line of people outside the candy store. Seventy-eight customers had been invited—either by word of mouth or by the posters plastered in many of the other storefronts—to this very unusual open house.

Relieved that she didn't have to cut in line and explain she was only here to offer Charlene a bit of moral support, she was worried that the innovative open house was turning out to be a flop.

When she stepped into the store, Charlene's Aunt Dorothy sat up straighter in her chair, just inside the door, and greeted her right away. "Hi, Ellie. Charlene didn't mention you'd be coming today."

"Miss Gibbs! I didn't expect you to be here. You must be feeling as good as you look."

The elderly woman chuckled and held tight to the basket of bows on her lap. "On good days, yes. On bad days, no. Today's a good day. Have you got your order form?"

"I didn't order a gift basket. I'm just stopping by to say hello to Charlene. Is she in the workroom in the back?"

"She just went down to the basement with Daniel to get more baskets, and left me in charge. This is the first lull we've had since she opened the door at nine o'clock."

Relieved that people had indeed shown up, Ellie smiled. "I can wait a few minutes to see her."

"Take a look around while you're waiting," Dorothy urged.

Ellie smiled and scanned the showroom, amazed by the transformation. Two days ago, when she had visited Charlene here to cheer her up, the showroom had been totally empty. Now it was full again, but it scarcely resembled the cozy little store it had been before the accident. To her left, half a dozen baskets sat in front of the boarded-up window. Two rows of tables, lined up end to end and loaded with Easter candy, created a wide aisle down the center of the store. Customers could walk along the length of each row to select their candy, much as they would select food from a buffet at a wedding reception. The only remnant of the store Sweet Stuff had been was the hutch and shelving, which now held a variety of stuffed animals. In the back, where the counter used to be, several tables held rolls of cellophane. This was where Charlene most likely wrapped the gift baskets once the customers had finished filling them.

"It's so clever to have the customers come in and fill their own baskets," she commented.

"That was Daniel's idea. He told me about a farmer he knew once who took sick at harvest time, so his wife painted up a sign that said Pick Your Own, stuck it into the ground and set out some bushel baskets and a tin box where folks could put a donation. So Charlene decided to have a Fill Your Own Basket open house for all her customers who'd placed orders for Easter."

"Isn't Charlene worried that people will take more than they should?"

Dorothy Gibbs chuckled. "They probably will, but there's so much candy, there's still bound to be some left. Besides, they have to take their baskets over to Charlene to get them wrapped up. That should keep most folks from being too greedy. Here—while you're waiting for Charlene, fill up a basket," she insisted, and pressed a white bow with lavender polka dots into Ellie's hands. "Take one of those baskets over there and tie the bow on top. That's how Charlene knows the customer gave me an order form. Then just wander around and take whatever you want for yourself and your mother, too."

"I couldn't do that. I didn't place an order, remember?"

"Don't argue with an old lady, especially when she's in charge," Dorothy teased. "And tell your mother I've been thinking of her and praying she'll be feeling better soon."

"Mother's actually doing much better. Thank you."

Miss Gibbs smiled. "I'm glad. I've known your mother for a good long while, you know."

"Yes, she mentioned that."

"We weren't close friends, since she was a good four years ahead of me in school. But I do remember how much she wanted to be a teacher. She must be especially proud of you."

Ellie clutched the bow a little tighter. "She wanted to teach?"

"It was all she ever talked about. Of course, back in those days, not too many girls in Welleswood went off to college. There was plenty of work in the factories nearby, though. But as I recall, your mother had learned how to type in school, so she ended up working in Doctor Ingram's office, which used to be right on the avenue where the dentist is now."

"Yes, she's mentioned that," Ellie murmured. "She always said how much she really liked her job."

"She probably did a good job, too, which didn't help much in the end. Doctor Ingram still fired her."

Ellie's eyes widened. "He fired her?"

"Right on the spot."

"Why?" Ellie asked, anxious to learn the part of the story her mother had left out.

"The same reason other girls got fired from their jobs when they worked in offices. She got engaged. From what I heard, Doctor Ingram told her she'd have to leave when she got married anyway, so he didn't see any reason why she should stay, and sent her home the first day she wore her engagement ring to work."

"That wasn't fair. Was it even legal?" Ellie asked, appalled that any woman would lose her job simply because she chose not to remain single.

"I couldn't tell you if it was legal or not, but it happened all the time. Oh, dear. Here come a few customers. Go ahead and fill up that basket. Charlene should be back before you're done," she said before turning her attention to two women Ellie didn't recognize.

While Miss Gibbs explained the system to the newcomers, Ellie wandered over to the baskets and selected one with a white cotton lining. But she was preoccupied with the information Miss Gibbs had given her about her mother.

Why hadn't her mother ever mentioned wanting to become a teacher? Or talked about wanting to go to college? Ellie couldn't remember when she had not wanted to be a teacher herself. She had never played house as a child. She'd always played school. Yet her mother had never said a word about sharing the same career dreams as Ellie. And why hadn't her mother mentioned being fired from the job she always said she'd loved so much?

Was there some connection between the way her mother constantly criticized her and the fact that Ellie's dream had come true, while her mother's hadn't?

Ellie didn't know, but she intended to find out. Not today, she decided as she approached the candy table. Tomorrow. She would wait until tomorrow, when she and her mother would spend the day together. During their drive to the shore, Ellie would have the perfect opportunity to broach the subject with her mother and maybe, just maybe, they might be closer by the time they got home again.

Chapter Twenty-Five

"Done, done and done!" Ellie said as each of the three pages emerged from the printer in her home office, just as the clock ticked the first hours of the new day.

She was bleary-eyed and exhausted, but she wore a huge grin as she stored the lesson plans in her briefcase. By working nonstop since supper, she had managed to get every bit of her work done, and now she would have the entire day to spend, guilt-free, with her mother. After shutting down her laptop, she arched her back and stretched her muscles.

She debated whether to leave the empty snack plate, which had held three pink marshmallow chicks from the basket she had made at Sweet Stuff, and her empty water bottle until morning, or take them downstairs to the kitchen. Eventually, she grabbed them both since she had to go downstairs anyway. Her mother had still been up reading at eight o'clock when Ellie had gone down to get her snack, and she wanted to check the doors to make sure her mother had locked up before going to bed.

While Ellie descended the steps, she realized the light was too bright to be coming from the night-light she kept in the living room now that her mother was living with her. Once she reached the landing where the staircase turned, she saw the floor lamp next to the chair where her mother had been reading had not been turned off. Considering how often her mother criticized her for wasting electricity, she thought it odd, but assumed her mother had simply left the light on for Ellie.

That is until she turned and saw the light coming from beneath the door to the small den she had converted into a bedroom for her mother.

Since her mother always insisted she couldn't sleep unless her bedroom was in total darkness, Ellie sensed immediately that something was amiss. Praying silently, she started toward the door on tiptoe to avoid startling her mother.

She thought she heard a faint sound coming from the room, and with every step, the sound grew more and more distinct. It sounded alarmingly like a groan of pain or distress. With her heart racing, Ellie set the empty plate and bottle on a chair and hurried forward.

"Mother? Are you all right?" she whispered, in part because she didn't want to frighten her mother in case she was just having a bad dream, but mostly because the lump in her throat made it hard for her to speak any louder. She pressed the palms of her hands against the door, but when she leaned forward and turned her head to hear better, the door started to creak open.

"El-lie."

The sound of her name was scarcely above a whisper, yet held the undeniable roar of pain and desperation. She pushed the door open, rushed inside and immediately experienced absolute fear.

The sheets and blanket on the bed were in total disarray, but her mother was not in the bed. She was lying on her side on the floor in front of a bedside table. With her hands clutching her nightgown at the base of her throat, her face was ash gray, and her eyes were dull with pain. Her breathing was shallow and ragged.

"H-help me, El-lie."

Ellie rushed to her mother's side, dropped to her knees and put her face close to her mother's. "I'm here now. I'll help you," she crooned, further alarmed to see her mother drenched in perspiration. There was no sign of blood or trauma, which indicated her pain was most likely the result of another, more severe, heart attack.

Her mother closed her eyes. "H-hurts."

"I know. I'm going to call for an ambulance," Ellie replied. She rose to her feet and reached for the cordless telephone on the bedside table, spying the Total Care bracelet sitting beside it. Her hands were shaking hard and her heart was palpitating, but she managed to tap in nine-one-one on the first try. She explained the emergency to the dispatcher, and hung up.

Praying, Ellie lowered herself back down to her mother's side. Her mother was now lying very still with her eyes closed.

"The ambulance will be here in a few minutes," Ellie whispered, and wrapped her hands around her mother's. Frightened to find them cold and stiff, Ellie gently massaged them. "Don't try to speak," she said when her mother said something Ellie could not understand. Then her mother took several shallow breaths and her eyelids fluttered, but she didn't try to speak again.

While the sound of distant sirens grew louder, Ellie pressed her forehead to her mother's and continued to pray. *Father of all comfort and mercy, please look upon us now and grant my mother the gift of Your healing touch and Your loving presence. Comfort her fears and ease her pain,* Ellie's tears flowed freely down her cheeks.

Her mother stirred and opened her eyes. Tugging one hand free, she laid it gently against Ellie's cheek. "Loved," she murmured. "Al-ways loved. If…" She sighed, as if the effort to speak was too great, and closed her eyes again.

Ellie choked back more tears and waited, but the rest of her mother's words remained unspoken. "I love you, too," she whispered, praying silently with her heart that the tomorrow they had both planned to share together had not come too late after all.

With her mother gravely ill, Ellie had not been allowed past the waiting area outside the emergency room at Tilton General Hospital, where her mother had arrived by ambulance shortly after two o'clock on Sunday morning. Several hours later, after being told her mother had suffered a major heart attack, Ellie was also told she could finally see her.

She followed the directions the nurse had given her to the coronary care unit, or the CCU, on the main floor, where her mother was listed in critical condition. Even when pressed, however, the doctor hadn't been able or willing to tell Ellie if her mother would recover, and Ellie was not certain what to expect.

When Ellie arrived at the CCU, wearing a green plastic visitor's pass given only to immediate family members, she read the instructions on the double doors at the entrance and pressed a red button on the wall to her right. On her left was a small waiting room, which was empty—not surprising at this hour.

As the double doors swung open, a man in wrinkled blue scrubs with a stethoscope around his neck came through another set of doors several feet directly ahead. He had silver hair, and walked with authority. Ellie assumed he was a doctor until he got close enough for her to read *R.N.* after his name on his employee badge.

"Mrs. Waters?"

"Yes," she replied, surprised that he knew her name.

"They called me from the E.R. to tell me you were on your way, so I thought I'd meet you here. I'm Raymond Tanner. I've been assigned to take care of your mother," he said, but did not extend his hand. "Is this your first time visiting someone in the CCU?"

She nodded.

"We take extra precautions with visitors here," he explained as he led her to a small room off to the side. He opened the door and turned on a light, and she could see it was a bathroom. "Before you visit your mother, we'd like you to wash your hands. Everything you need is right in here. Once you've done that, you can come through the second set of double doors. I'll be waiting there to take you to your mother."

"Is she…is she all right?" she asked.

His gaze softened. "She's resting comfortably. We'll talk more once you're inside," he replied before leaving her.

Ellie went into the bathroom and shut the door. After hanging her purse on a hook, she walked to the sink. When she caught a glimpse of herself in the mirror, she quickly looked away. She was not surprised to see that her face was red and puffy from crying, but it was the fear and exhaustion in her eyes that upset her the most.

She splashed cold water on her face, hoping that would help, then she washed her hands with the liquid antiseptic soap and dried them before grabbing her purse.

As he had promised, Raymond Tanner was waiting on the other side of the second set of doors, in a very large room divided by curtains into patient cubicles along two walls.

"Your mother is right over here," he said, keeping his voice low. He led her toward a far corner.

"In the CCU, the nurses each have responsibility for two patients, because the care required is very intensive," he explained. "We're a bit slow right now, so I only have your mother assigned to me, but that could change at any time. As far as I know, Peggy O'Hara will be working the day shift with your mother. Feel free to speak to either of us about any concerns you might have."

He slowed his steps. "Do you have any questions before you see your mother?"

She shook her head, unwilling to let questions delay her any longer. But when she was led toward a bed where an elderly patient was breathing on a ventilator, she felt her heart drop. She looked at the frail, aged woman lying there comatose—her mother—and gulped back tears.

Between the whoosh of the ventilator, the beep of monitors and the IV line, Ellie had the impression her mother was alive only because of the technology that surrounded her. "Why can't she breathe on her own?" she asked.

Nurse Tanner moved to stand opposite Ellie on the other side of the bed. "We're trying to ease the burden on her heart, at least for the first twenty-four hours or so. We've got her sedated so she's able to rest more comfortably and so she won't fight the ventilator."

"Can she hear me?" she asked.

"Probably not, although I've had a few patients tell me later that they could hear well enough. But they weren't able to respond, of course, so you might want to keep that in mind and keep what you say very positive. I'm sure she feels your presence, though."

Ellie swallowed hard. "How…how long will she be… like this?"

He reached down and tucked the end of her mother's hospital gown over her shoulder again. "The first twenty-four to forty-eight hours are the most critical after any heart attack."

This time Ellie had to clear her throat before she could swallow hard again. "May I stay with her?"

"Of course. But you might be better off going home and getting some rest," he said. He pulled a business card and a pen from his pocket and wrote something down before he handed her the card. "Here's the number for the CCU so you can call here directly. Ask for me or for Peggy O'Hara, depending on what time of day it is. We've got your cell phone number, and we'll call you, day or night, if there's any significant change in your mother's condition."

Ellie tucked the card into her purse. "I'd like to stay with her, at least for a little while."

"That's fine. There's a chair at the end of the bed if you'd like to sit down."

"Thank you. I think the sign said I could only visit for fifteen minutes each hour. Is that right?"

"Don't worry about what the sign says. Come when you like and stay as long as you like, at least until your mother…stabilizes," he said gently. "Would you like me to pull the curtain so you can have some private time with your mother?"

Touched by his sensitivity, Ellie nodded, unable to speak as she tried to absorb the reality that the time for private moments with her mother was ebbing away. Once she and her mother were secluded behind the curtain, Ellie set her purse down on the chair. When she saw a stack of cloths and a pitcher of water on the overbed table, which had been pushed to the side, she moistened one of the cloths and wiped her mother's brow.

Fearful that her mother might never be conscious again to talk to her, Ellie set aside all but the heaviest burden of her heart. After whispering a prayer that her mother would hear her, if only with her spirit, she leaned close and pressed a kiss to her mother's pale, cool cheek. "There's so much I need to say," she murmured, "but most of all, I want you to know that I'm sorry, Mother. I'm so sorry, and I—I wish…I wish I could have been the daughter you always wanted me to be."

Chapter Twenty-Six

Hour by hour, day by day, Ellie's mother rallied.

By Monday night, she was actually breathing on her own again. She was weak, but slowly recovering, much to the amazement of her doctors. The following day, both of Ellie's sons, Alex and Richard, arrived, and stayed until Wednesday afternoon, when they flew back to their homes again. Early Thursday morning, Rose Hutchinson left the Coronary Care Unit for a private room in the regular cardiac unit on the fifth floor of the hospital.

Once Ellie was satisfied that her mother was resting comfortably in her new room, which was not until just after lunchtime, she finally ended her four-day, nearly round-the-clock vigil at the hospital. She had scarcely left her mother's bedside, and had only gone home occasionally to shower and change, take in the mail and feed the turtles before heading straight back to the hospital.

On her way home, Ellie stopped at the high school several hours after both the students and staff had left to begin their ten-day spring break, which traditionally coincided with Easter. She let herself into the building with a master key, and only stayed long enough to pick up the work her students had done in her absence and collect the papers overflowing in her mailbox.

Ten minutes after she got home, she collapsed into bed and slept through the night for the first time since her mother had been rushed to the hospital.

When she woke at 10 a.m. the following day, it was Good Friday. She was tempted to snuggle back under the covers, but she doubted she would get any sleep until she ate something to make her stomach stop growling. She also needed to get back to the hospital. If her mother was still making good progress, Ellie hoped to visit for a while, leave for three-o'clock services and return to the hospital until visiting hours ended at eight.

After showering and dressing, she went into her home office to play the phone messages that had accumulated over the past four days. Most of the calls were from well-wishers. Charlene had called twice, and Ellie added her name to the list of people she needed to call back. She played the last message, which had come at nine o'clock that morning, wondering how she could have slept right through it.

"This is Gail Brown in the social services department at Tilton General Hospital. Please call me back regarding your mother's transfer. My number is—"

Ellie pressed the delete button. She had already met with Gail Brown after her mother had been transferred from the CCU to the regular floor. Twice. As far as Ellie was concerned, if Gail Brown needed more help wading through the insurance and related paperwork, she would simply have to wait until Ellie got back to the hospital. Besides, she had told everyone at the hospital, including Gail Brown, to call on her cell phone instead of the house phone, but as happened so often, that directive had been ignored.

She tucked the list of people to call in the corner of the

blotter on her desk, confirmed with a quick glance that the land turtles had not emerged from hibernation yet and went downstairs to the kitchen. After existing on cafeteria food for so many days, she treated herself to a cheese omelet and whole wheat toast. She checked the voice mail on her cell phone while she ate, and deleted a message from Gail Brown that was nearly identical to the one she had left on the house phone. Feeling badly for assuming the woman had not called her on her cell phone, she grabbed an apple to eat later and drove back to the hospital.

Despite all the time she had spent with her mother, Ellie really had not had the opportunity to have any sort of serious conversation with her. Until late Monday night, her mother had been sedated and on a ventilator. After the ventilator had been removed, her mother's voice had been very raspy, and she had complained about having a sore throat the entire time Alex and Richard had been there.

Her mother had been able to talk more easily by the time she had been moved into her private room, but the constant traffic of doctors, nurses, aides and technicians had made it almost impossible to speak privately for more than a few minutes at a time. Even when they were alone, her mother seemed to be almost withdrawn, if not outright distant, and Ellie sensed she was now finally facing the reality of her own death, and trying to come to terms with it.

Unfortunately, her mother had never mentioned hearing what Ellie had said to her that first night in the CCU, and Ellie had not had the courage to ask her about it.

Grateful that her mother had survived this second heart attack, Ellie prayed that her mother would grow even stronger over the next few days and be able to come home while Ellie was on break from school. By then, Ellie hoped to learn if there was any hope at all of establishing peace between them before her mother died.

* * *

Ellie arrived at Tilton General Hospital and got her visitor's pass in the main lobby. Instead of stopping at Social Services to speak to Gail Brown first, however, she went into the gift shop, bought a pot of white hyacinths, her mother's favorite Easter flower, and took the elevator to the fifth floor.

Since her mother had been hospitalized so frequently in the past several months, Ellie knew her way around well. She didn't stop at the nurses' station to ask for directions to room 528 as she passed by, but it would have done her little good if she had. There wasn't a nurse or an aide in sight.

When she got to her mother's room, the door was closed. She stopped, reluctant to enter and interrupt if a doctor was inside examining her mother. She leaned closer and listened hard. When she didn't hear any voices or movement inside, she knocked once and waited. When she got no response to her second knock, she assumed her mother might be sleeping and opened the door very slowly. Once the door was open and she slipped inside, however, Ellie's heart skipped a beat, and she began to tremble.

The bed was empty, stripped right down to a plastic-covered mattress.

All of the cards her mother had received, which Ellie had pinned to the bulletin board above the headboard, had disappeared. The box of tissue and the plastic pitcher and cup that had been on the overbed table were missing, too.

Her mother was gone.

Ellie backed out of the room in fear, disbelief and confusion. When she ran into something, she swung around and found herself staring at Cindy Morgan, the young nurse Ellie had confronted when her mother had been discharged earlier than expected after her first heart attack. The memory of that mix-up, when no one had remembered to call Ellie on her cell phone, was still vivid.

Latching on to the faint hope that the call from Gail Brown might have been to tell Ellie that her mother had been transferred again today, she choked out, "My mother. Where's my mother?"

"Oh, you're Rose's daughter. It's Mrs. Waters, isn't it? I've been off on vacation, so I didn't know until this morning that your mother had suffered another heart attack."

Fear had formed such a huge knot in Ellie's chest that she fought to breathe, and clutched the pot of flowers hard against her body. "My mother. I can't find my mother."

"She transferred to a sub-acute unit early this morning. Didn't Gail Brown call you?"

Ellie's heart rate dropped back to double time. "I had a couple of messages to call her," she admitted, "but I haven't gotten back to her yet. I wanted to see my mother first. What floor is the sub-acute unit on?" she asked, mentally kicking herself for assuming the transfer Gail Brown had been referring to had been her mother's transfer out of CCU. This time, however, she had no one to blame for the mistake but herself.

Cindy put her arm around Ellie. "You're as pale as those flowers you're practically strangling. Why don't you let me get you a glass of water and I'll have Gail Brown come up to speak to you."

"I don't need any water, and I don't need to speak to Gail Brown. I need to see my mother," Ellie insisted, and pulled free.

"I know you're upset, and I'm sorry for the apparent miscommunication, but your mother's fine. In fact, she was doing so well, the doctor agreed to release her to the sub-acute unit at Havenwood Care Center, where she can build up her strength with some physical therapy before she goes back home with you again."

"Havenwood? She's not here in the hospital?"

"Not since about eight-thirty this morning. I'm sure she's in her room by now. If you like, you can call her from the nurses' station before you leave."

"No. Thank you. I—I have to go," Ellie stammered, and headed back out to the elevator, too distraught to wonder for more than a second how this caring, compassionate nurse could be the same one who had been so cavalier with her the last time they had talked.

From the outside, Havenwood Care Center, which was located some fifteen miles from Welleswood, looked exactly like what it was—a nursing home.

Inside, however, the main lobby of the single-floor struc-ture was as beautifully decorated, in soothing earthtones, as a hotel lobby. Thick tweed carpet muffled Ellie's footsteps as she approached a receptionist sitting behind a stylish walnut desk.

The middle-aged woman, who wore her red hair swept up in a chignon, greeted her with a toothy smile. "What lovely flowers. And they smell so good, too! Which one of our guests are you visiting today?"

"Rose Hutchinson. She's new. I'm sorry, I don't know her room number."

"Sign in right here. I'll check for you," she said, and slid a register and pen toward Ellie.

While Ellie signed in, the woman tapped the keyboard of her computer. "She's in room three-oh-five in the Audubon wing. Go right through the double doors on your left, follow the corridor along the courtyard and turn left when you reach the activities room. You can't miss it."

Ellie hesitated. "Do I need a pass?"

"Not at all. Just remember to sign out when you leave," she said before turning to answer the telephone.

Once Ellie went past the double doors, she quickly reached the activities room, where several residents were working on jigsaw puzzles, knitting or just chatting together. She turned left and started down the corridor, where the carpet gave way to a tiled floor. She found Room 305 halfway down the hall.

Since the door to the room was partially open, she merely knocked lightly on her way inside, and braced herself to be berated for not being here earlier. Straight ahead, beyond the empty bed that had been covered with a pretty bedspread, she saw her mother sitting up in bed, talking with a petite young woman not a day over twenty-five, with light brown hair that fell in ringlets halfway to her waist. Dressed in pale pants and a denim blazer, the young woman was holding a clipboard, obviously taking notes.

"Here's my daughter now," her mother said, and smiled as Ellie approached.

Although her mother still appeared very frail, she looked almost serene, a marked change that Ellie noticed at once.

The young woman immediately held out her hand as Ellie approached. "Hello, I'm Roberta Morris. I'm one of the social workers here at Havenwood."

Ellie shifted the flowers so she could shake hands. "Ellie Waters."

Her mother smiled and held out her hands. "Are those for me, I hope?"

"Yes. I'm sorry I didn't get here earlier," Ellie replied, then handed the pot of hyacinths to her mother and kissed her cheek.

Her mother held the hyacinths up to her face, closed her eyes for a moment as she took a long whiff, and smiled. "Thank you. Now I know it's Eastertime. Set these right there on the table, will you?" she asked, and handed the flowers back to Ellie with a broad smile on her face.

Ellie set the flowers on top of the gleaming bedside table, which matched the mahogany headboard. She noted the snow-white chenille bedspread on the bed and was impressed by the homey feel to the room.

"Since your mother just arrived today and will be staying with us until she's strong enough to go home again, I was just going over some admission details with her. We're nearly finished," Roberta said before turning to face Ellie's mother. "Would you like to continue with your daughter here? Or would you like me to ask her to leave?"

Ellie braced herself, expecting her mother to dismiss her. Instead, her mother reached up and took Ellie's hand. "Ellie is all I have. I'd like her to stay."

Moved by her mother's words and her gesture, Ellie didn't question the transformation in her mother's attitude. She simply embraced it.

"Fine, then. I know this will be the most difficult part, but it's something we need to discuss. Please take your time before you answer my questions, and if you need more time, just say so. No one here will be upset or angry if you change your mind later, either. Okay?"

Her mother took a deep breath and nodded.

Roberta continued. "I just need to confirm what the social worker at the hospital wrote down before you left there," she murmured, her gaze softening. "According to the admissions form, you've requested a DNH—Do Not Hospitalize. That means if you become ill again, you'd like us to monitor you here and keep you as comfortable as we can, but you do not want us to send you back to the hospital, even if your illness is life-threatening. Is that right?"

Ellie's mother tightened her hold on Ellie's hand. "Yes, that's what I want," she whispered.

Ellie's throat constricted.

"You also specified that should your heart stop beating, you do not want us to engage in any measures to resuscitate you, to start your heart again. We call that DNR—Do Not Resuscitate. Do you agree that's what you want us to do?" she asked gently.

"Yes, I do," her mother said, without a heartbeat of hesitation in her voice. "I do," she repeated firmly.

As the social worker left the room, her mother looked Ellie

directly in the eye. "Don't worry about all that," she said. "We both know that it's time for me to make those kinds of decisions. But I also know it's time for us to talk…because…because while I know I haven't been the mother you've deserved, I want you to know that you have always been the daughter I so deeply wanted to have."

Chapter Twenty-Seven

Ellie clutched her mother's hand like a lifeline that held her fast, while her heart pounded hard and steady and her mind echoed with the long-awaited words her mother had spoken. This was the new beginning in their relationship that Ellie had prayed for. It was the dream that she had kept alive with faith and hope, the balm that soothed the bitter hurts and crushing disappointments of the past.

And Ellie knew that, in this same moment, another prayer had been answered—her mother had been given the strength to face her impending death without fear. It was a miracle of transformation in the troubled relationship of a mother and daughter, and a gift of grace for a woman facing the transition from one life to another.

"I'm not sure what to say, except that I love you," Ellie whispered, glancing down at her mother and gently squeezing her hand.

Head bowed, her mother laced her fingers with Ellie's and sighed. "After you left the hospital yesterday, Reverend Fisher came to see me. I'm afraid we talked clear through till evening. I hope his wife isn't put out with me, even though he did call to tell her not to hold supper for him."

"I'm sure she understands there are times when he's needed and he can't avoid being late. She's been a pastor's wife for a long, long time," Ellie reassured her mother.

"And I've been a Christian for a long, long time, but that doesn't mean I've always acted like one and lived like one," her mother confessed and shook her head. "Dying is scary business, Ellie."

Ellie swallowed the lump in her throat and struggled to find words of comfort, but everything she thought to say sounded hollow. Instead, she asked, "What scares you most?"

"It's not the dying itself," her mother replied. "And I'm not afraid of what happens after I die, because I believe in God's promise that anyone who believes in Him will enter His kingdom. But I am afraid of dying without…without ever having the chance to tell you that I'm sorry," she whispered, before looking up at Ellie. "I'm…sorry. So very sorry…for everything. I don't expect you'll ever be able to forgive me completely for not being the kind of mother I should have been, but…but I'd be able to die in peace if I thought you might one day come to understand why I've always been so negative and so critical of everything, and forgive me. Just a little."

Overwhelmed by her mother's apology and her request, Ellie let the tears roll down her cheeks, wondering why it had taken so long for the two of them to set aside their differences and simply love each other.

Since Ellie had never had a daughter, her only knowledge about the nature of the mother/daughter relationship was the experience she had had with her mother. After raising two sons, however, she did know that she had never felt any need to compete with them or to compare herself to them, the way she had done her whole life with her mother. Whether that was typical for mothers and daughters did not matter. Not now that Ellie had realized that her mother was not solely responsible

for the difficult relationship they had always shared. Ellie
bore responsibility, too, and it weighed heavily on her heart

"I—I never made it easy for you," she admitted.

Her mother sighed again and rested her head against Ellie's
arm. "If you hadn't been so strong, you would have ended up
bitter and resentful like me. I was so blinded by my own
misery, I made you miserable, too. But you were so smart and
so strong, you succeeded, in spite of me."

"At what price?" Ellie whispered as her mother's words
stripped away the pretense of her own motives to succeed as
a wife and mother, but most of all as a professional educator
then as department head and ultimately, perhaps, as a supervisor. She had been driven to succeed, not to please herself
but to prove she could go far and beyond the limited world she
thought her mother had created for herself as a homemaker.

Ellie swallowed hard. "I was foolish, too," she admitted
"I was so busy trying to prove I could be a better wife or a
better mother or that I could have a career, as well as a family
that I forgot to love, respect and appreciate you the way a
daughter should. I'm sorry. Please say you can forgive me, too
Just a little," she said, and prayed God might also forgive her

"Oh, Ellie…"

And then, for several minutes, they both wept cleansing
healing tears of sorrow and regret, and of love and forgiveness

Ellie wrapped her arm around her mother's shoulders and
Ellie pressed a kiss to her cheek. "Dorothy Gibbs told me the
other day that you always wanted to be a teacher," she
prompted, hoping to hear the details of her mother's life she'd
never known.

"She's right. I always did."

"Then why didn't you become a teacher?"

Her mother sighed. "Life was different back then. At the
time, very few young women had the opportunity for both a
career and a family. We had to choose, and in my father's

house, there was no choice at all. He refused to waste a dime on college for me because he believed a woman's place was in the home. Period. Not that I want you to think your grandfather was an ogre. He wasn't," she insisted. "He was just a man of his time, just as I was a woman of mine and you are of yours, which is something Reverend Fisher helped me to understand when we talked yesterday."

Her mother sniffled, reached for a tissue and wiped away her tears. "I actually applied for a partial scholarship, but once my father got wind of it, he told me I'd better find a way to afford the rest of the tuition and have money to pay for room and board at home, too. So I got a job with Dr. Ingram, right on the avenue."

"Where the dentist is now?" Ellie asked, to encourage her mother to continue.

"That's right. After a few years, I'd even saved up enough money to start college, but the summer before the fall semester started, I met your father. He was here visiting his cousin for the summer."

She stopped to clear her throat. "We were young and stupid, Ellie, but we were crazy in love. One thing led to another and… Well, you'll find out after I'm gone, anyway, when you go through my papers…"

"Find out what?"

Her mother tensed for a moment before she answered. "We got married late in October that year. You were born six months later in April."

Ellie stared at her mother. "Six months later? That can't be right. You and Daddy got married a year and six months before I was born," she argued, repeating what she had been told all her life.

"That's what we told you when you were old enough to ask about such things. It's why we never wanted to make a fuss about our anniversary," her mother countered.

Ellie wanted to disagree again, until she recalled being told rather pointedly that her parents wanted absolutely no part of a huge twenty-fifth wedding anniversary party she had wanted to have for them, since they hadn't had a big wedding.

"You were pregnant with me when you and Daddy got married," Ellie murmured, voicing the obvious, and recognizing one more element behind her difficult relationship with her mother.

"I found out I was pregnant a week before my classes started, and we announced our engagement right away. I got fired from my job immediately, not that it mattered much. Your father and I got married in a quiet ceremony a few weeks later. When you were born, you were such a tiny little thing. You didn't even weigh five pounds. Most folks thought you'd just arrived earlier than you should have, but I imagine there were others who suspected you were conceived before the wedding."

She paused and twisted her hands together. "And so now you know the shame of it. I know that times have changed and there's not much shame attached to anything today, but time can't change the fact that a sin is a sin. Your daddy and I sinned, Ellie, but even though we both took our sin straight to God and asked Him to forgive us, neither one of us ever had the courage to tell you."

Ellie looked down at her frail and aged mother with tenderness. "It doesn't really matter when I was born," she murmured, saddened that by becoming pregnant before being married, her mother had carried a heavy burden of shame for so long. The fact that her mother had been forced to get married instead of going to college to become a teacher also explained much of the resentment her mother had harbored against Ellie. "You chose life for me and you chose to get married and raise me. Not all young women who found themselves in similar circumstances would have done the same," she insisted.

"No, they wouldn't," her mother replied, "but if I had truly believed then, as I do now, that God had forgiven my sin, I wouldn't have been so jealous of you when you went off to college to live the life I'd wanted for myself."

"I couldn't have done that without your help," Ellie stated. Looking back, she clearly remembered now that it was her mother, not her father, who had helped her to fill out her college applications. She reminded her mother of it now.

"I'd forgotten about that," her mother said, gazing down at her hands.

"So had I," Ellie admitted. "I wish I'd known then how hard it must have been for you to help me."

"I wish I had been able to tell you, but I couldn't. I just couldn't. Then the years flew by. You graduated from college, started teaching and you had your work and the students. Then you met Joe and got married, and the children came along and you had a home of your own. A real home. After you were gone and your father died, all I had left was a house filled with bitterness, disappointment and guilt, and no matter how many times I tried to decorate and redecorate that house, nothing could ever change the fact that I'd failed you most of all."

Her mother turned and looked up at Ellie again with tear-stained cheeks. "I love you, Ellie, and I've always been proud of you. You're a gifted teacher and you were a wonderful wife and mother. No matter what I've said or done in the past, please remember that…after I'm gone. Please."

"Always," Ellie promised, and held her mother tight in her arms. "As long as you remember that no matter what I might have said or done, or how upset I might have been with you, I've always loved you. Always," she whispered, knowing that all they both really needed to know was that they loved one another and were loved in return by their Creator.

Amen.

Chapter Twenty-Eight

The day before Easter, Charlene shuffled across the lawn to the front door of Aunt Dorothy's house, determined to carry all her packages in a single trip. Juggling five shopping bags and her purse without dropping anything, took a fair bit of energy, and she had little to spare.

After spending the last few days running Aunt Dorothy to three doctor appointments, to the lab and the pharmacy, Charlene had to squeeze all her own errands to prepare for Easter into one day—today.

She had been playing telephone tag with Ellie ever since Ellie's mother had gone back into the hospital, but she hoped the Easter basket she had left on Ellie's porch would brighten her holiday a bit. She doubted, however, that anyone else would appreciate receiving a basket filled with little pieces of chocolate shaped like octopuses. Unfortunately, Charlene had not been able to get a hair appointment, but she decided she would fix her hair as nicely as she could tomorrow instead of wearing a ponytail.

Overtired and eager to get inside to relax and hopefully reclaim a bit of Easter spirit, Charlene almost groaned out loud when she spied Agnes Withers heading straight for her.

Keeping a smile on her face used up the last ounce of her patience, which meant she had none left to deal with whatever gossip or problem the elderly neighbor was bringing her way.

"This is great! You can save me some steps," Mrs. Withers said as she hurried toward Charlene, carrying a small brown lunch bag. "I stopped to wish Dorothy a happy Easter while you were out, but I forgot to give her this. I even wrote myself a note," she admitted.

While pausing to catch her breath, she looked at Charlene and frowned. "Oh, dear. You seem to have your hands full already," she said before she stuck the bag inside one of the larger bags Charlene was carrying. "There. That should do it. Tell Dorothy I'll call her when I get back. My son's coming any minute to pick me up. I'm spending the holiday at his home in Lancaster," she explained. "Happy Easter to you and that sweet husband of yours," she said, then turned and hurried back to her house.

Charlene was so taken aback that the encounter had contained neither gossip nor complaint, that by the time she murmured "Happy Easter" in reply, Mrs. Withers had already gone back inside her house.

Charlene dragged herself, her purse and her five bags into the living room, along with her remorse for misjudging her aunt's neighbor, and shut the door. She immediately glanced over to the sofa. She saw her aunt lying there resting with her lap shawl across her legs, and returned her smile. "Well, I'm finally back, and I'm not stepping a foot out of this house again until tomorrow morning," she announced, removing her coat and laying it across the back of a chair.

Her aunt chuckled, started coughing and propped herself up on her elbow until she stopped. After grabbing a tissue and wiping her lips, she added the tissue to a pile already on the coffee table, and lay down again.

"Let me get you some water," Charlene offered, worried

that all the running around they had done over the past few days had been too taxing for her aunt.

Aunt Dorothy waved away Charlene's offer. "I'm okay now. I'm just plain tuckered out. I thought I'd get a nap in earlier, but Agnes stopped by to see me. Daniel's still working out back. I tried to tell him he didn't have to get the rest of the backyard done by tomorrow, but he's as stubborn as you are. Did you remember to drop off my note to Max Duncan?" she asked.

"I did. He wasn't home, but I gave it to the receptionist in the Towers office. She said she'd give it to him as soon as he gets home. If he's not back before she closes the office, she promised to slip it under his door," Charlene explained.

She tried not to sigh, but adding a stop at the Towers to drop off a note to the man who had yet to call on Aunt Dorothy seemed very odd and completely unnecessary. Since he had called several times this week, she could not imagine why Aunt Dorothy couldn't tell him on the telephone whatever she had written in the note, but Charlene didn't want to pry or deny any request from Aunt Dorothy, who asked for so little.

"Good girl. You didn't run into Agnes on your way in, did you?"

"As a matter of fact I did," Charlene said. She plucked the brown sandwich bag out of her shopping bag and carried it over to her aunt. She had suspected there might be a plastic baggie with a treat Mrs. Withers had brought home from some event, but the bag felt too light. "I'll set it here so you can look at it after your nap," she said, and set it on top of the coffee table.

To her surprise, Aunt Dorothy sat up again, shoved the lap shawl off her legs and slowly swung her feet to the floor. "There's something in here for you and Daniel, too," she said. She opened the bag and neatly laid out the contents on top of the table: three sticks of balsa wood, maybe five inches long and as wide as a drinking straw, three smaller pieces half that size and long, thin strands of something that looked remarkably like strips of palm.

"These are for sunrise services tomorrow. Since we couldn't get to Good Friday services yesterday because I had that doctor's appointment, Agnes was kind enough to pick all this up for us."

Charlene furrowed her brow. "What exactly is that for?" she asked. Although she assumed the materials would be assembled into crosses, she didn't know how they would be used during the service.

"Crosses," her aunt replied. "Come sit next to me. I'll show you how to make them so you can show Daniel."

Charlene sat down next to her aunt.

Though her fingers trembled a bit, Aunt Dorothy managed to lay a smaller stick across a larger one to form a cross. She held it together with one hand, selected a strand of palm from the table and wrapped it around the two pieces of wood where they crossed. When she finished, she laid the cross in the palm of her hand and held it up. "See? It's easy enough to make a cross for tomorrow. It's the prayer that comes after making your cross that's harder sometimes, but that's the most important part."

"What prayer?" Charlene asked.

"Oh, dear. I keep forgetting that you and Daniel haven't been to our sunrise services before. I guess I jumped ahead a little. Our sunrise services are held in the park down by the river. When we first get there and it's still dark outside, we get to lay our crosses on the ground at the base of the big cross that's been erected for the service. But we can't do that until we look back over the past year and pray to God to forgive us for what we've done wrong, and for all the things we didn't do that we should have done."

Charlene swallowed hard. Even at a quick glance back over the past year at her relationship with Daniel, she saw things she regretted doing, as well as others she should have done to make their marriage stronger.

Her aunt folded her fingers around her cross and sighed wistfully. "When the sun first rises and shines on that big old cross and all those little crosses piled beneath it, you can almost see the light of Jesus shining down on us, and you know that through His death and glorious resurrection, He's fulfilled His promise to lift us all from the darkness of our sins and from death itself."

She paused and took Charlene's hand. "I sure do like the way Daniel's eyes twinkle again when he looks at you, and I'm real proud of how you two worked together at Sweet Stuff. But you both need better glue than that to keep your marriage strong. Make your crosses together tonight. Pray together," she urged.

Charlene squeezed her aunt's hand. "I'll ask him," she said, adding that promise to one she had already made to herself after she and Daniel had talked about working together to revive their marriage the day of the accident at her store.

Between all the preparations for her open house and watching over Aunt Dorothy last week, Charlene and Daniel had not had any real private time together before he had gone back home again last Sunday night. Since then, he had spent the entire week back at work, and she had spent her week either at the store making sure her customers got their gift baskets, or running Aunt Dorothy around.

Daniel had driven straight here from work last night in order to finish Aunt Dorothy's yard, and he and Charlene had had no time or opportunity to discuss the next step in their efforts to revive their marriage. But Charlene knew that unless they asked God to guide them, those efforts were doomed to fail.

Aunt Dorothy, however, had just given Charlene a very fitting way to broach the subject with Daniel—one she hoped would bring them together again through their faith.

Aunt Dorothy tried to stifle a yawn, but failed. "I think I'll take that nap now," she said.

Charlene moved off the sofa and helped her aunt by lifting her legs onto the cushions and covering them with the lap shawl again.

Still clutching her cross, Aunt Dorothy laid her head on her pillow and closed her eyes. "You won't forget to ask Daniel, will you?"

"I won't forget."

"Good. It probably wouldn't hurt to dab on a little toilet water, too," she murmured, and drifted off to sleep.

Chapter Twenty-Nine

Between wrapping her gifts after Aunt Dorothy went to bed and cooking ahead for tomorrow, Charlene did not finish up in the kitchen until after eleven o'clock that night. By then, the refrigerator was stuffed—fuller than the small turkey would be tomorrow when she put it into the oven to roast. The cake she had baked and iced was on top of the refrigerator, stored under an old-fashioned aluminum dome. And the Easter basket Charlene had made for Aunt Dorothy was on the counter, covered with a shopping bag, just in case Aunt Dorothy woke up and wandered out into the kitchen before morning.

While Daniel finished packing the car with everything they would need for tomorrow's sunrise service, Charlene lifted the bag, peeked at her aunt's Easter basket again and grinned. She had had to look through dozens of supply catalogues before she had found the tiny, gray stuffed elephant wearing an Easter bonnet. Thanks to express delivery, the elephant was now snuggling between two raspberry donuts from McAllister's. An elephant pin and matching earrings were wrapped in separate boxes, and dietetic candy from Sweet Stuff completed the assortment of goodies.

Satisfied, Charlene let the bag drop back into place to

cover the basket. She had one wrapped gift for Daniel on the kitchen table, but there was another one tucked in her pocket. She couldn't decide whether or not to give it to him. She was setting out the wood and strands of palm Aunt Dorothy had given to her earlier when her husband came back inside.

"I think we're finally all set for tomorrow morning. The three lawn chairs all fit in the trunk. I put new batteries in the flashlights and left a note taped to the steering wheel to remind us to bring along Aunt Dorothy's lap shawl," he said as he removed his coat and hung it on the back doorknob before walking over to the table. "What's all this?" he asked, frowning. "Where did you get—"

"The present is from me to you for Easter. The rest is for something Aunt Dorothy asked us to make," she replied. After taking a deep breath, she repeated what her aunt had told her about making the small crosses. She also explained that during services in the morning, the individual crosses would be an opportunity for them to set aside their sins and find forgiveness, as well as renewal, as Easter dawned.

"We've both been really busy getting ready for Easter and we haven't really been able to talk more about what we're going to do next to…to make our marriage really work, but unless we start now, I'm afraid we never will," she admitted. "I know it's late, but Aunt Dorothy was hoping we could make our crosses tonight. Together. If you want to," she added, hoping and praying that he, too, would want to celebrate the joy of Easter tomorrow truly as one again.

When he glanced away, her heart trembled, but just when she thought he was going to break her heart, he looked back at her. His gorgeous blue eyes were glistening with tears. "I've been afraid all week that maybe you'd changed your mind about…about us."

"I wouldn't do that. I couldn't," she insisted, blinking back tears of her own.

"Is making those crosses really something that you want us to do, or are you doing this just to make Aunt Dorothy happy?"

"I want us to make our crosses together and I want us to pray together. You said we could do that again, but we never did," she whispered. "If we're both serious about rebuilding our marriage, I think we need to start right now by asking God to help us. With prayer."

"Show me how to make the crosses," he said, and moved closer to stand beside her.

She nodded, unable to speak for the lump in her throat. After she picked up two pieces of wood, she wrapped a strand of palm around them until the little cross was secure. Then she closed her fingers around it.

Following her lead, he made a cross of his own, which he clutched in one hand.

Impulsively, she opened his hand and laid her cross atop the one he had made, and covered them both with the palm of her hand. When she looked up at him, she saw his love staring back at her. "Pray with me," she whispered, and bowed her head.

He cleared his throat. "Father, we come to You together to ask that You forgive us both for taking one another for granted. Through Your beloved Son, You have shown the world the meaning of pure love, and through Your spirit, You have given us all the strength to follow Your Word."

When he paused, Charlene added to her husband's prayers. "Guide us, Father, as we rebuild our marriage. Keep us close to You when we wander apart. And tomorrow, when the sun rises in the east to announce the glorious victory of righteousness over evil, fill our hearts with Your love, that we may share that love with one another. Amen."

"Amen," Daniel whispered, and pulled her into his arms.

He hugged her so tight she had to pull away to draw a breath, then he leaned forward and stole a kiss. And then another.

She chuckled, wondering what would have happened if she

had had time to dab on that perfume behind her ears, and remembered the present for him she had stuck in her pocket. "Here," she said, handing him a Turkish Taffy that she had salvaged from her store. "Happy Easter, Daniel," she said, hoping he would remember the first time she had offered him the candy.

Grinning, he took the candy, but immediately shoved it into his own back pocket. "Since I'm not wearing a helmet, I think it's better if I put it away before you get any ideas about using my head to crack it into pieces," he teased.

Delighted that he remembered, she grinned back at him. "I've got something else for you," she said, and leaned over to get his present from the table, handing it to him. "Open this."

Looking a bit surprised, he backed away. "Hold on to that. I'll be right back," he said, and rushed out of the kitchen and through the dining room. When he returned, he handed her a gift that was identical in size and wrapped in the same pink-and-purple-striped paper as the gift she had picked out for him.

They opened their respective presents simultaneously, but she was the one who laughed first when she saw that he had bought her the same book she had bought for him—a collection of scripture verses meant to be shared by couples. "I don't believe this," she whispered as she ran her fingers over the cover.

"I do," he replied. "Great minds think alike."

"Great *couples* think alike," she corrected. "What should we do now? We really don't need two copies of the same book."

"Maybe we do," he said, and set his book on the table. "We can keep one copy here to read together on the weekends, and I'll take the other one home. That way, during the week after I get home from work, I can call you and we can pray together over the phone."

"Good idea."

He grinned. "I thought so."

"Aunt Dorothy still needs our help, although none of the doctors seem to be able to tell us how much time she has left," she said. "While living apart during the week isn't exactly a good way to rebuild a marriage, I don't see that we have much choice."

"Maybe we won't have to be living apart. At least, not for long," he responded, to her surprise. "I was thinking about having both of us move in with her. Permanently."

She furrowed her brow. "Both of us? How? You can't commute back and forth. Not after working ten hours a day."

He pecked her cheek. "I'll make some coffee. Why don't you get that cake you hid up there on top of the refrigerator and cut a few slices. I don't know about you, but I need a snack. We can talk over cake and coffee."

She gasped. "I can't cut the cake now. It's for Easter."

He grinned and turned her around to face the clock. "See? Easter is only five minutes away. Before the coffee is even ready, it will officially be here," he teased.

She leaned back against him, looked up and kissed his cheek, knowing that the promise of a new day for them had already begun.

"That clock's running awfully slow," Aunt Dorothy announced. "Happy Easter!"

Startled, Charlene felt her husband jump, too. When she stepped out of his embrace and turned to look toward the dining room, Aunt Dorothy was shuffling toward them. In addition to a broad smile, she was wearing the ankle-length winter coat she had laid out for the sunrise service, with a scarf tied around her head and slippers on her feet. She was also holding Charlene's coat in one hand and a flashlight in the other.

Aunt Dorothy grinned at both of them. "I'm glad to see you two so happy."

"We are, but it's hours too early to leave for the service," Charlene said, hoping Aunt Dorothy had merely misread the digital clock next to her bed, and wasn't disoriented.

Aunt Dorothy handed Charlene her coat. "We're not

leaving for services. We're going out back. I've been lying in bed watching the clock for hours. I've been so excited about seeing what Daniel did back by the creek that I haven't been able to sleep a wink. Once I saw it was just about midnight and I still heard your voices in the kitchen, I decided to get up and see if you wanted to come outside with me."

Chuckling, Daniel grabbed his coat from the back doorknob. "I've got the other flashlights packed in the car already. I'll be right back," he told them before slipping outside.

"You two seem to have patched up your troubles. I'm proud of you both," her aunt whispered.

Charlene blushed, wondering how much her aunt had overheard. "We really have. Thank you. We—"

Daniel opened the back door, interrupting her. "Ready?"

Aunt Dorothy took Charlene's arm. When they were outside, their flashlights guiding their steps, they followed Daniel, who used a larger flashlight to spotlight their surroundings.

The air was cold, but there was no wind. Dazzling stars splashed across the night sky and a half-moon cast a wan light upon the earth. The woods were thick with trees, but the bushes along the wide pathway leading to the creek had been trimmed back. Their steps crunched as they walked side by side on a thick bed of stones toward the sound of moving water.

When Daniel raised his flashlight, illuminating a concrete bench that faced the creek, Aunt Dorothy yelped excitedly: "Look! There's the bench. You found it, Daniel!"

"Actually, that's a new bench," he said. "I only found the base for the old one, and it was pretty much ruined." As they approached the bench, he moved his flashlight to the right, revealing a white wrought-iron table with matching chairs. "Now that the weather is about to warm up, I thought you might want to sit out here with your friends when they visit."

"What a lovely idea. It's perfect. And if the day warms up, we can have brunch right here, too. Thank you," her aunt murmured, and plopped herself down in the middle of the bench. She sat still for a few moments, looking straight at the creek, where a narrow strip of moonlight stretched across the surface of the water. She let out a sigh. "I've been dreaming and dreaming about sitting out here again for a very long time, but I never thought I would," she admitted in a low voice.

Charlene moved closer to her husband and took his hand. "Thank you. I love it, too."

Before he could answer, Aunt Dorothy stood up and started waving her flashlight around. "I've got a surprise waiting for the two of you around here somewhere. There! Shine your lights right over there," she said, pointing her flashlight off into the woods to their left.

When Charlene turned and pointed her flashlight in the same direction, she blinked twice to make sure she wasn't seeing things that really weren't there. "A bike?"

"Two bikes," Daniel said, shining his light next to Charlene's.

"The red one is for you, Charlene. The blue one is Daniel's. Since the two of you seem to need things to do together, I thought you'd enjoy biking. I know I always did, at least in my younger days. There's a biking path along the river, you know, and lots of folks ride around town, too."

Charlene chuckled, reminded once again that her aunt was never to be underestimated. "How did you ever get these bikes back here?"

"I didn't. Max Duncan did. His son-in-law owns the bike store on the avenue, which I'm sure you didn't know. Annie was going to drop the check off for me at the store, but she kept forgetting. That's why I had you drop it off in my note to Max at home. I couldn't very well ask you to drop it off at the store. That would have ruined my surprise."

"Max Duncan?" Charlene gasped. "He's not… I mean, he didn't… I thought…"

"Max wasn't calling me to ask if he could keep company with me. He was trying to help me pick out the bikes over the telephone because I wasn't up to going to the store. Annie and Madeline were just helping me convince you otherwise so you wouldn't get wind of what I was planning and ruin my surprise."

When Aunt Dorothy looked at Daniel, however, her smile quickly slipped into a frown that matched the one he wore. "What's wrong? Don't you like my present?"

"I do," he assured her. "It's a great idea, but there's only one problem. I—I don't know how to ride a bike," he admitted sheepishly.

"Mercy! How old are you?"

"Sixty-one."

"Then it's long past time you learned. Why don't you get those bikes and bring them closer to the house while Charlene and I go inside and get that snack you wanted ready," she suggested, and took Charlene's arm again. "What kind of cake did you say you made?"

Charlene caught her husband's gaze and smiled. She was no longer certain whether they were taking care of Aunt Dorothy or whether she was taking care of them, but, in the end, it didn't really matter. Right now, the three of them were taking take care of one another.

And whether she and Daniel rode together, as Aunt Dorothy hoped, or not, as long as they prayed together, their love and their marriage would only get stronger and stronger.

Chapter Thirty

Retiring from teaching turned out to be easy.

Four days after Easter, Ellie met with her supervisor at his home to tell him about her future plans. The following day, a Friday, while school was still officially closed for spring break, Ellie left the principal's office shortly after noon, immediately following their brief but poignant meeting.

She did not have to return to either her office or her classroom. She had emptied her personal files and removed her personal belongings earlier that morning and had stored them in the trunk of her car. Everything else she had left for her successor, the young substitute teacher who had so capably taken over Ellie's class schedule during her recent absences.

With her mind untroubled and her heart content, she walked out of the school. She was confident she had made the right decision to retire, both for herself and for her students, because it felt right and it felt good. She had touched many lives over the course of her career, and she, in turn, had been touched by her students and their families. Not every memory was a good one, but each memory was precious, and she was grateful to be taking them with her as she crossed the staff parking lot for the last time.

The sun was exceptionally warm today. If she had not been on her way to pick up her mother from Havenwood Care Center, she would have put down the top on her convertible in a heartbeat.

Instead, she opened all four of the windows, took one final glance at the building where she had spent all of her professional life and pulled away. Filled with a sense of freedom and relief, she embraced her new identity as a daughter—a good and loving daughter.

She drove across the avenue and through the side streets until she reached the river, where she turned to follow the winding road to Havenwood. She passed the large wooden cross that had been erected for sunrise service last Sunday. She had attended Easter services at the care center with her mother this year, but seeing the cross in the park reaffirmed her belief that He would guide her through the bittersweet weeks—perhaps months—ahead with her mother, as well as whatever future she might create for herself when she was once again alone.

Although she had talked to her mother about nearly everything else, she had not shared her decision to retire with her yet. The process of retirement had actually been complicated by the emergency leave she had taken in order to care for her mother for the remainder of the school year, but the result was the same.

For whatever time her mother had left, Ellie intended to be with her every moment, and she planned on revealing that today after they got home.

When she walked into the lobby at Havenwood, she was surprised to see that the receptionist was not at her desk, but her mother was sitting in one of the chairs close to the fireplace. She was even more surprised when her mother stood up, clad in a pair of soft gray slacks and a pale lemon sweater set. Her coat and purse were lying on the chair beside her.

"Do you like my new look?" her mother asked.

"Do you?" Ellie replied.

"If I'd known how comfortable I'd be wearing slacks, I wouldn't have waited all these years to try them," her mother replied.

"Where did you get them?" Ellie asked, wondering what her mother had done with the dress Ellie had brought yesterday for her to wear home.

"Phyllis brought this outfit in this morning. She took the other one home with her," she explained, and looked down at her feet. "The oxfords might not look that swell, but they're comfortable, and you don't notice them so much if I'm wearing slacks. My physical therapist said they'd do just as nicely as sneakers, which is just as well. I'm not ready to wear those yet."

"You look terrific," Ellie offered, and she meant it. Although her mother was still a little pale and had lost weight, her color was good and her eyes were bright and clear.

"Thank you. I'm feeling pretty spiffy, although by the time I walk to the car, I'll probably need a nap to recover. Not that I'm complaining. I'm pleased as I can be to be able to walk out of here."

"Me, too," Ellie murmured. "Can we just leave or do I have to sign you out?"

Her mother picked up her coat and purse. "All done, and I've got all the papers in my purse, along with some new prescriptions. All you have to do is go back to the nurses' station to let someone know I'm leaving."

"I'll be right back," Ellie promised.

She returned to the lobby less that five minutes later. "We're all set. I'm parked right in front. Would you like me to bring the car closer to the entrance doors so you don't have to walk so far?"

"I'll manage. Walking is good therapy. Besides, you're right here."

"That I am," Ellie said.

They looped arms, and Ellie patted her mother's hand. Outside, her mother stopped for a moment, raised her face to the sun and smiled. "I had an idea it would be warm. I'm glad I don't need my coat," she said, but frowned when they resumed walking and approached Ellie's car. "Why isn't your top down on your car?"

Ellie's eyes widened. "You want the top down?"

"Absolutely," her mother said quickly. "Don't you?"

"Sure, but you always said that it was too dangerous to ride in a convertible with the top down."

"Well, I've changed my mind. Put the top down, Ellie," she insisted, "and stop looking at me like I've had a brain transplant. I've got a bum heart. That's all. I survived my second heart attack, but the next one will probably be my last, which means I don't have all that much time left to do all the things I've always wanted to do before I die."

"Fair enough," Ellie replied, and got into the car. Once she'd put the top down, she got out again to help her mother into the passenger seat. Back in the driver's seat, she noticed that her mother had taken a piece of paper out of her purse and was crossing something off. "What's that?"

"My wish list," her mother replied, holding it up and waving it in the air.

"You actually made a list?" Ellie asked, a bit unnerved by the idea of it, and that it appeared quite long.

"One of the social workers helped me." She slipped the list back into her purse.

While Ellie backed out of the parking space, her mother laid her head back, closed her eyes and tilted her face to the sun again. "Riding in a convertible with the top down was number five on my list. Wearing slacks was number eleven."

Ellie chuckled. "How many wishes are there on that list of yours?"

Her mother laughed. "Probably too many. Why?"

"Just curious," Ellie replied. "Is there anything else we can do on the way home?"

Her mother sat up straight and turned toward her. "There's one thing, but I don't want to take up any more of your day than I already have. With all the time you've spent with me this week, I'm sure you have errands of your own you need to do. Or papers to grade."

Ellie kept her gaze focused on the road, but cleared her throat. "Actually, I was going to talk to you about that when we got home. I stopped at school on my way to picking you up," she said, and slowed down for a stop sign.

"But school's closed," her mother argued. "Never mind. I forgot. You have a master key."

Ellie glanced at her mother. "Not anymore. I turned in all my keys today, along with my retirement letter."

Her mother looked away for a moment before she stared down at her lap. "You didn't have to retire just to take care of me."

Ellie checked her rearview mirror, saw that there was no other car behind her for several blocks and reached over to take her mother's hand. "I didn't retire for you. I retired for us and for me. There's a whole list of things I want to do with you, too, you know. Maybe I haven't written them down like you have, but that doesn't mean I haven't thought of things we should do together or things that I'd like to do for myself, for that matter."

"Name one," her mother said, lifting a brow.

Ellie checked her rearview mirror again, saw another car approaching and looked both ways before accelerating. "Okay, I will. I want to go parasailing this summer when I go to South Carolina to visit Alex and my grandsons."

"Parasailing?"

"You know, you suit up in a harness and there's this parachute type thing that lifts you up into the air when the motor-boat pulls you through the ocean."

"You're not serious! You could get killed," her mother exclaimed.

"That's right. Or I could have the time of my life."

"True," her mother admitted. "Is everything on your list so dangerous?"

"Not at all. I want to get more active at church, for one thing."

"What's on your list for us to do together?" her mother asked.

Ellie looked into her rearview mirror, met her mother's gaze and smiled. "That's easy. Anything you want to do with me."

"Anything?"

"Anything," Ellie replied.

"Then take me home to my house. We won't stay long," she promised.

Fifteen minutes later, Ellie pulled up in front of her mother's house and turned off the ignition. "Do you want to tell me what we're doing here?"

Her mother shook her head. "Not yet. Let's go inside."

Eager to find out what was coming, Ellie helped her mother out of the car and held on to her as they walked up the sidewalk. When she stepped inside, she bent down to remove her shoes, but stopped instantly, amazed to see that her mother was walking right across the living room carpet...wearing her shoes.

"Mother! Your shoes!"

Her mother glanced down at her feet for a moment. "Oh, dear, I'm wearing shoes and I'm walking across my carpet. Imagine that," she said, looking at Ellie and grinning. "I can't tell you how many times I wanted to walk around this house in my shoes instead of acting like a fussbudget all the time. Come on. Join me. It's about time we had a little bit of fun here in this house, although if any of the neighbors could see us getting all excited about wearing our shoes indoors, they might send us both away for a while."

"You're serious."

"Absolutely. This is wish number sixteen—I want to walk around my own house without taking my shoes off. I could show you the list if you don't believe me."

"No, I—I believe you."

"Good. Then you can help me take care of another wish, too."

Ellie chuckled as she walked across the carpet toward her mother. "I'm almost afraid to ask what that is."

"Lights, Ellie. I want to turn on every light in this house! And I want you to help me."

"Why? So you can yell at me again for wasting electricity, just for old times' sake?" Ellie asked, wondering if this wish business wasn't getting out of hand.

"No," her mother argued. "I want you to turn on as many lights as you want and leave them on, just once, without hearing me yell at you."

"But why?" Ellie asked, wondering if there weren't other, more important issues from their past that needed mending.

"Because I can't change how you grew up, and I can't change the fact that I was so hard on you," her mother whispered. "After I'm gone, when you're working in this house clearing out my things before you put it up for sale, I don't want you to hear echoes of me yelling at you all the time. I want you to remember being with me today and laughing and being silly together."

"How silly?" Ellie teased, if only to keep tears at bay.

"This isn't silly enough for you?"

"Not unless we sing while we walk around with our shoes on and turn on the lights," Ellie insisted, and looped her arm with her mother's. And so they began, walking slowly around the house, going from room to room, singing their hearts out as they turned on the lights together, chasing away the hurtful memories of the past and creating new ones, strengthened by the most important light of all—the light of faith they each carried in their hearts.

Epilogue

As the other mourners milled about in small groups near the cars lined up in the cemetery, Charlene stood at the grave site at the head of the coffin, while Daniel made arrangements for all of Aunt Dorothy's friends to be taken back to the house for light refreshments.

It was late September, but the sun was shining as brightly and warmly as it had all summer. While Charlene was filled with gratitude for all the love and wisdom that Aunt Dorothy had shared with her over the past six months, and for the love of her husband, it was knowing that Aunt Dorothy was now safe in the arms of her Creator, sharing in the glories of eternal life, that warmed her heart most of all.

She glanced at the elephant pin she had added to the flowers on top of the coffin, down at the pin that she wore, and smiled. Shortly before her death, Aunt Dorothy had insisted that Charlene keep the candy tin filled with memories and jewelry. Rather than storing them away to collect dust, Charlene had gotten Aunt Dorothy's permission to take the three engagement rings and Aunt Dorothy's birthstone ring to the jeweler.

Using the stones from all the rings, as well as the diamond

from Charlene's mother's engagement ring, the jeweler had fashioned a lovely pin of four diamonds clustered around the amethyst stone. Charlene had worn the pin for the first time on her aunt's birthday ten days ago. She wore it again today to honor the generations of strong women in her family, but most especially for her Aunt Dorothy, a woman who had lived life with humor, grace and faith.

"Thank you," she whispered, knowing how hard it was going to be to go back home where her aunt would not be waiting for her.

When she turned to leave, Ellie suddenly appeared and put her arm around Charlene. "I'm sorry I missed the funeral. My plane got delayed," she managed, pausing to catch her breath.

Charlene smiled and hugged her friend. "It's all right. I really didn't expect you to come all the way back for Aunt Dorothy's funeral. Especially with your mother passing so recently. You should have stayed in South Carolina, visiting with Alex," she said as they started walking to join the other mourners.

"Actually, I left there last week to spend some time in Dallas with Richard, but I wanted to come," she replied. "You cut your hair! Is that a perm, too?"

Charlene ran her fingers through her hair. "Actually, once I had it cut, the waves appeared. Go figure. All these years, I had naturally curly hair and didn't know it."

"Well, you look terrific, but how are you feeling?" Ellie asked.

"Empty. Drained. But blessed. Truly blessed to have had the time we did with Aunt Dorothy."

"She was quite a lady, wasn't she?"

"That she was," Charlene said. "I'm going to miss her a lot."

"I know," Ellie murmured. "I miss my mother, too, but I'm really grateful that we had a chance to spend some time together before she passed. How long are you and Daniel going to stay here in Welleswood before moving back home again?"

"Why?" Charlene teased. "Now that you're retired and

traveling back and forth to visit your sons all the time, I wouldn't think you'd be spending that much time here."

"Oh, yes, I will. To tell you the truth, the more I travel, the more I want to be in Welleswood. My best friend has a store here, you know, and I have lots of plans for us. Of course, it would be easier if she didn't live so far away and have to spend so much time commuting, but—"

"This best friend needs her best friend, too," Charlene said. "Actually, while you've been away, Daniel and I decided we both wanted to live here, and Aunt Dorothy was very excited and very pleased that we wanted to keep her house. Right after Daniel put in his retirement papers last month, one of the commissioners here asked him if he was interested in being head groundskeeper at Welles Park."

"He did?"

"It's not official yet, but Daniel should be approved for the post at the next commissioners' meeting."

"But I thought you said he liked living in the country," Ellie queried.

Charlene gave her friend another hug. "He did, but he likes living here even better. So do I," she murmured. "So do I."

* * * * *

DISCUSSION FOR QUESTIONS

1. Chocolate, chocolate, chocolate! What is there about chocolate that most women just love? Do you love chocolate, too, or is there something else you enjoy eating that makes you just as happy?

2. With so many women working full-time today, like Ellie and Charlene, how do they and their families meet the needs of their aging parents or relatives? How is this different for single women, compared to those who have spouses?

3. What is so unique about the relationship between mothers and their daughters, and how is that bond strengthened and tested as both women age?

4. Forgiveness is a strong theme throughout CARRY THE LIGHT. Why is it that many people find it easier to forgive others than themselves?

5. Aunt Dorothy had the opportunity to share the stories behind the family heirlooms she was passing down to Charlene. Are their heirlooms in your family with stories that should be told? Have you told those stories to your loved ones?

6. Though happily married for many years, Charlene and Daniel faced a crisis in their marriage once their "nest" was empty. How can couples anticipate the changes in their marriage as their children leave home, and how can their faith help them?

7. Every time Ellie returned to the home where she grew up, she was surrounded by memories. Not all of them were happy ones. What memories do you have of growing up? If some of those memories are painful, as Ellie's were, what have you done to come to terms with those memories?

8. Both Charlene and Ellie have careers where they nurture others. Charlene cares for her customers while Ellie has devoted herself to her students. Through your work or your volunteer work, whom do you nurture, and how does your faith help you?

9. Both Charlene and Ellie have children who have moved away from the area, a common experience for many women today who grew up in a time when children were more likely to settle nearby after they married. How does this impact the relationship between parents and their grown children, as well as their grandchildren?

10. Although both are women of faith, Charlene's aunt and Ellie's mother face the prospect of death very differently. Is there a right way or a wrong way? Why or why not? Does faith really make a difference?

ACKNOWLEDGMENTS

As always, I am indebted to my entire family and network of friends for their support, but for this book in particular, I want to thank my sister, Carol Beth Hatz, R.N., for sharing her wisdom and professional experience, as well as her editorial skills, with me.

Carol has been a registered nurse for over twenty-five years. She has spent most of that time caring for the elderly in a variety of settings, and currently works as a hospice nurse. With help from Gizmo, her late, trained physical-therapy dog, Carol has brought comfort, understanding and compassion into the lives of many, many people. She is looking forward to training her new puppy, Magyver, to be a therapy dog, too.

Her help during the writing of this book has been immeasurable; however, any mistakes I have made rightfully belong to me.

Thanks, Carol!

AUTHOR'S NOTE

According to the American Heart Association, heart disease, specifically coronary heart disease, which leads to a heart attack, is the number one killer of women in the United States. For more information about heart disease for both men and women, please visit the American Heart Association at www.americanheart.org.

Featured in previous books in the Home Ties series, the Shawl Ministry is a wonderful ministry that has spread through the country. For more information, please visit the wonderful folks there at www.shawlministry.com

Readers can find the recipe for German Chocolate Cake online. Mother always used the recipe for this cake that was on the back of the box of Baker's German's Sweet Chocolate. For the recipe, go to: www.kraftfoods.com/BakersChocolate/recipes.htm. Once there, do a recipe search for Sweet German Chocolate Cake and choose the third recipe for Original BAKER'S GERMAN's Sweet Chocolate Cake. There is a link there for the coconut-pecan filling and frosting, too. You can also ice the sides of the cake with your favorite chocolate frosting for a total chocolate delight. Enjoy!

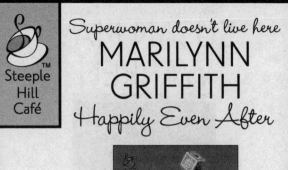

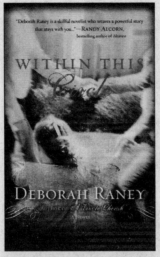

From Christy Award winner

Vanessa Del Fabbro

comes the third installment in
her South African–set series.

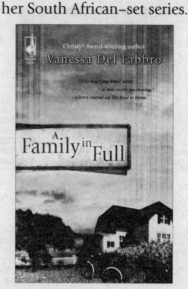

A Family in Full

Follow the stories of the two heroines of
Sandpiper Drift as they complete their families
in the fictional small town of Lady Helen,
South Africa.

Steeple
Hill®